The BRAVE and The LONELY

ROBERT VAUGHAN

Exclusive Distribution
by
PARADISE PRESS, INC.

This book is dedicated,
with affection,
to my publisher, editor, and friend:
Jim Bryans

High in the crystal blue sky over western Europe, a formation of 64 B-17G bombers beat their way through the rarified stratosphere toward their target, deep inside war-torn Germany. Most of the bombers sported flamboyant names, and many had tiny bombs painted on the fuselage to indicate the number of previous missions flown. The name of one of the planes was *Truculent Turtle Two,* and beneath the name, which was done in script, there was a cartoonist's rendition of a large turtle, wearing an officer's service hat which was crushed at the sides by an oversized headset. The turtle stared ahead with a ferocious scowl, and guns bristled from beneath his chin and from his shell in approximately the same places guns were bristling from the bomber itself.

Just behind the turtle there were three painted rows of ten bombs each, and one row of eight, denoting a mission history which began with the great Black-Thursday Schweinfurt raid of 16 months earlier, and ended with an attack on Berlin in the previous week. Behind the rows of bombs there was more information:

A/C SERIAL NUMBER: 324459
FOR RESCUE CUT HERE

Fire Extinguishers Located at Stations
115, 430 and 610

Service this Aircraft with 115/145
Crew Chief: T/Sgt. Donald L. Weaks
Pilot: Captain Martin W. Holt

Martin Holt had also been the pilot of the original *Truculent Turtle,* in which he flew 16 missions before being shot down over France, coming back from a raid. Those missions weren't reflected in the bombcount on the side of this aircraft, so Martin's personal total stood at 54, making him one of the most experienced pilots in the entire Wing.

Inside the *Truculent Turtle Two,* Martin pulled and tugged at his oxygen mask in a feverish effort to relieve the discomfort of the sweat. Though the outside air temperature was minus forty degrees, the close-fitting mask had caused his face to sweat, and the sweat had gathered and pooled at the chin cup of the mask, irritating him with its unbearable itching. Martin wanted to jerk the mask off and wipe his chin, but he couldn't. He didn't dare remove the mask because they were flying at 25,000 feet, and at this altitude his lungs could burst if they were denied the equalizing pressure of the forced oxygen.

"I mustn't think of it," Martin spoke aloud. He often spoke aloud during the long flights, but as he didn't key the mike button, none of the other members of his crew could hear him; thus he was able to engage in this habit without the embarrassment of being discovered. "If I can just get my mind off the problem, the problem will go away," he said. "I must think of something else. It's worked before, it will work again."

Martin scanned the sky around him, looking out at the planes which were flying in the standard "combat box" formation. As missions went, this was a relatively small effort. Martin had been in raids which consisted of more than three hundred airplanes. But that was in '43 and '44, when there were still many targets worthy of such operations. This was the fifth of January, 1945, and there were very few German cities which had not been reduced to rubble by nearly three years of bombing around the clock, Americans by day and British by night.

The target for today's mission was Nurnberg.

"It is a psychological target," General Busby, their Group Commanding General, had told them at three o'clock this morning, when they gathered in the briefing room, still clinging to paper cups of coffee, and trying to fight off the damp, penetrating English cold.

"Did you say it was a *psychological* target, General?" one of the pilots asked.

"Yes, I did."

"Excuse my ignorance, sir, but what the hell is a *psychological* target?"

Several of the others laughed nervously at the pilot's question, but they listened to the answer, because he had asked the question many of them wanted answered.

"It is simply this," General Busby replied. "The Nürnberg marshalling yards have all been destroyed, the factories have been neutralized, and there are no military installations there. But the city is one of the most important cities in the entire Nazi psychological make-up, home of the rallies and all that. We feel we can undermine their will to fight by reducing the city to rubble. That would hasten the end of the war."

Martin thought about General Busby's words. He had bombed the submarine pens at Wilhemshaven, the aircraft factories at Wurzburg, the ball-bearing plants at Schweinfurt, and the rocket bases at Peunde. The fighter and flak resistance over those targets had been terrible, and on many of those missions, the Americans lost more than one third of their attacking force. But Martin could see a reason for those attacks, and he felt justified in dropping the bombs. To Martin's mind, the psychological attack on Nürnberg was little more than the wholesale slaughter of civilians, and he did not like to think about that.

Martin looked over at his new co-pilot. His former co-pilot had been given his own airplane and Martin had drawn a second lieutenant from Iowa who would be flying his very first mission. His name was Walter Kindig, and his biggest fear had been that the war would end before he was able to drop any bombs on Germany. Kindig had been positively elated ever since they took off from Wimbleshoe early that morning.

Wimbleshoe, Martin thought. A typical English name, like Staffordshire, and Ingersall Hall. Like Allison Cairns-Whiteacre. Where was Allison right now, this very moment? Was she thinking of him at this very moment, the way he was thinking of her? Could love really bridge time and distance, better than a radio, so that people who were in love were never really apart, no matter how far their distance from one another?

Then there was Yolinda. They were never really together, no matter how close the distance. What was she doing now, this very minute? In Illinois, it was still before dawn, so she was probably in bed. Alone?

"Oops, sorry, Cap'n," Kindig suddenly said, referring to a rather severe bounce the plane made.

Martin was letting Kindig fly, and Kindig was having a difficult time of it. Martin had said nothing, nor had he made any corrections. Kindig was just now learning what all the experienced pilots knew. Trying to maintain position, heading, and altitude in a bomber stream was nearly impossible. The air, which looked so clear and innocent and smooth, was actually a boiling cauldron, storm-tossed by the hurricanic forces of all the airplanes pushing through it. There were propeller washes, wing-tip vortices, and turbulent wakes which rolled back with a gale force of two hundred miles per hour, and the bombers bobbed and bounced like corks on the wildest sea.

It wasn't fair to the other members of the crew to let Kindig continue to slide all over the sky. Martin knew that some of the men were already filling their air-sick bags, even the most seasoned veterans. Martin could have prevented much of that by taking over the controls. But Martin also knew that Kindig might have to bring the ship home alone. That wasn't a pleasant thought, but it was one which had to be faced. It was better to let Kindig experience this now, with him here to act as a back-up, than to experience it for the first time with Martin no longer able to help.

"Cap'n, maybe I should ease back on the power," Kindig suggested, interrupting Martin's thoughts.

"No," Martin said. "We need all the power we can turn up if we are going to stay with the stream. If we drop back, we'll be left behind and there's nothing the Germans like better than to pounce on a straggler. Just stay with it, Walt, you're holding her alright."

"It's not holding her that I'm worried about," Walt said. "It's the fuel. We're down to under 8,000 pounds."

"Don't worry about it," Martin said easily. "We always burn a lot more fuel going to the target than we do coming back. It's all been computed for you by the boys with the slip-sticks."

"That's good," Walt said, "because I was beginning to sweat it."

No, Martin thought, though he didn't give voice to his thoughts. Now isn't when you sweat it. The time to sweat it is when you are below a thousand pounds of fuel and you still have an hour to go. That's when you sweat it.

Martin turned his head to look at the leading edge of the left wing. Behind the blur of the spinning propellers he could see the lusterless, glare-reducing brown of the inside of the engine nacelles, the black of the wing de-icing boot, and the red and yellow unit I.D. stripe at the wing tip. The rest of the aircraft was unpainted, polished aluminum. The first *Truculent Turtle* had been painted olive drab, as had all the bombers early in the war. Then someone with a slide-rule figured that they would gain ten miles per hour cruising speed and decrease fuel consumption by as much as fifty pounds per hour if they didn't paint the planes. Now they were all polished aluminum, with only such paint as was required for markings and identification.

Let's see, Martin mused. The fuel is being expended at the rate of 1600 pounds per hour now. During our climb we increased fuel consumption, so that during the first hour and a half, we gobbled up 3600 pounds. That means that so far we have used 10,000 pounds. That only leaves 8,000 pounds but as our weight goes down, our consumption decreases. Minus bombs and minus fuel, we should only use 960 pounds in our final hour. . . .providing we encounter no abnormal headwinds, or pick up any holes in our fuel tanks, or. . . .

"Cap'n, I have a fix," Manny said, cutting through the static of Martin's earphones. Manny was Manny Byrd, the only other member of Martin's crew who was still with him from the original *Truculent Turtle*. He, like Martin, was a captain, and he was the navigator.

"Go ahead, Manny," Martin said.

"We are 180 miles out on a 285 radial from target. Our ground speed is 205 miles per hour, and ETA to the aiming point is 52 minutes."

"Roger. Pilot to crew, we are 52 minutes from target. Be on the alert."

"You would think the krauts would've hit us by now," Kindig said anxiously, scanning the sky for any sign of fighter aircraft.

"Not yet," Martin said. "Since the P-51s with the long-range tanks have been escorting us all the way to the target, the Germans have refined their tactics. Now they pick us up on radar, collect a wolf-pack of fighter aircraft, then vector them to us at the exact point which will allow them the maximum engagement time for fuel expended. They've got it down to a science, believe me. And wait until you see their jets."

"I've seen pictures," Kindig said. "They showed us film of the jets while I was still in flight school, back in the States. Have you seen the jets? I mean for real?"

"Yeah, I've seen them," Martin said. "You'd better believe I've seen them. That is, as much as anyone has seen them. They go by so fast you can't blink, or they'll be gone."

"Wow, wouldn't it be something to fly one of those babies?" Kindig asked. "Wouldn't you just love to fly something like that though? Why the hell don't we have jets?"

Jeez, Martin thought. Is he really that brave? Or is he just too damned dumb to be afraid? No, he isn't too dumb, he is just too green. Was I ever that green?

Martin closed his eyes and leaned his head back for a moment. It was impossible for him to have ever been that green. He was born experienced, conceived at 25,000 feet as the result of a symbiotic coupling between a Wing Commander and a B-17G. He had been nursed on hydraulic fluid, and weaned on raw oxygen. He took his first steps in the hell-hole aft of the cockpit, and he was toilet-trained at the relief tube. There had never been a life before this life, had there?

Gradually, with the steady beat of the engines providing a hypnotic insulation against all else, the disjointed thoughts in Martin's brain began to take form and substance. With effort, he was able to recall a past which was before over-revved engines and runaway props, screaming men and hammering machine guns, coagulated blood and frozen vomit. Then a smile came to Martin's lips as he recalled another, more innocent time. He remembered Standhope College, and Thanksgiving Day of 1941....

1

"Good afternoon ladies and gentle-
men, this is Roy Carter, bringing you a play-by-play
description of this 1941 Thanksgiving day football game
between the undefeated Ohio Normal Lions, led by their
All-American tackle, Brad Phillips, and our own
Standhope Warriors, with All American halfback, Martin Holt. It's a crisp, cool day under the bright, blue sky,
and Shackleford Jackson stadium is filled to near capacity for this game. Below the pressbox here, I can see an
ocean of orange and black, Standhope's school colors.
Across the way the visitors are waving flags of green and
white. Standhope's record, coming into this game, is five
and two, but I spoke to Coach Gillis a short time ago,
and he says that Holt has recovered from his knee injury,
and the Warriors are ready and anxious to take on the
Lions. So, who knows? There may be joy in Mount
Eagle tonight.*

Shackleford Jackson Stadium, Shaky Jake the
students called it, sat in a natural bowl in the
north end of the college town of Mount Eagle,
Illinois. From the top row of the wooden bleach-

ers, one could look out across the rolling, park-
like campus of Standhope College, beyond the
grey and red buildings, down to the Mississippi
River, sparkling silver in the bright afternoon sun.

Thurman E. Holt inched his white Buick along
slowly up the drive toward the stadium parking
lot gate. The car in front of him had an Ohio
license plate, and green and white banners were
thrust out each of the windows and tied to the
radio antenna. The people in the car were laughing and cheering for Ohio Normal. "Lions' growl,
Lions' growl, wow, wow, wow!"

The car passed a group of Standhope students,
boys and girls, and the Standhope students made
a train, and returned a cheer of their own: "Victory, victory is our cry. V-I-C-T-O-R-Y. Are we in
it? Well, I guess. Will we win it? YES, YES, YES!"

"Here are the starting lineups for the Standhope War-
riors," the radio announcer was saying, and Thurman reached down to turn the radio off.

Dottie had been sitting in the back seat, watching the students cheer and jeer each other, and
when Thurman turned the radio off, she leaned
over the seat back. "Oh, Daddy, don't you want to
hear the announcer say Martin's name?"

"He just said it," Thurman said. "He said All-
American halfback, Martin Holt."

"But he didn't say his name in the lineups,"
Dottie insisted.

"Yes, dear, let's listen to the lineups," Nancy
said.

"Okay," Thurman agreed, turning the radio back
on. "I know better than to try and hold out against
both of you."

Thurman rolled down the window as they approached the gate. "Hello, George, are you ready

for the last game?" he asked, as George, the gate guard, leaned down and smiled at them.

"Well, Professor Holt, I was beginning to wonder if you were going to make it today."

"Did you ever know him to miss a game?" Nancy asked.

George laughed. "No ma'am, you've got a point there. The professor's been one of our strongest supporters, even before your boy started playing. Just go on over to the faculty parking area, prof, you know where it is."

"Thanks, George," Thurman said. "Happy Thanksgiving."

"And the same to you," George yelled back as the Buick pulled away.

"Daddy, do I really have to sit with you and Mom? It's so em-*bar*-rassing," Dottie said. "Just everyone is here today, and there I'll be, sitting with my parents."

"Dottie, we have a box right on the fifty yard line," Thurman said. "Now you tell me where in the Sam Hill you would rather sit?"

"Anywhere but with my parents," Dottie said. "Really, Daddy, don't you understand how a woman feels about something like this?"

Thurman laughed. "I'd scarcely call you a woman, honey, you're still in high school."

"Yes, but I'm seventeen and I'm a *senior*."

Thurman sighed. "And my little bird is ready to leave the nest, right?"

Dottie recognized the acquiescence in her father's voice, and she renewed her efforts to persuade him. She was full of life, with a figure which was a perfect blend of womanly curves and girlish innocence. She had light brown hair, shot through with sunbursts of gold, so that in certain light it appeared almost blonde. Her eyes were hazel, with flecks of silver, and her skin was smooth and clear. She had a small, button nose, and she wrinkled it now, in the way that she used to when she was much younger and discovered that, somehow, a wrinkled nose seemed to work magic in getting her way with her father.

"Oh, please, Daddy, a day like today, it's just too perfect to have to be cooped up in a little box."

"Very well," Thurman said.

"Oh, thank you, Daddy," Dottie squealed in delight, and she leaned over the seat to hug his neck, just as he was parking the car.

"But remember, we are all going to grandma's for Thanksgiving dinner after the game, so I don't want to have to look for you," Thurman admonished.

"I'll be right here by the car," Dottie promised, and she opened the door and melted into the crowd before Thurman and Nancy were even out of the car, moving quickly as if afraid that he might change his mind.

"She's going to have to soon, you know," Nancy said, as she and Thurman entered the stadium through the press entrance. Thurman was an associate professor of English at Standhope College, but he was also publisher of the Mount Eagle *Crier*, a daily newspaper with a circulation of ten thousand, and it was the newspaper which occupied most of his time, and provided him with most of his income.

"She's 'going to have to soon' what?"

"Leave the nest."

"I know," Thurman said. "They'll all three be gone then." He put his arm around Nancy and pulled her to him as they walked down the inclined boardwalk through the tunnel to field level. Ahead of them was a patch of blue sky, the blurred color and movement of the fans on the opposite side of the field, and the bright green with white stripes of the field itself. They could hear the hollow thumping sound of footballs being kicked, and an orange-shirted player ran across the opening for a brief moment. "Where has the time gone?"

"If the kids only knew how little time there really is," Nancy said.

When they exited the tunnel, they emerged into a world of sound and color. They moved toward the box which Thurman, with the combination influence of an associate professorship, and the power of the press, had managed to wrangle from the college, and they were greeted by friends and acquaintances along the way.

"How's Martin's leg?" one anxious fan called. "Will he be at full strength today?"

"His leg's fine," Thurman assured them. "He was running full speed all week with no problems."

"I hope so," the fan replied. "If we ever needed him, we need him today. Ohio Normal hasn't lost a game all year long. And that Brad Phillips is awfully good."

"Not only that, they beat us pretty good last year too, if you recall," another fan put in.

"Oh, I recall all right," the first fan said. "I lost ten dollars." Those around him laughed at his admission.

"Did you bet twenty today to recoup your loss?" someone else asked, and there was more laughter.

"Ladies and gentlemen, would you rise please for the Star Spangled Banner?" the field announcer asked, and the entire stadium grew quiet as fifteen thousand people stood and faced the flag.

Charles Holt had the heat balm and tape laid out on the tables, ready for the half. There would be at least three ankles to tape, and half a dozen bruises to treat, so it was always necessary for him to leave the field at about five minutes before the end of the half in order to be ready for them. Since he had become student trainer to the football team he had yet to see an entire game. He didn't mind it, though, because at least this way he was part of it. Not like Martin, of course. Martin was big and fast and strong, and Coach Gillis once told Charles that Standhope was fortunate that Martin chose to go to school here because he was the only All-American Standhope ever had. Charles was proud of his older brother, and he felt no jealousy at all. There was nothing he could do about it, so he never dwelt on the capriciousness of genetics which left him small and wirey and his brother endowed with all the physical attributes—strength, agility, speed, and then, just to cap off a good job, genetics had added sandy hair, blue eyes, straight teeth and nose, and a smile that every co-ed in school dreamed about.

"One of the three of us has to be the intellectual," Charles once said, when someone had commented about how handsome his brother was, and how beautiful his sister was, and how unlike either of them he looked. Of course, they hadn't said it to be cruel, they were just unthinking, and with someone less secure, it would have been a devastating blow. Charles accepted it as a compliment for his sister and brother, and he took pride in that.

He was right when he said that he was the intellectual of the family, though that didn't imply by any means that his siblings were lacking in the mental department. Both Martin and Dottie were excellent students, always in the top of their class. But Charles was "exceptionally bright," his father liked to point out, and he had known from the fourth grade of school what he wanted to do with his life. He was going into academe, the world of scholarship and higher education. He would become a physicist, one who was totally committed to academic research. He was going to study atomic theory, because there was much room for discovery, and he would become an expert in the field, seeking knowledge as its own reward.

The door to the dressing room was banged open, and the players lumbered through like elephants on rampage, huge, padded young men with dirty faces and grass-stained uniforms. Their cleats clattered on the concrete, and they moved sullenly around the room, then settled on the floor, leaning back against the wall. One of them threw his helmet against the lockers in disgust.

"Charley," Martin said, limping over to the table. "See what you can do about this, will you?" He dropped his pants, then hopped up on the table with his bare legs hanging over the side.

Charles didn't even have to ask what was wrong. He could see it. The right knee was swollen to half again its normal size, and it was already beginning to turn blue.

"Martin, you can't go back out on this knee," he said. "I'd better tell Coach Gillis, you'll—"

"No!" Martin said, and he reached out and grabbed Charles by the shoulder, squeezing it so tightly that it hurt. "Don't say a word about this, Charley. I mean it!"

"But Martin,"

"Not a word," Martin said. "Wrap it. Just give me some tape to support it, I'll be all right."

Charles sighed, then began wrapping the knee, winding the tape so that the leg could still bend at the knee, but bracing it against any lateral movement. "What's the score?" he asked.

"Nineteen to seven."

"Nineteen?"

"They scored again just before the half," Martin said.

"How's the boy?" Coach Gillis asked, coming over to the table then. "Did you hurt the knee again?"

"Just a little bruise, coach," Martin said, grimacing as Charles worked. "I'll be all right."

Coach Gillis looked at the knee, and Charles could tell by the expression in his face that he knew Martin was lying. Charles could also tell by the expression that Coach Gillis was going to accept the lie. "Good, good," he said. "I need you out there, Holt. Don't let me down."

"I won't," Martin said.

"There," Charles said, after he finished the wrap. "If this doesn't do it, nothing will."

Martin hopped down from the table and pulled his pants up, then laced and buckled them into place. He took a few tentative steps, and though he tried to hide the limp and the wince of pain, he was unable to do so. Nevertheless he smiled, then reached over and patted Charles on the shoulder.

"Charley, my boy, you are a genius," he said. "I feel solid as granite."

"Oh, yes, I'm sure you do," Charles said, sarcastically. "Martin, if you take a good hit on that leg, you go down, do you hear me? Don't try and break any tackles. You could hurt yourself."

"Believe me, brother," Martin said with a small smile. "If Brad Phillips hits me on this leg, I will go down, you can count on it."

"Good," Charles said.

"Okay, guys, listen up," Coach Gillis said, and the orange and black clad young men who called themselves "Warriors" looked toward the blackboard to see what, if anything, they could do to pull this game out of the fire.

"Thirty-two to seven," one of the girls a couple of rows behind Dottie said disgustedly. The crowd was filing out in earnest now that the game was over, though many had begun leaving several minutes earlier, when it was obvious that Standhope had no chance of getting back into the game.

"What was wrong with Holt?" another fan asked. "He ran like an old woman or something. He couldn't do anything right today."

"Yeah, and he missed a field goal that I could have made," another said.

"Then why didn't you go out there and kick it?" Dottie asked hotly, turning to fix the disgruntled fans with her most severe glare. "It's awfully easy to stay up here and criticize."

"Dottie," Jim said, laughing. "Take it easy, they don't mean anything by it. They are disappointed because we lost."

"Well, don't they think Martin is disappointed too?" Dottie said. "I just don't like to hear anyone talking about him."

"Listen, Martin is a well-known personality," Jim

explained. "Anyone who is famous is going to have people talk about them, and some of it is going to be bad."

"Famous?" Dottie said. She laughed. "Martin's not famous."

"Maybe he isn't famous like Mickey Rooney is famous, but to college football fans he's famous."

"I suppose he is, isn't he?" Dottie said. She smiled proudly. "I guess I was just thinking of him as a brother."

"He is your brother," Jim said. "And that's why you have a certain responsibility to, well, to sort of share him with other people."

"I'll share him," Dottie said. She looked at Jim coquettishly. "But I won't share you, Jim Andrews. You belong to me, and me alone."

Jim looked around in quick embarrassment, then back to Dottie, who had seen his embarrassment and was revelling in it.

"Dottie, don't say something like that when someone might hear you. You could cause a lot of trouble."

"Pooh, do you think I care if anyone hears?" Dottie said. "I want them to hear. I want everyone to know that I am in love with Jim Andrews."

Jim blushed, and put his fingers on Dottie's lips, as if trying to hold back the laughter which was bubbling out from her.

"You know how your father feels about us," Jim said.

"Daddy likes you," Dottie said. "He's said so. He said you were the brightest young man and the best worker ever to work at the *Crier*."

"Yes, but he also said that he would not approve of us going steady until you graduate from high school."

"Well, that's just six more months, and I'm not going to change my mind in six months," Dottie said.

"Nevertheless, if Professor Holt found out, if he even *suspected* that we were secretly engaged, he'd.... well, there's no telling what he might do. I have him for my Lit class, and sometimes I get the idea that he's looking right through me, right into my brain, and he can see what secrets are hidden there. It's spooky."

"Never you mind, Jim Andrews. I'll handle Daddy when the time comes. I've always been able to have my way with him."

Jim laughed. "Dorothy Holt, I'd like to see the man you couldn't have your way with."

They had been coming down from the upper part of the bleachers, and now they were at the entrance of the tunnel which led out to where Dottie's father had parked the car. They stopped there.

"Are you going to Susan's party?" Dottie asked.

"Susan's party? I don't know, I hadn't heard anything about it. I haven't been invited."

"Yes you have, silly," Dottie said. "I'm inviting you right now."

"But shouldn't Susan—"

"Honestly, Jim, use your brain," Dottie said. "The whole reason Susan is giving the party is to give us a chance to be together more than the one time Daddy allows a week. Now, the party is tomorrow night. I'm going with Carl Fisher, but he is really Susan's date, see, because Susan's father is as much an old fogey as mine is and he won't let her date the same boy more than one time a week either. Then, when we get to the party Carl will be with Susan and you will be with me. Good idea, isn't it?"

Jim laughed. "You ought to consider a life of crime," he said. "You'd be good at figuring ways to get around the law."

"I know," Dottie said, smiling brightly at him. "I'll see you tomorrow night at Susan's party. And don't forget Saturday night. We are going to the show."

"If I get off work in time," Jim said.

"You'll get off work in time," Dottie said. "I'll make Daddy let you off."

"Oh, here you are," Thurman said, coming to the tunnel opening at just that moment. The stands were nearly empty by then and Thurman, who always stayed to visit with people after every ball game, was just beginning to leave. "I was wondering if we would see you again."

"Oh, Daddy," Dottie said, startled by her father's sudden appearance. "Look who I just happened to run in to! Oh, and listen, can't he come to work early Saturday morning so he can take off early Saturday night? It's ever so important."

"Hello, Jim. So you want off Saturday night, do you? That's when we put the Sunday paper together."

"I know," Jim said. "I wouldn't want to cause any problems."

"It won't be a problem, will it, Daddy?"

"I think it can be arranged," Thurman said.

Dottie smiled and hugged Thurman. "Oh, thank you," she said. She turned to Jim. "See, I told you it would be all right.

"Thanks, Professor Holt," Jim said.

"Isn't it a marvelous coincidence that out of

fifteen thousand people you just happened to run into Jim?" Thurman said to Dottie as they left.

"Yes, isn't it, though?" Dottie said. "Daddy, don't you think we could invite him to Thanksgiving dinner? He's an orphan and he has no one—"

"He isn't an orphan," Nancy interrupted. "His mother is still living . . . in sin," she added pointedly. "She's in California with that man who has the audacity to call himself a preacher. She's living with him."

"She's married to him, Mama," Dottie explained.

"That preacher had a wife and four children when that woman took him. You can't tell me that God recognizes their marriage."

"Maybe God doesn't," Thurman chuckled, "but the state of California does."

"Anyway, she is in California, and Jim's father is dead, so he has been living in the college dormitory for the whole time he's been in college. Don't you think it would be nice to invite him?"

"Dear, I'm not sure it is good for you to see too much of Jim," Nancy said. "You know, blood will tell, and if—"

"Oh, Nancy, don't be silly," Thurman interrupted. "Jim is a fine boy. He's a decent, intelligent, hard-working young man, and if Dottie is going to see anyone then she can see Jim. I do think she is too young to see so much of him, though, and I wish she would at least wait until she graduated from high school before she started thinking about one young man. But, Dottie, remember, this is your grandmother's dinner, not ours, so we have no right to invite anyone."

"Can we invite him over to our house for dinner sometime?" Dottie asked.

"We'll talk about it later," Nancy said, showing

by the tone of her voice that she was rather cool to the idea.

They were to the car then, and Dottie sighed and slipped into the back seat. "Are we going to wait for Martin and Charles?" she asked.

"No," Thurman said. "Charles has the panel truck from the newspaper. The boys'll come over in that."

"I'm glad it's them and not me," Dottie said, wrinkling her nose in disapproval.

"You're glad it's them and not you what?" Thurman asked.

"Coming over to Grandma's in a panel truck. It's bad enough to have to go to Grandma's on Thanksgiving Day, but it would be awful to arrive in a truck that says, 'Read the Mount Eagle *Crier*'. I would die of embarrassment. I would just die."

"What do you mean it's bad enough to have to go to your Grandma's for Thanksgiving dinner?" Nancy asked with a hurt tone in her voice. "Why, Grandma would be terribly hurt if she ever heard you say something like that. She loves all you children so, and I thought you loved her."

"I do love Grandma, Mom," Dottie said. "That's not it, it's just, oh, I can't explain, Mom. If you don't understand, I just can't explain. But grandparents are so. . . . so embarrassing."

"Like parents are embarrassing?" Thurman asked, with a smile.

"Yes," Dottie said. "Oh, Daddy, you do understand, don't you? I mean, what if the other kids knew that we were going to Grandma's?"

"I've got a news bulletin for you, honey," Thurman said. "All kids have parents and grandparents. It is biologically impossible to be on this planet without them."

"Thurman!" Nancy scolded.

"What? Dear, Dottie is a very attractive seventeen-year-old girl. If she doesn't have at least a rudimentary understanding of biology, and how children are brought into the world, then we are going to be in trouble."

"You wouldn't be in trouble, *I* would be the one to get in trouble," Dottie said lightly, enjoying the opportunity to joke in such an adult fashion with her father.

"Please," Nancy said, turning to look out the window of the car. "I don't want to talk about this anymore. We are going to Grandma's for Thanksgiving dinner, and you are going to enjoy it, young lady. And you are going to let Grandma know that you enjoy it. Do I make myself clear?"

"Yes, Mom," Dottie said and as she settled back into the back seat, she saw her father's face in the rearview mirror. He was looking at her and smiling, and when he caught her eyes in the mirror he winked, and she winked back.

Sometimes parents aren't all that bad, she thought.

2

"**M**artin, have you put those parts in the cleaning solvent yet?"

Martin raised up from the workbench and brushed the shock of hair back from his forehead. When he did so he left a small smudge of grease, but it was indistinguishable from the other smudges of grease already on his face.

"Piston, rings and valve assembly," Martin said. "I put 'em in about fifteen minutes ago. You think they should come out now?"

"No, we'll give 'em another fifteen minutes or so, then I'll take care of 'em. I have something else for you to do if you don't mind."

"No, I don't mind," Martin said.

"It's out here, on the flight line. You'd better put on your jacket, it's a little chilly."

Martin walked over to the side where his jacket hung on one of the many nails that had been driven into the hangar wall. Above his jacket was a faded poster with a drawing of an airplane and an oversized pilot sticking up from the cockpit with his neck twisted around and around like a screw. "Look all around you!" the caption cautioned.

"Mr. Turner, do you want your jacket too?" Martin asked, seeing Turner's jacket right beside his own.

"Yeah, you might as well throw it to me," Turner answered. "How's the knee holding up?"

"It's a little sore," Martin admitted. "I'm glad football season is over."

"Too bad about that last game. I would have really liked to see you fellas beat Ohio Normal."

"They were a better team," Martin said.

"Maybe, but if your leg hadn't bothered you, we might've had a shot at it."

Martin was following Turner across the hangar floor as they talked. He had started working at the airport on weekends during the summer, in exchange for free flying lessons and flying time. He hadn't even told his parents about it, because his mother heartily disapproved of flying and Martin knew that it would just cause a scene if she knew.

Martin loved the airport. He loved the smell of airplane dope and fabric, of gasoline and oil, and he loved to look at the airplanes, the squat, sturdy-looking biplanes and the sleek, graceful monoplanes. He liked to hear Turner tell stories too. Logan Turner had been a member of the Hat and Ring Squadron during the World War, and sometimes Martin would close his eyes during the stories, and see the fog-shrouded aerodromes of France, and hear the drone of engines as the squadron went up to meet the Red Baron's dawn patrol.

Turner slid the door open, and Martin followed him through. The small Piper Cub was still parked on the apron where they had left it a couple of hours earlier when they had come back from Martin's flying lesson. They were going to wheel it back into the hangar.

"We'll have to open the door further than this," Martin said. "She won't go in."

"She's not going in," Turner said. "At least, not yet."

"Oh," Martin said, noncommittally. He looked up and down the apron. The Cub was the only airplane in sight. "What else do you need done out here?" he asked.

Turner pointed to the little Cub. "I'd like one more hour put on the Cub·so we can pull her in for an inspection," he said.

"Good," Martin said. "You mean we're taking her up again?"

"No," Turner said.

Martin looked at Turner with a question in his eyes.

Turner smiled. "We aren't taking her up, son. *You* are."

For just an instant, Martin wasn't sure that he heard correctly. But the smile on Turner's face was unmistakable. "Mr. Turner, you mean me? I'm taking it up alone? I'm going to solo?"

"Well, that's what they call it when you fly all by yourself," Turner said. "I think you're ready for your first solo. What about you?"

"I'm ready," Martin said. "Yes, I'm ready. I know I am."

Turner pointed to the plane. "Well, there she is. It's all yours."

"Oh," Martin said, excitely. "Oh, this is great! Thanks, Mr. Turner. Thanks a lot!"

Martin ran toward the little yellow plane with a smile as big as all outdoors on his face. He put his hand on the cowling and patted it lovingly, then he looked inside. He could smell leather and canvas, and he could feel it rocking gently in the wind. He stood there, letting the moment sink in. He was going to solo! He was really going to solo!

"You aren't having second thoughts, are you?" Turner called.

"No, sir!" Martin replied, and he climbed into the back seat, because the weight and balance of the Cub dictated that it be flown solo only from the rear. "Will you prop me, Mr. Turner?"

Turner chuckled. "Do you know any other way of getting her started?"

Martin turned on the fuel, primed the engine, and cracked the throttle. He sat there while Turner pulled it through, then Turner yelled, "Contact!"

"Contact," Martin replied, moving the mag switch to left magneto, because that was the only magneto with an impulse coupling.

Turner gave a quick twist to the propeller, and it caught right away. Turner stepped aside and held his hand up with his thumb and forefinger forming a circle, and Martin opened the throttle.

It seemed like it took forever to taxi down to the end of the runway, but finally he was there. He swung the nose around into the wind, then, suddenly, he was ready. Before him stretched a long, wide, grass strip, lined on each side with yellow painted baskets. Far ahead of him, the baskets seemed to merge, squeezing out the runway as if telling him that he had only so much of it and then no more.

Martin pushed the throttle all the way forward and the little airplane started down the runway with its engine growling loudly. The tail came up, and then, without Martin consciously lifting it from the runway, the main wheels also broke ground, and he was flying!

"Yippee!" Martin shouted at the top of his voice, and he had the idea that his shout could be heard by Turner, even above the sound of the engine.

Martin pulled back on the stick and the airplane began to climb. He was even with the hangar now, and he looked off to his left and saw Turner walking slowly back into the hangar. He was amazed at how small Turner looked, at how high he had already climbed. The end of the runway passed under him, and then the highway, and across the highway the cattlebarn, and beyond that, fields of winter wheat. The town of Mount Eagle was passing under his left wing, and he turned, keeping it under his left wing as he circled slowly around it.

Martin saw the Mississippi, and a string of barges going downriver, and the bridge which led over into Missouri. He also saw the campus, and Shaky Jake stadium. The lines from the last football game were still visible from up here, and that surprised Martin, because before the game was even over the players were having trouble making out the yardlines. It looked as if the lines had been freshly applied, but Martin knew that they hadn't. It must be some sort of optical illusion, he decided, so that the lines, when seen from a distance above, seemed sharpened.

Mount Eagle was a pretty town from the air. There were several hills and many trees, and though the hills were brown and the trees were bare now, the town was no less pretty because of it.

Martin found Elm Street, then saw his house. It was a big, two story brick house, with a huge back yard. The house had been built in 1908, and it was built for a very large family. There were six bedrooms upstairs, and one bedroom downstairs. Though Martin and Charles were both going to college now, it seemed ludicrous to pay money to live in a dormitory and leave their own rooms as unused as the three which stood empty now, so both boys had agreed not to move out of the house.

Flora was hanging out the wash in the backyard. "Hello, Flora, look up here," Martin said, waving at the black maid who came in every day. She didn't live in because she had a husband and eight kids to look after at home.

Seven blocks away from the house, about three minutes by car and longer when there was traffic on Malone Boulevard, was the building of the Mount Eagle *Crier*. From up here the distance was covered in less time than it took to think about it, and as Martin continued the slow turn around the town he could see his father's Buick parked outside the building. The Saturday paper had already been delivered, and they were not making up Sunday's paper. The Sunday paper was printed late Saturday night and delivered early Sunday morning. The presses wouldn't even start to roll until ten P.M. tonight, and by then Martin would be there to run them.

All three of the Holt children had worked at the newspaper from the time they were old enough to empty wastebaskets. As boys, Martin and Charles had both delivered the newspapers, even the Sunday morning papers, which meant riding their bicycles through the streets of their route in the dark hours between three and five A.M. In the summers the route was pleasant, but the winters were hard.

Dottie had never delivered papers, but she had worked her way up from emptying wastebaskets, through "copyboy" to typesetting, and she pulled her own weight. Martin and Charles had gone through a natural selection of jobs as they grew older. Martin loved machinery, and had a knack with all mechanical things. He gravitated toward the press room, and was as good a press operator as could be found in the state. Charles, on the other hand, was a writer. He wrote all the sports, and even put in a book-review column. Despite their exposure to the newspaper, or perhaps because of it, neither Martin nor Charles had ever expressed a desire or even a willingness to go into the profession after graduation. But Jim was studying journalism in school, and wanted to go into newspaper work when he graduated.

Martin was all the way down to the south end of the town now, and he could see the Semmes's house. Professor Semmes taught history, and he was a close friend of Thurman Holt. Professor Semmes also had a daughter, Yolinda, and she was more than just a friend to Martin.

Martin had seen all of Mount Eagle from the air before, many times in fact, but this was the first time he had ever seen it from the vantage point of being all alone. It was a sense of power such as he had never before experienced. From here he could see to all four corners of the town. None of the town's 7,000 inhabitants could do a thing without him seeing. It was as if he were Ruler of the World. . . . or at least, the King of Mount Eagle. It was a wonderful, heady, powerful feeling, and he wished for a moment that he had some of his brother's poetic ability so that he could express what he was feeling. He wanted to tell Charles and Dottie all about it, but most of all he wanted to tell Yolinda. He wanted to share with her the exultation of flying. Such a thing, he knew, was beyond his poor powers, so it was better not to dwell on it. It was better just to absorb and enjoy the moment, while it was here.

"Thanks again," Martin said, stepping out of Turner's truck in front of the newspaper office. "I'll never forget today."

"You earned your right at it, kid," Turner said. "Are you sure you can't make it out tomorrow afternoon?"

"No, I've got a big exam coming up Monday, and Yolinda is coming over to study with me."

Turner smiled, and stuck half a well-chewed cigar into his mouth. "Can't say as I blame you any for that," he said. "Yolinda's a hell of a lot prettier than anything I got to show you out there."

"Much as I like airplanes, I'm afraid I have to agree with you there," Martin said. He waved as Turner slipped the truck into gear, then drove away.

"You're thirty minutes late," Dottie said when Martin stepped inside.

"I'm sorry," Martin said. "We got hung up. Is Dad upset?"

Dottie smiled. "He doesn't even know it. He left before you were supposed to be here and he hasn't come back yet."

"I'll make it up to you," Martin said.

"I know you will," Dottie said. "Jim came in early and he has already gone. I'm going to a movie with him, and I want to get home in time to get ready. I need someone who will set the datelines for tomorrow's paper."

"Oh, come on, Dottie, you know I don't like to mess with that stuff. Can't you find something else for me to do?"

"Please, Martin," Dottie said, and she wrinkled her nose at him as she would her father. Martin laughed. "Hey, that rabbit-nose trick doesn't work with me, kid," he said. He sighed. "Oh, all right, I'll do it, I guess. What is tomorrow's date, anyway?"

"Sunday, December 7, 1941."

"I know the year," Martin said sarcastically.

"Yeah? Then why is it that the last time you did the dateline you made it 1914?"

"I was just checking to see if anyone really read the dateline," Martin said.

Dottie pulled the bottom drawer of her desk open and took out her purse. "Thanks, Martin," she said. "Thanks a lot."

"All right," Martin replied, going toward the type boxes. The datelines had to be set by hand, because the linotype machine they had wouldn't set type small enough for the date line. Martin turned and pointed toward Dottie just as she was leaving. "But I don't want you thinking your bunny-rabbit nose changed my mind."

"Ha!" Dottie said. "You say it doesn't work with you, but it has every time." She slammed the door before Martin could reply.

Charles came into the room then, and he laughed when he saw Martin struggling with the type to set the datelines.

"She talked you into it, did she?"

"Yeah," Martin said. "Hey, Charley!"

"No, thank you," Charles said, holding out his hands. "I've got to set copy from the A.P. wires. Unless you would like to do that."

"Shit," Martin said. "You know what the old man thinks about my editing. 'Boy, can't you tell the wheat from the chaff? Don't you know what to keep from these stories and what to throw out?' I just use what I have until I run out of space, that's all. How the hell do you do it?"

"How do you keep that blasted press running?" Charles replied.

"A lot easier than I could handle those stories. What's hot off the wires?"

"Envoys Kurusu and Nomura are still talking with Secretary Hull in Washington," Charles said.

"Hey, that's wonderful news," Martin said sarcastically. "Who the hell are Kurusu and Nomura?"

Charles laughed. "Martin, if I didn't know better, I'd swear that you never saw a newspaper in your life. Kurusu and Nomura are special delegates from Japan. They are holding critical talks in Washington now, trying to resolve the differences between our two countries."

"What do they want?" Martin asked. "Their assets to be unfrozen, oil and metals to be shipped to them, and our blessing for them to take over all of Asia?"

Charles looked at Martin in surprise. "Well, maybe there's hope for you after all," he said. "You do know there is more to the paper than the sports page."

"Yeah, I got all that from *Terry and the Pirates*," Martin said.

"I never knew you read those things, I thought you just looked at the pictures," Charles teased.

"I like the way he draws those Oriental girls in dresses with long slits up the side," Martin said.

"I'm going to get a Coke. Do you want one?"

"No, I'd better not."

"Why not, you aren't in training now," Charles said.

Martin laughed. "No, I guess I'm not, am I? Thanksgiving was my last football game. What do you think about that?"

"What do *you* think about it?"

"The truth? I'm glad it's over. Grass drills, head-to-heads, wind sprints, seems like I've been doing that for most of my life."

"Then you won't be turning pro," Charles said. It was more of a statement than a question.

"Hell no," Martin said. "Whatever made you think that I might?"

"Coach Gillis said there were some people down from the Chicago Bears to look at you earlier in the season. They saw you against Southeast Missouri Teachers College. You were awfully good in that game. The money's good in the pro's. Eight games, five hundred dollars a game, you could make $4,000 in just eight weeks."

"Huh, uh," Martin said. "Four weeks to get ready and four weeks to get over it. Add that to the season and it's sixteen weeks, and I don't want to take sixteen weeks out of my life before I get started. Anyway, what is all this? I never thought you'd be trying to talk me into going pro."

Charles smiled. "I'm not," he said. "I just like to be reassured that you mean what you say when you say you won't do it."

"I mean it," he said. "There, I got these things done. Now all I need is for someone to come along and knock this tray off on the floor, scattering them all to hell and gone."

"Did you have a good afternoon out at the airport?"

"Oh, no!" Martin said, hitting himself in the forehead with the heel of his hand. "I almost forgot. How could I forget? How could I forget the most exciting moment of my life?"

"What?" Charles asked. "What happened?"

"Charley, I soloed!" Martin said, his eyes beaming in excitement. "I, Martin William Holt, soloed on this, the sixth day of December, in the year of our Lord, nineteen hundred and forty-one."

"Really?" Charles said, catching some of the enthusiasm from Martin. "Tell me about it. What was it like?"

"It was like nothing I've ever experienced before in my life," Martin said. "It was better than making a touchdown, or intercepting a pass, or kicking a forty yard field goal. It was exhilarating and thrilling and—"

"Insane," Thurman said suddenly. Both boys looked around to see their father standing there.

"Dad, I didn't hear you come in," Martin said.

"Be glad it was me and not your mother," Thurman said. "If she thought you were up in an airplane it would just about drive her crazy. And if she thought you were flying one by yourself, I don't know what she would do."

"Dad, she's going to have to get over that," Martin said quietly. "It's what I want to do with my life."

"What do you mean it's what you want to do with your life? You mean you want to fly an airplane for a living? What are you going to do, become a mail pilot, or a barnstormer, or something like that?"

"If that's what it takes," Martin said. "But, eventually, I would like to become an airline pilot."

"An airline pilot? You've gone to college to become an airline pilot? You don't need a degree to be an airline pilot. That's like being an engineer on a train, or driving a bus. It's ... it's beneath you."

"No, it isn't beneath me, Dad," Martin said. "It's all out there, before me. Airplanes are getting bigger and faster and more complicated. They have huge flying boats which cross the ocean now, and it's going to take educated men to fly them. That's what I'm going to do, Dad. As soon as I graduate from college."

Thurman leaned against a desk and looked beyond his two sons, into the darkness of the pressroom where the press now stood silent. In this light the silver of his hair took on a grayer look, and the lines around his eyes seemed more pronounced. He was only 49, but as he realized that the last, tenuous line of control over his son was being severed, his age seemed to descend on him with amazing suddenness.

"I, uh, had always thought," he started, then he cleared his throat. "That is to say, I'd always hoped that one of you might want to.... to...." He raised his arm in a sweeping gesture, taking in the newspaper.

"Dad, you've got thirty more years or so to run this paper," Martin said with an easy grin. "That gives us all time to make our own lives, and still come to some decision about the paper. It's not like the paper's going to close down when I leave, is it?"

"Not bloody likely," Thurman said, smiling so quickly now that the melancholy passed as if it had never appeared. "You ever pulled your finger out of a bucket of water? That's about how big of a hole you'll leave here. Now, quit standing around and gabbing on my time. We've got a paper to get out."

3

The peace of God, which passeth all understanding, keep your hearts and minds in the knowledge and love of God, and of his Son Jesus Christ our Lord; and the blessing of God Almighty, the Father, the Son, and the Holy Ghost, be amongst you, and remain with you always. Amen."

The organ began the postlude immediately after the blessing, and the congregation of St. Paul's Episcopal Church rose from their kneelers and greeted those around them.

"Why, Nancy, how perfectly beautiful you and Dottie are this morning," Mrs. Abernathy said, turning around from the pew in front of them. "And your boys, my, they are such handsome young men. I know how proud you are of them, and how proud you are that they came to church with you today."

"Yes, I am proud of them," Nancy said. "You can't always get the young people to go to church as much as they should, but they came of their own accord this morning."

"We didn't want to miss a Sunday in Advent," Charles said.

"Well, we're mighty glad you came," Mrs. Abernathy said. "I still remember when you two boys were acolytes. My, how sweet you looked in your little red vestments."

Someone a pew away hailed Mrs. Abernathy, and she excused herself and went to talk to them.

"Let's go quick, before she comes back," Dottie said under her breath, and both the boys laughed.

"Martin, you'll have to take the family home, then come back for me in about an hour," Thurman said. "Father Percy wants to have a vestry meeting."

"A vestry meeting? Whatever for? Didn't you just have one two weeks ago?" Nancy asked.

"Yes, but there's a bad leak in the roof of the rectory and we have to authorize the repair."

"Oh, dear," Nancy said. "I have a roast in the oven. I can't keep it in much longer, it will overcook and dry out."

"You go ahead and start dinner without me," Thurman said. "I don't want to ruin your roast."

"No," Nancy said. "We'll hold dinner for you. This is Sunday, and a family should eat together on Sunday."

"I'll be dead of starvation in an hour," Dottie said. "The rest of you'll have to go on without me."

"We will," Charles said. "But we'll say a prayer to your memory."

"Mom," Martin said. "I invited Yolinda to have dinner with us today. I hope that's all right."

"Of course it's all right," Nancy said. "Yolinda is a very sweet girl and she's welcome in our home anytime, you know that."

"Why is it that Martin can invite Yolinda anytime, but I can't invite Jim?" Dottie pouted.

"Because Martin is older than you are," Nancy said. "Besides, it isn't proper for a girl to invite a boy. Martin, if you are going to go get Yolinda, perhaps you'd better take us home now so you can get on over there."

"Mom, I probably won't be back until it's time to pick up Dad," Martin said. "We have some studying to do, and we have to plan our afternoon."

"You mean you have some smooching to do, don't you?" Dottie teased.

"Dottie!" Nancy scolded.

Martin pulled the bell rope beside the front door of the Semmes' house, and he could hear the bell echoing from inside. A moment later he heard footsteps, then the door opened and he saw Yolinda standing there, smiling up at him.

"You got over here fast," she said. "We just got back from church. Come on in, I'll be ready in a moment."

"Okay," Martin said, stepping inside the door. He looked into the living room and saw Professor Semmes reading the newspaper. "Good morning, sir."

Professor Semmes looked around the paper and saw that Martin was dressed in a suit and tie.

"I see you're wearing a suit," he said. "Did you go to church this morning?"

"Yes, sir."

"Have you folks learned your Latin yet?"

"I beg your pardon?"

"Pay no attention to him," Mrs. Semmes said, coming into the hallway from the kitchen. She was wearing an apron, and smelled of baked bread. "He says Episcopalians are nothing more than

Roman Catholics who can't speak Latin. He was just joking with you."

"How's your knee?" Professon Semmes asked, folding the paper and putting it aside.

"It feels pretty good," Martin said. "I wouldn't want to play a ball game on it right now." He smiled. "And, I'm glad I don't have to."

"It's a shame about the Thanksgiving day game. That tackle they had, what was his name?"

"Phillips, sir. Brad Phillips."

"Phillips, yes. He hit you pretty hard there once, didn't he?"

Martin laughed. "He hit me hard several times," he said. "No matter which way I turned he was in front of me. I'm glad I won't be running into him again."

"I'm ready," Yolinda said, coming down the stairs just then. Yolinda had dark brown, almost black hair which fell in waves around a pretty, heart-shaped face. Her eyes were brown and flashing, and her complexion was dark and lovely. She was high-bosomed and slim-hipped, but with enough of a pinch in at the waist to give her a curvaceous figure.

"You two have a nice time," Professor Semmes said, picking his paper back up as they left the house.

"We don't have to be there for an hour," Martin said as he backed out of the driveway. "Dad's at a vestry meeting. We'll pick him up then, and go home."

"What are we going to do for an hour?" Yolinda asked.

Martin looked at her and smiled. "Guess?"

"Martin, no," Yolinda said. "You know what will happen. You'll wind up getting all frustrated, and upset, and just plain angry. Then you'll pout the rest of the day and—"

"Hold it," Martin said. "Look, all we have is an hour, not even that now. You know I'm not going to try and get you to do anything in an hour, now, don't you?"

"Well," Yolinda said, weakening a little. "I don't know. You know how you are."

"Listen, I cross my heart. All we're going to do is sit there and look at the river and listen to the radio. Nothing else, I promise."

"Nothing?" Yolinda said.

"Nothing."

Yolinda smiled coquettishly. "That's liable to get pretty boring, isn't it? I mean if we do nothing at all."

"Well, maybe we'll do something," Martin said. "A little something."

Martin stopped the car on a bluff that overlooked the river and he reached down to turn on the radio.

"No, not yet," Yolinda said, stopping his hand before it reached the dial. "Let's just sit here and listen to the river for a while. Roll the window down."

"You'll get cold."

"You can keep me warm," Yolinda said.

"Good idea," Martin agreed with a big grin. He turned the window crank until the window was down, then he put his arm around Yolinda and pulled her against him.

"Listen," Yolinda said quietly.

Outside, they could hear the muted, undying whisper of the river as it rolled south majestically.

"I love that sound," she said.

"And I love you," Martin said. He put his hand

to her cheek and turned her face so that her lips were brought up to his, then he kissed her, gently at first, then deeper, and deeper still, tasting the cherry taste of her lipstick, the slight mint of her toothpaste, and, most exciting of all, the unique taste which was just her.

Yolinda had never gone all the way with Martin, but she had allowed him several liberties with his hands, and Martin believed he had never petted with a more exciting woman. His hand went under her blouse and lay against her skin, so smooth and incredibly hot, despite the open window. Yolinda didn't offer any resistance as his hand moved up, then under the bra where it cupped the warm mound of flesh, tipped by a straining nipple, and pulsating with life and with desire, as raw-edged and hungry as Martin's own.

"Martin, please," Yolinda managed to say, though her voice betrayed her desire as surely as her breathing and the temperature of her skin. "Please, we can't do this."

"I love you, Yolinda," Martin said. "I want you. I need you." Martin's hand came out from under the bra, and moved back along the burning skin until it slipped under her panties and then through the exciting tangle of hair to the hot, moist center. He felt Yolinda's body jerk once, as if she had felt an electric shock when his finger came in contact with the slickened little piece of flesh which hid itself in the creamy folds of her womanhood.

"No," Yolinda whimpered. "No, Martin, please, we mustn't, we can't, don't do this," she was almost crying. She twisted away from him, away from the hand and the finger which was causing her to melt like so much hot wax. She turned on the radio. "Let's listen to some music," she said. "Martin, if you love me . . ."

Martin sighed, then pulled his hand away and leaned back in his seat.

"I'm sorry, Martin," Yolinda said. "Really, I'm sorry. But I just can't . . . we shouldn't,"

"I know, I know," Martin said. He put his arm around her and pulled her to him. "Listen, I'm the one who should be sorry. I promised you nothing like this would happen and then I . . . but . . . damnit, Yolinda, I love you, and I want you, and I've never wanted anything in my life like I want you."

"I love you too," Yolinda said. "But please, can't we wait? At least until after we graduate. That's not much longer."

"It's a lifetime," Martin said. "It's like two lifetimes."

". . . . *Hickham Field*," the radio said, just warming up. *"Civilian casualties in Honolulu are also said to be high, as the planes bombed that city indiscriminately. Wait, this just in . . ."*

"That's not music," Yolinda said, reaching for the dial.

"Hold it," Martin said, reaching down to stop her hand. "Hold it, what is this? Listen to this."

"It has now been confirmed," the radio announcer said. *"It has been confirmed, that the airplanes which bombed the United States Naval base at Pearl Harbor, and the United States Army at Schofield Barracks and Hickman Field, were Japanese carrier launched planes. Even as Japan had their peace envoys in Washington, D.C., they were launching an attack against the American territory of Hawaii."*

"Hawaii?" Martin said. "My God, Hawaii has been bombed! The Japanese have bombed Hawaii!"

"What?" Yolinda said. "I don't understand. Why would they do that?"

"Why?" Martin said. "Because they are a bunch of yellow-bellied cowards, that's why! Those dirty, sneaking. . . . they've attacked the United States of America! This is war, Yolinda! Do you realize that? We're going to war! There's no way out of it now."

"Martin, no," Yolinda said. "Oh, my God, what if . . . what if you have to go?"

"Have to go? Honey, there's no way anyone is going to keep me out of this one. I'm going."

Martin started the car, then backed out of the parking place and started back down the bluff toward the street. "It's not a whole hour yet, but Dad is just going to have to leave early. Once they hear this news, they'll probably break up the meeting anyway."

Martin drove quickly through the streets of the town. The town was strangely quiet, even for a Sunday. Finally he reached the church.

"Come in with me," he said, reaching for Yolinda's hand.

"No," she said, pulling back. "I don't want to barge in on anything."

"We're not barging in on anything," Martin said. "As soon as I tell them the news, that meeting is over and you know it. Besides, I want you to meet the man who is going to marry us."

"Marry us?" Yolinda said. "Martin, are you asking me to marry you?"

"Yes," he said. He took both her hands in his then, and looked at her with eyes which were open all the way to his soul. "Yes, Yolinda. I'm asking you to marry me. Will you marry me?"

"I . . . I. . . ." Yolinda started, then she laughed a little. "I don't know whether to laugh or cry."

"Do neither, or both if you wish," Martin said. "Just tell me that you'll marry me."

"When?" Yolinda asked.

"After I complete flight school."

"Flight school?" Yolinda asked, her face screwed up in an expression of confusion. "What do you mean, flight school? Flight school where?"

"In the Army Air Corps," Martin said. "They won't take married men for the cadet course, but we can get married just as soon as I graduate and receive my wings. I'm going into the Air Corps, Yolinda. I'm going to be a pilot. They'll be needing lots of pilots now."

"But this is so sudden," Yolinda said. "The Air Corps, getting married . . . it's all so sudden."

"The war was sudden," Martin said. "Look, I didn't know the Japs were going to bomb Hawaii. Hell, nobody did, so we weren't able to make any plans. Believe me, there are probably thousands of men and women just like us, right this moment, all across this country, having to make the same major decisions. Now honey, I've made all the decisions but one, and I can't make that one. You'll have to make it. Will you marry me, or won't you?"

"I'll marry you, Martin," Yolinda said. She went into his arms. "I'll marry you."

They were standing that way, embracing each other, when the front doors to the church opened and Father Percy, Thurman Holt, and the other men of the vestry came outside.

"I'll think you'll see that we made the right decision," one of the vestrymen was saying. "It's better to put on a whole new roof now, than to start a series of fixups, which will only have to be replaced someday anyway."

"I suppose you are right," Father Percy said. "It's just that I hate to spend so much money right now."

"This is a little public for that sort of thing, isn't it?" Thurman said, as they approached Martin and Yolinda.

"I suppose it is, Dad," Martin said. "But you'll understand when I tell you the news."

"What news?" Thurman asked. He looked at the two young people, and Martin could tell by the look in his face that he was expecting to be told that they were engaged. Well, he would tell him that, but not until he told him the other, the news that was shaking the world right now.

"The Japs have bombed Pearl Harbor, Dad," Martin said. "We're at war."

"What? What's that you say?" one of the vestrymen asked.

"I said the Japs have bombed Pearl Harbor. They bombed it this morning while we were in church. While the whole world was in church, or asleep, or something."

"Where is Pearl Harbor?" another vestryman asked.

"It's a U.S. Navy Base in Hawaii," Thurman said. "It's on the island of Oahu, near Honolulu. I visited it once, years ago. It's a beautiful, beautiful place. And you say the Japanese bombed it? But how? Pearl Harbor is in the middle of the Pacific Ocean. There's no airplane in the world that can carry bombs that far and return."

"They came from aircraft carriers," Martin said. "Come on, listen to it. It's all over the radio."

Thurman opened the door to the car and turned

on the radio. He left the door open and the others gathered around to listen as well. There was absolute silence until the tubes warmed up and the radio came on.

"*. . . .unconfirmed reports say that the Battleship Arizona has been badly hit, with heavy loss of life. Several other ships have also been heavily damaged, though the identity of the ships and the extent of damage is not now known. Sources close to the White House say they expect the President will ask Congress for a Declaration of War, possibly as early as tomorrow. And now, repeating, at 7:55 this morning, Honolulu time, carrier based Japanese airplanes bombed and strafed United States Army and Navy bases on the island of Oahu, in the Hawaiian Islands. There has been a heavy loss of life, both among the American military and the Hawaiian civilians. We are informed that the United States military reacted quickly, and shot down several of the invaders, but not before the Japanese had succeeded in their sneak attack. The entire island has been put on alert for possible landings by the Japanese, and the West Coast has been alerted for a possible air, land or sea attack within the next 24 hours. San Francisco, Los Angeles, San Diego, and Seattle are under martial law at this time.*"

"How could this have happened?" one of the vestrymen asked. "My God, didn't we have anyone awake out there?"

"Does your mother know yet?" Thurman asked.

"No," Martin said. "That is, I don't know if she knows or not. Yolinda and I just heard it on the car radio."

"We'd better go to her," he said, pulling the door shut.

The others went to their own cars then, most

too stunned to say anything. Thurman was nearly halfway home before Martin spoke again.

"I'm going in, Dad," he said quietly.

"I imagine a good number of you will be going in," he said. "You'll probably be drafted as soon as you graduate."

"I'm not going to wait for the draft," Martin said. He took a deep breath. "I'm not even going to wait for graduation. I'm going in now, tomorrow."

Thurman looked over at his son and started to say something, then he just sighed and looked straight ahead. "I can't make your decisions for you," he said.

"I've decided to go into the Air Corps. I'll go to flight school just as soon as I can, and after I finish flight school and have my commission and my wings, Yolinda and I are going to get married."

"You're asking an awful lot of her, aren't you?" Thurman said.

"What do you mean?"

"You are asking her to marry you, then stay at home while you go off to fight. And you have to face it, son. You may not come back."

"No, don't say that, please," Yolinda said, gasping quickly.

"It has to be faced, girl."

"He's right," Martin said. "Yolinda, I won't hold you to your promise of a while ago. There is a chance that I won't come back. I have no right to make you go through that."

"Silly," Yolinda said softly. "Do you think it would make any difference whether we were married or not? Darling, I will be thinking of you every moment of the night and day for as long as you are gone whether we are married or not. If . . . if you don't come back, I shall be as crushed by it whether we are married or not. At least, this way, we'll have our marriage to cling to. Don't you back out on me now, Martin Holt. I won't hear of it."

"I won't back out," Martin said, putting his arms around her. "I promise, I won't back out now.'

4

I've never liked train stations," Nancy said. She wiped her eyes with a handkerchief. "Now I know why."

The Holt family was sitting on the hard wooden benches of the Mount Eagle train station. It was three-fifteen in the morning, and outside, snow was falling. A pot-bellied coal stove roared cheerily in the middle of the waiting room, and as the Holts were the only ones in the waiting room, they had chosen the seats nearest the warmth.

Martin was sitting on the bench next to his mother, and Thurman was on the other side. Charles was at the far end of the bench, with his legs stretched out and his hands thrust into his pockets. Dottie was looking through the window at the glowing, green light which stood beside the silent railroad tracks.

"I wish I could have gotten a train at a decent hour," Martin said. "But I would have had to leave yesterday morning at eleven in order to make the right connections. This way, I at least got one extra day before I had to go."

"And we had Christmas and New Year's together," Thurman said. "Don't forget that. There were many families who weren't together this Christmas."

"I wonder," Nancy said. "Will we ever have another Christmas together?" She began to cry again, and Martin comforted her.

"Of course we will, Mom," he said.

"The light just changed to red," Dottie said. She came back from the window and sat next to Martin, who put his arm around her. "That means the train is coming, doesn't it?"

"I guess so," Martin said.

The door to the waiting room opened, and a man, wearing a coat, gloves, and stocking cap, stomped his feet on the floor, leaving dirty little pieces of snow. "She's about two miles out now," he said. "The one brown suitcase was all the baggage?"

"Yes," Martin said. "I guess they'll be giving me most of what I need, once I get to Kelly Field."

"Kelly," Nancy said disgustedly. "Named after some Irish Catholic, no doubt."

"We mustn't be bigoted, Mother," Martin said, smiling, and squeezing her with his arm.

"It's too bad Yolinda couldn't have come this morning," Dottie said.

"We said our good-byes last night," Martin replied. He kissed his sister on the cheek. "Besides, if Yolinda had come, I couldn't be holding you like this now, could I?"

"I suppose not," Dottie said. "But believe me, when Jim leaves, I won't let him come down to the railroad station all by himself in the middle of the night, while I'm home warm in bed."

"Dear, I wish you would quit talking about Jim as if there were something between you two," Nancy said. "You are still a school girl, and you obviously have a school girl crush. It is not good for you to take it so seriously. Perhaps you should stop seeing him for a while."

The sound of the approaching train whistle reached them then, and Charles stood up and looked through the window toward the track. "Here it is," he said quietly, though it wasn't necessary for him to make the observation.

The windows of the station began to rattle, and then the very floors of the station house began to shake. They could hear the train quite clearly now, not just the whistle, but the rush of steam, and the roar of steel, rolling on steel. The dark outside the windows was suddenly bathed in a bright light, and the falling snow glistened like diamonds in the beam of the headlight. Then the engine roared by, its giant wheels pounding with such force that everything in the building, including the people, felt its power.

The fireman was looking toward the station as the engine rolled by, backlighted by an orange glow which could have been the fire, or the cab lights. The coal tender was next, shining black in the reflected lights from the platform, then the baggage car, then the passenger cars. There was not one light showing through the first two passenger cars, but from the third car on, lights shined from within, and as Martin and the others moved onto the platform, they could see the passengers inside. Some had their heads back and their eyes closed, while others rested their chins on their hands and stared tiredly through the window at this way-station in their journey.

The conductor stepped down from one of the cars and put a boarding stool on the snow covered platform.

"Careful of the snow now," he said solicitously, as Martin and the others walked toward the train.

"Just one passenger, Elmer," the station attendant said. The attendant had Martin's suitcase in his hand, and he started toward the baggage car. The door to the baggage car slid open, and the suitcase was handed up, then the door slid closed.

A hiss of steam escaped from beneath one of the cars, purpled in the station light, then drifted away.

"Martin, you will write?" Nancy said.

"Of course I will," Martin said, and he hugged his mother for a long moment, then hugged Dottie, who had also started to cry. "I thought you weren't going to cry," he scolded.

"I can't help it," Dottie said.

Martin kissed each eye, as if kissing away her tears, then he saw Charles, and he reached out to take Charles's hand. "At least you aren't crying," he said.

"Hey, what do you mean?" Charles said. "Look, I'm glad for the opportunity to be the big brother around here. I'm taking over your territory, see," he said, effecting a tough guy accent like Humphrey Bogart.

Martin took his father's hand, and the two men stood for a long moment, looking at each other without speaking.

"I've no words of wisdom for you, son," Thurman finally said. "Only that we love you and we'll miss you, and we pray that you come back safely to us."

"I will, Dad," Martin said. "I promise, I will."

"You need to get aboard, son," the conductor said. He had recognized a soldier going off to war, and his tone, though insistent, was gentle.

Martin turned away from the others and went quickly to the step, then up into the car. From the platform they could see him through the windows as he walked to the middle of the car, finally selecting a seat on the other side.

The train gave two quick blasts of its whistle, then started away. The puffs of steam were loud, and the echoes returned from the nearby bluff. The cars jerked, then jerked again, and finally began rolling out, first at the pace of a swift walk, then a brisk sprint, until finally the last car whipped by swiftly, and the green and red lanterns hanging on the back of the rear car moved up the track quickly, until they dimmed, and disappeared in the swirling snow.

They heard one last mournful whistle as the engine approached the crossing of highway 51, nearly half a mile away, and then the train was gone, almost as if it had never been there. Above and behind them there was a buzz and a click, and the semaphore light which had been shining red turned to green, so that the snowbanks on either side of the track glowed in a soft, emerald hue.

Thurman felt a lump in his throat, and he fought hard to swallow it. He was not a man given to showing his emotions, and now, with his family gathered about him, he certainly had no intention of breaking down. And yet, the stinging in his eyes and the hurting in his throat could easily give way to tears if he let it. He was thankful for the cold weather, because that helped him keep it all in.

"Let's go," he said quietly, and he started across the platform toward the car before anyone could speak to him or look at him.

The windshield and windows of the car had

become covered with snow, and Thurman used his hat to brush the snow away.

"Thurman, that's your good hat," Nancy scolded.

"Mom's all right, kids," Thurman said. "She's already stopped worrying about Martin and started worrying about my hat."

It was a joke, not a very funny one, but enough to enable everyone to laugh, even Nancy, and it relieved some of the gloom which hung over the entire family.

"I don't know about the rest of you," Dottie said as she shivered in the back seat of the Buick. "But I, for one, am getting back into bed as soon as we get home."

"Would you like me to cook some breakfast?" Nancy asked Thurman.

"No," he said. "No, there's no reason to stay up, is there?"

"I guess not. It's just that . . . well, with Martin awake, I feel . . ."

"Mom, Martin's asleep already, I can promise you that," Charles said. "He can sleep anywhere and anytime."

"That's the truth," Thurman said laughing. "Do you remember the time I took you boys duck-hunting down near Cairo, and we put Martin over on the corn blind, and all the ducks came to him and we kept wondering why he wasn't shooting?"

"Yes," Charles laughed. "And then you sent me over there to see what was wrong and he was sound asleep."

"And do you remember . . ." Dottie said, and she told another story, then even Nancy got into the scheme of things and told her own, "remember when" story, so that by the time they arrived back at the house, they were all laughing.

It was nearly half an hour before the bathroom had been used for the last time and all the lights were out and all the doors closed to the bedrooms. Thurman was in bed, feeling the delicious warmth of cover in winter, and he stuck his arm under Nancy's pillow then moved it, so that she came to him with her head on his shoulder. He could feel her body against his, covered by the long silk nightgown she wore. Nancy was 44 years-old, and she wore the same size dress now that she had worn when they were married. Her breasts had never been too large, which had been decidedly to her advantage during the '20s, when jazz-age fashion flattened the bosom. She had worried about it during the '30s when sweaters and full figures became the fashion. Now, however, her small breasts had become an asset again, because they had not broken down and sagged with age.

Thurman could feel the warmth of her breasts, and the contrasting textures of her pelvis as she lay against him; the sharpness of the pelvic bone, the softness of the flesh, and the cushion of hair, through the silk.

Thurman turned toward her then and kissed her deeply, then, slowly, bunched the nightgown up in his hands, lifting it so that her flesh was against his flesh and there, in the early morning darkness, they made love.

Thurman rolled the paper out of his typewriter, and read through the editorial he was running in the next day's paper.

Last week, President Roosevelt signed an order authorizing the evacuation of all Japanese-Americans living on the West Coast. Mr.

James Omura, representing Japanese-Americans before a Senate sub-committee, asked the question, "Has the Gestapo come to America?"

Mr. Omura had every right to ask that question, and those people whose lives are being disrupted, whose property is being confiscated, and whose every freedom is being denied, have every right to feel oppressed. We are now engaged in a great World War, fighting, we say, for our basic freedoms. But I would ask every American Citizen, what freedom is more basic than the right not to be penned up in prison?

You may counter by saying that these American citizens have not been sent away to prison, but rather to 'Assembly Centers', and 'Relocation Camps'. But I say to you that any American citizen (and why should we call them Japanese-Americans, any more than we say German-Americans, or English-Americans?) who is relocated against his will has had his basic freedom denied.

These are troubled times, I'll admit. It is not an easy thing to send sons off to war. I know this, because I have sent my own son to war. He is now in training to become a pilot in the Army Air Corps. I am proud of Martin, as I am proud of all America's sons who are in uniform. But I say that we should deport ourselves as a country in order to preserve the dignity of all our citizens, and act in a way that will enable our fighting sons to be proud of us.

Let us not oppress these innocent people!

"Charles," he called. "Set this for tomorrow's paper, would you?"

"Sure, Dad," Charles said, taking the editorial. He glanced at it as he started toward the linotype machine, then he stopped and read it through in its entirety.

"You're going to get some flak over this one," he said.

"I know," Thurman said. "It was being discussed in the barbershop this morning, and I was amazed at how many in there agreed with the policy."

"How many?"

"All of them," Thurman said, smiling sheepishly.

Charles chuckled. "No one can accuse you of taking the easy way out," he said.

"What do *you* think about it?"

"I think it's a great editorial," Charles said. "It gets right to the point, and it—"

"No," Thurman said. "I mean what do you think about the fact that our government is doing this to the Japanese-Americans who live out there?"

"I think it's wrong," Charles said. "I think it's a few prejudiced people, playing on the fears of many, to bring this about, and I am sorry to see that the President has been taken in by it."

"Well," Thurman said. "I'm glad to see that I have support in my own house at least."

"But you didn't go far enough," Charles said.

"I didn't? What do you mean?"

"What about the colored?"

"The colored? What about them?"

"Dad, do you realize that a colored person who doesn't know someone can't even get something to eat in this town? If a troop train of colored soldiers stopped down at the station, they would all starve to death."

"Oh, I doubt that," Thurman said easily.

"Do you? Didn't you read about those Italian prisoners who were brought to the United States, and who were traveling out to a prison camp in the west on the same train as some colored soldiers?"

"No," Thurman said. "I mean, I knew that we had accepted some prisoners from the British, but I didn't read the story."

"The prisoners were on the same train as colored American troops. The train stopped in a small town, about like Mount Eagle, and the prisoners were taken into the station restaurant where they were fed a meal."

"Well, they do have to eat, you know, even if they are enemy prisoners."

"That's the point," Charles said. "Our colored troops have to eat too, but the restaurant wouldn't feed them. They wouldn't even close down for an hour or so to feed them. Do you know what the colored troops had to eat?"

"No."

"Apples," Charles said. "The army bought a truckload of apples from a farmer and passed apples out to the colored soldiers, while the Italian prisoners of war sat in the station restaurant and had a hot meal."

"That's wrong," Thurman said. "The army should have made some arrangements for them to eat."

"That needs to be changed," Charles said. "That's as great an injustice as this is." Charles held up the editorial.

"Perhaps you're right, son," Thurman said. "Perhaps you're right. But we can't change all the ills of the world in one fell swoop. The colored people have had two hundred years of oppression. It would take a mighty social upheaval to reverse that trend. It will come. I have every confidence that it will come, even within my lifetime. But this other thing, can't you see? We are embarking right now down a wrong road. We are just now starting a policy which is evil in tone and tint. Now is the time to stop this, while it is still new and can be killed at birth. Not two hundred years from now."

"I guess you're right," Charles said. He smiled. "Perhaps I'm a Don Quixote."

"It's all right to be a Don Quixote," Thurman said. "If there were no Don Quixotes, this world would be over-run with windmills."

"There's Mom," Charles said.

Thurman looked toward the door and saw Nancy coming in. She was wearing the latest "military cut" dress, with a feathered pillbox hat, and she was moving quickly, in that way she affected when she had a million things to do.

"You look lovely, Nancy," Thurman said.

"Thank you," she said, almost breathlessly. "I have to go right back out. You can't *believe* all the things I have to do this afternoon. The garden club has been debating for over a month now about whether or not we should have our annual spring dogwood festival—"

"Well, of course you should have it," Thurman interrupted. "Why shouldn't you?"

"Well, the war and all," Nancy said. "After all, I suppose a case could be made against engaging in frivolity during such a time."

"Nonsense," Thurman said. "The whole town turns out for the dogwood festival. I can't think of any better time to have it. There is such a thing as keeping up morale on the home front too, you know."

"That's what I said," Nancy said "And finally, this afternoon, we had a vote and we will have the dogwood festival."

"That's wonderful," Thurman said.

"And I have been elected chairwoman," she said proudly. "They said that since I had argued so eloquently on its behalf, that it would only be fitting for me to have the job."

"My dear, I've never been prouder of you," Thurman said.

"I've always wanted to be chairwoman, at least once," Nancy said. "I have so many ideas I want to put into effect. I just wish that, well, I just wish it could have been under different circumstances."

"No," Thurman said, and he walked over to his wife and kissed her. "This is the best possible time for you. The dogwood festival never needed you like it will need you this year. You will make the festival something people will remember for years, I know you will."

Nancy smiled broadly at his compliment, and it looked as if she might even blush. She was positively radiant, and for a moment, she wasn't the 44-year-old mother of three grown children at all. She was the 19-year-old girl Thurman had first seen selling chrysanthemums outside the gates of the Standhope College football field, long before Shaky Jake stadium was built.

"Why . . . why are you looking at me like that?" Nancy asked, smiling curiously at him and brushing a strand of hair back from her forehead. "What is it?"

"Have I ever told you that I think you are beautiful?" Thurman asked. "I like the emerald fire in your eyes, and the touch of autumn in your hair."

"My hair is turning gray," Nancy said.

"No, it isn't," Thurman said. "It's still like it was the night of the homecoming dance."

"You're an old fool," Nancy said, but she said it in such a way that let him know that she was pleased with his comment. "But you're my fool," she added, kissing him before she left.

5

Nancy stood in the door between the dining room and the living room, and looked at the chairs she had arranged in rows for the meeting. She crossed her arms, then raised one finger to her jaw, crooked her head, and looked at them critically. Behind her, Flora was busily putting cookies, canapes and small pastries on the table, placing them on the silver trays, and arranging the trays in such a way as to show off the lace tablecloth to its prettiest advantage.

"I don't know, Flora, what do you think?" Nancy asked. "Do you think I should leave these chairs like this, or should I put them around the edge of the room?"

"Yes'm, you could put them around the edge of the room," Flora said. "That would be nice."

"And yet, this is a working meeting," Nancy said. "I'm sure that if I leave the chairs like this, the ladies will know that I mean business."

"Yes'm, that's true all right," Flora said. She hadn't even looked toward the living room, and in fact, knew that her employer didn't really want an answer, but was just using her presence as an excuse to think out loud.

"I think I'll leave them the way they are," Nancy finally decided.

"Yes'm, I think that's best," Flora said. Flora stepped back and looked at the table. The center-piece was a three-tiered silver tray, laden with colorful cookies and pastries. To each side of the centerpiece there were long, rectangular silver trays laden with canapes, while scattered around the trays were silver plates of various sizes and designs bearing mints and jellied fruits. On the sideboard a large silver punchbowl sat, holding the pink lemonade, awaiting the ice mold which would be put in at the last moment.

Nancy turned and saw the table and smiled at Flora.

"You have been such a dear, Flora. I just don't know what I would have done without you. Every-thing looks so lovely."

"Miz Holt, when they leave here, they gonna know they was in a fine home," Flora said, then she started back into the kitchen.

It is a fine home, Nancy thought. One might even say a gracious home, and she felt a sense of pride that she had helped make it so. They had bought the house shortly after Martin was born. It was much bigger than they needed then, and as things turned out, much bigger than they ever would need. But Thurman had plans for a large family . . . at least six children, he used to say, and he wanted the house so they would be ready.

There were to be no more children after Dottie was born. It had been an extremely difficult birth, and there were complications. As a result of the complications, the doctors said, she would no longer be able to bear children.

For quite some time after Dottie's birth, Nancy had a feeling of having failed Thurman in some way. She felt as if she were somehow less than whole, and when Thurman would try to come to her in the middle of the night, she would often beg off, claiming a headache, or tiredness, or some other malady. Sex without the possibility of procreation was somehow wrong, she thought, even though she and Thurman were man and wife.

Divorce was a very rare thing then, especially if children were involved, so there was very little chance of Thurman ever divorcing Nancy as a result of her abandonment, but Thurman eventually found the comfort he needed in the arms of another woman. Thurman had accepted the fact that Nancy would never again share her bed with him, and he was adjusting to it. Ironically, it was the other woman who saved the marriage.

Her name was Leah Davis, and she was a school teacher. There had been more to it than a mere, casual affair, at least as far as Leah was concerned; she was hopelessly in love with Thurman. Leah soon discovered that though Thurman cared for her, and respected her, was still in love with his wife. She also discovered why, if he was in love with his wife, he would carry on an affair with her. When she discovered that she had no hope of his ever divorcing Nancy and marrying her, she applied for a position in another town. Before she left Mount Eagle, however, she paid a surprise visit to Nancy.

At first, Nancy pretended that it was a casual visit, and she smiled and gossiped as if that was all there was to it. Then came the bombshell.

"Let's quit trying to fool each other, shall we, Nancy?" Leah said, setting the teacup down and smiling sweetly at her.

"Fool each other?" Nancy replied. "Why, whatever could you be talking about?"

"You know perfectly well what I'm talking about."

"No, really, I—"

"Then you are even a bigger fool than I thought," Leah said. "And I thought you were the biggest fool I've ever known."

Nancy looked at the floor and tried hard to keep the tears from welling up in her eyes, but she couldn't. They pooled over, then spilled down her cheeks.

"You know what I'm talking about, don't you?" Leah asked quietly.

"My husband has been . . . visiting . . . you, hasn't he?" Nancy said.

"Visiting me? Nancy, he's been sleeping with me."

Nancy raised a napkin to her eyes and dabbed at them.

"Is he . . . is he going to divorce me?" Nancy wanted to know.

"No," Leah said. Leah waited for a moment, as if she expected Nancy to reply, and when she didn't, Leah went on. "Lord knows, he should divorce you. He has every right to. But he won't. And do you know why?"

"The children," Nancy said quietly.

"No," Leah said. "He won't divorce you because he loves you. Can you believe that? After what you've done to him? He still loves you."

"I . . . I haven't done anything," Nancy said.

"That's just it," Leah replied. "When is the last time you let your husband come to you the way a husband should come to his wife? When is the last time you were intimate?"

"That . . . that's none of your business," Nancy said hotly.

Leah chuckled, a quiet, knowing chuckle. "That's where you're wrong, dear. It became my business. Thurman came looking in my bed for what he couldn't find in yours. And I gave it to him, and I would have gone on giving it to him forever if I thought there was ever any chance of his leaving you for me. But I know there's no chance. Oh, there's a chance he'll leave you, all right. In fact, there's more than a chance. I would say that the odds are he will leave you, but not until it's too late for me. What I can't understand is, if you don't love him anymore, why don't you tell him? Why don't you let him go in peace? Why are you slowly killing him by breaking his heart, little piece by little piece?"

"But I do love him," Nancy insisted. "I love him very much."

"Oh? All I can say is you have a strange way of showing it. If you really loved him, you wouldn't make him feel like some . . . unclean thing . . . at night."

"You don't understand," Nancy said. "I can't have any more children, the doctor—"

"My Lord, Nancy, are you so stupid that you think there is nothing left, just because you can't have children? You already have three beautiful children, now have each other. No two human beings can be closer than a man and woman during such moments of intimacy. Thurman lives in this house with you, and he is helping you raise your three children, but he has been closer to me than to you for the last year. Do you think that is right?"

"No," Nancy said.

"Then do something about it. Go to him tonight. Tell him that you love him, show him that you love him. Let him know that you will never turn him away again, and I swear to you, Mrs. Holt, you will be happy for the rest of your life."

Nancy didn't say anything for a long moment. She just sat there, quietly dabbing at her eyes.

"I have to be going," Leah said. "I'm catching a train this afternoon. Listen, Thurman has no idea that I came over here today. In fact, he has no idea that you even know or suspect about me. If you are smart, you'll never mention this visit to him, not ever. You'll just stop being a fool, and go to him before it is too late."

Nancy still didn't answer, so Leah stood up and started toward the door. "Yes," she said. "Well, I may have wasted my time here this afternoon, but I had to try. You see, even though he doesn't love me, I love Thurman, and I had to try and do something to save him. I hope you understand."

Leah put her hand on the door.

"Wait," Nancy called.

Leah stopped and looked around.

"I, uh," Nancy said, and again she dabbed at her eyes with the napkin. "I want to thank you. I know it was difficult for you to come over here."

"Difficult?" Leah said. "From my point of view, it was insane."

"Nevertheless," Nancy said. "I appreciate it."

That very night Nancy went to Thurman, approaching him as shyly and with as much trepidation as she had on their wedding night. Thurman was surprised, and happy, and so pleased by it that he didn't even notice how difficult it was for Nancy. But over a period of time Nancy finally overcame the personal difficulty she had encountered, until she was able, once again, to know the tenderness, the pure joy, of being a wife in fact as well as in name.

Nancy never mentioned Leah's name to Thurman, nor ever told him one word about the visit.

The doorbell rang, rousing Nancy from her thoughts, and as she heard Flora coming from the kitchen to answer it, she called out, "I'll get it."

Edna Semmes was at the front door. Edna was Yolinda's mother, and though she and Nancy had been friends for years, there was an even greater closeness between them now, with the announced engagement of their two children.

"I know I'm a little early," Edna said. "But I thought I would come over to see if there was anything I could do to help." Edna had the same dark hair and eyes that Yolinda had, though her hair was frosted with a great deal of gray. Nancy wished Edna would dye her hair with one of the new rinses which helped retard the gray, she just knew Edna would look better, but when she mentioned it once, Edna just said that people start to get gray in their forties and she wasn't going to worry about it.

"Well, there's nothing to do to get ready for the meeting, actually," Nancy said. "Flora has taken care of everything." Nancy held her arm out toward the dining room, and Edna walked in to look at the table.

"Oh, my, what a beautiful table," Edna said. "And the silver. That's your grandmother's silver, isn't it?"

"Yes," Nancy said proudly. "My grandmother lived in Jackson, Mississippi during the Civil War, and she had to take all the silver out and hide it when the soldiers came through. I wouldn't take anything in the world for it."

"I don't blame you. It is absolutely beautiful. Oh, by the way, did you hear about Corabeth Masters, and that Evans boy?"

"Corabeth? You mean Jean's daughter?"

"Yes. My dear, she eloped with Jerry Evans," Edna said.

"No, you don't say!"

"It is the gospel," Edna said, holding up her hand as if she were swearing an oath. "I heard it at the beauty parlor not fifteen minutes ago."

"But Corabeth is still in high school," Nancy said. "She's Dottie's age."

"I know, and of course they won't let her finish now. I understand the school board has already written a letter to Jean saying as much."

"Whatever possessed her to do such a thing?"

"Jerry Evans is in the Army, as you know, and he is home on furlough before he goes overseas. He came by the house and picked her up as if they were just going to a movie, and instead he took her down to Piggott, Arkansas, where they have a regular marriage factory. You know you can get married immediately in Arkansas and they say they do a regular business of it in Piggott. Poor Jean is simply heartbroken."

"I can well imagine she would be," Nancy said.

"I am so proud of Yolinda and Martin, and the sensible way they are doing things," Edna said. "Why, this gives us time to plan a fine church wedding and everything."

"You are being such a dear to let Father Percy

marry them in the Episcopal Church," Nancy said. "You don't know how much I appreciate that."

"Well, neither Arnold nor I have that strong a feeling about our own church. He feels, as do I, that one church is about as good as another, though he does enjoy teasing Thurman so about the "catholicism" of your church. And since Thurman is on the vestry, we felt it would only be fitting. What do you hear from Martin, by the way?"

"He has finished all of his basic training, and is starting on his flight training now," Nancy said. "It worries me to death, but I just have to live with it. There's nothing I can do about it."

"I admire the way you can divorce yourself from things you can't do anything about," Edna said. "Like that awful editorial Thurman wrote last week."

"The one about the Japanese being relocated?" Nancy asked.

"Yes. My, how his ears must be burning. I've heard people talking about that editorial all over town, and none of them—not one, mind you— agree with what he had to say."

"Thurman, and Charles, too, for that matter, have always been very sensitive to other people's suffering," Nancy said. "I'm sure it must be a very difficult thing for those poor people to be uprooted like that."

"A Jap is a Jap," Edna said. "Why, I heard that the Japs who lived in Honolulu actually lit large, burning arrows to point the way to the American ships, so the Jap planes could bomb them."

"You don't say," Nancy said, gasping and putting her hand to her mouth.

"Yes, it's the gospel. How else could they have managed to sink so many of our ships?"

"Well, I don't know," Nancy said. "I suppose people are upset with Thurman, but I try to never get involved with anything he writes." Nancy smiled. "I learned a long time ago that the editorial is his prerogative, and his alone. No one, not even I, has a right to interfere."

"Well, as I said, I admire your ability to divorce yourself from such things," Edna said. A car door closed outside, and both women looked through the door window. "Here come Millie and Sara. The others will be here soon. Oh, I'm so glad you are the chairwoman of the dogwood festival, I just know it's going to be wonderful."

"What do you mean the Japs lit large, burning arrows to point the way to the American ships?" Thurman asked, laughing.

"That's what Edna said," Nancy said, surprised that Thurman was laughing at her. "She swears it is true."

"Oh, *Edna* swears it is true?" Thurman said, and now he and Charles were both laughing. "And did they paint large signs in Japanese which said, 'these are ships' and put them on the ships?" he asked laughing.

"Well, I don't know," Nancy said. "And I don't understand why you two are laughing anyway. What is so funny?"

"Mom," Charles said. "Do you think the Japanese pilots really needed burning arrows to point the way to the ships? I mean, where else could they be except in the harbor? They sure wouldn't be in the sugarcane fields, would they?"

Nancy was perplexed for a moment, then suddenly she realized what they were laughing at and she joined them.

"I guess it is sort of silly at that, isn't it?" she said.

"No sillier than when she insisted that radio waves were changing the weather," Thurman said laughing.

"Or that President Roosevelt was going to declare himself king," Charles put in gleefully.

"I suppose Edna does come up with some rather strange ideas," Nancy agreed, laughing with them now. "But I like her, nevertheless."

"Well, it's a good thing you do," Thurman said. "After all, she is the mother of the girl who is going to be our daughter-in-law."

"Oh, that reminds me," Nancy said. "Corabeth Masters ran away and married Jerry Evans."

"Corabeth Masters? That's impossible—why, she's no older than Dottie," Thurman said. He laughed again. "Is this another one of Edna's 'gospels'?" and he held up his hand the way Edna did, anytime she insisted something was the "gospel".

"I don't know where Mom heard it, but it's true," Dottie said. Dottie had been just in the other room, working at a desk, tallying inches of advertising, and she came into the room with her family when she heard her mother talking about Corabeth.

"What do you know about it, dear?" Nancy asked.

"I know that Corabeth and Jerry went to Arkansas to get married," Dottie said. "They've had it planned for weeks, ever since they knew Jerry would be going overseas."

"How do you know all this?" Thurman asked.

"Because Corabeth told me," Dottie said.

"You mean you *knew* in advance, and you didn't *tell* anyone?" Thurman said, rather angrily.

"Who was I supposed to tell?"

"Well, her mother and father for starters," Thurman said.

"They would have stopped it."

"Of *course* they would have stopped it, that's the whole idea," Thurman said.

"Dad, I wouldn't do that," Dottie said. "Corabeth and Jerry have a right to get married if they—"

"A *right*?" Thurman exploded. "What do you mean they have a right? No one has a right to sneak off like a thief in the night without telling a soul."

"I don't agree with you," Dottie said. "This concerned Corabeth and Jerry and no one else."

"It concerned her parents," Thurman said. "Anyone will tell you that."

"Your father is right, dear," Nancy said. "Can't you just imagine how her poor mother and father must feel?"

"I would hope that they feel good about the fact that their daughter has a chance for some happiness before Jerry goes off to fight the war," Dottie said.

"That just shows how immature you are," Thurman said. "And God help me, Corabeth is your same age. Imagine, a child that immature, getting married. Charles, your sister has always listened to you, you tell her that Corabeth had no right to do what she did."

"I can't tell her that, Dad," Charles said quietly.

Thurman looked at Charles in quick anger. "What do you mean you can't tell her that?"

"I don't know all the circumstances," Charles said. "If Jerry is going off to fight the war, and if he and Corabeth are really in love, then who am I to say that they have no right? Who is anyone to say that they have no right?"

Thurman looked over at Nancy, and she could see the vein working in his temple. That vein always worked when he got angry, or upset, and she had learned long ago to be able to judge his moods by that distinguishing feature.

"They're your kids," he said disgustedly, throwing his arms up as if washing his hands of the whole thing. "Maybe you can talk some sense into them. I've got to go get the presses lined up. I sure wish Martin was here to do it for me, though the way things are going, he would probably side with his brother and sister."

Nancy watched Thurman push through the door then walk back into the press room. She looked over at Dottie, pouting defiantly, and at Charles, who had merely stated his own conviction, and she couldn't help but laugh. Her laughter, coming at such a tense moment, surprised Dottie and Charles, and they looked at her as if she had gone nuts.

"Why does he always say you are 'my' kids, when you do something which earns his disapproval?" she asked.

"That's Dad, Mom," Charles said, smiling now. "Generous to a fault, always giving credit where credit is due."

"He is a man who has strong opinions, and expresses those opinions in writing for all the world to see," Nancy said, "even when he knows he's running right into a hornets' nest. I suppose he can get used to his children having opinions contrary to his own. At any rate, Corabeth's marriage isn't our problem, and I see no reason why we should let it upset us, no matter how we feel about it. I say we call a truce, what do you say?"

"Agreed," Charles said. "Come on, Dottie, I need the lineage on today's edition. Get busy."

Charles and Dottie went back to their respective tasks, and the tension which had built up earlier passed on by. It did not escape Nancy's notice, however, that Dottie did not agree to the truce.

6

Charles sat in the window seat of his room, ostensibly editing his term paper, but in actuality looking out over the roofs of the sleeping town of Mount Eagle. His window was pushed all the way up to allow the soft, cooling breeze to drift through, and the scent of spring flowers perfumed the night velvet.

The dogwoods had been especially profuse this year, and the annual dogwood festival had been a smashing success, due in no small part to Nancy's efforts. She had promoted an art show in the park, despite everyone's objections to the idea. Art, they said, was to be enjoyed in a quiet gallery, not in a park full of screaming children. But the art was enjoyed—in fact, it was probably the most successful single feature in a very successful event. The lieutenant governor, their Congressman, and an Army general had all come, and a dozen bands participated in a patriotic music festival which lasted the entire day.

Charles had been particularly pleased for his mother, not only because she had finally gotten to do something that she had wanted to do for a long time, but also because while she was wrapped up in the planning and preparation, she had been able to get her mind off Martin. Charles had watched his mother's reaction everytime there was news on the radio or in the paper of an airplane crash somewhere. She would wilt, almost visibly, until she was certain that the crash didn't involve Martin.

At least she won't have to worry about me, Charles thought bitterly, and he thought of the doctor's report at his induction physical.

"A heart murmur," the doctor had said.

"A heart murmur? You mean I have something wrong with my heart?"

"As far as the Army is concerned you do," Doctor Presnell said. "The truth is, it's not anything to worry about really, but the Army won't take you if you have it. Son, you have a million dollar murmur there. There are thousands of men all over America who would give anything to have what you have. It's a golden ticket to 4F status."

"But I don't *want* 4F status!" Charles exploded. "Don't you understand?"

Doctor Presnell shook his head slowly. "Want it or not, you've got it," he said. "And there's nothing I can do to change it."

"Couldn't you overlook it?" Charles asked.

Dr. Presnell shook his head and smiled sadly. "Son, even if I did, it would be caught on the very first physical you had in the service, and then you would be discharged."

"It doesn't seem fair," Charles said.

Dr. Presnell put his hand solicitously on Charles' shoulder. "I know what you must be feeling now, Charles," he said. "Martin was the football player, you were the student trainer, he was the baseball player and you were the equipment manager, and now it's happening again."

"No," Charles said. "This is worse. At least I got to participate in football and baseball. I wasn't on the front lines, but I was useful. That's all I'm asking now. I know Martin will be flying and doing the actual fighting, but I at least want to be useful. There must be something I can do."

"Not in uniform, I'm afraid," Doctor Presnell said.

Charles had said nothing to his parents about the physical, but they found out about it as soon as the medical deferment came through the mail. Nancy was pleased about it, and she made no bones over it. "One son is enough for any family to be expected to send to the service," she said. Thurman had perceived Charles' disappointment, and came to his room that night, carrying a bottle of brandy and two snifters.

"Let's talk," Thurman said.

"All right, Dad," Charles replied. He moved a pile of books and papers off a chair so his father would have a place to sit, then he turned his desk chair around to face him. Thurman poured the brandy.

"Dad, that's your special brandy, the bottle that was bottled for Napoleon," Charles said. "Mom said the only time you had ever drunk from that bottle was at our christenings."

Thurman held the bottle up, and it caught the light and seemed to glow from within, as if it held captured fire. "I got this bottle in France, during the last war," he said. "It was in the cellar of a restaurant belonging to Monsieur Henri Garneau. Garneau had a son named Marcel, and Marcel had been captured by the Germans. They tried him for espionage, though of course the charge was ridiculous. Marcel was a French soldier, on a patrol behind the German lines when he was captured, but he had made the mistake of removing his officer's insignia. The Germans claimed he had removed his uniform, a technicality, of course, but one which they used to justify the death sentence."

Thurman poured a measured amount of brandy into each of the two snifters, then recorked the bottle and put it carefully on the window seat, away from any possible chance of accidental upsetting.

"My colonel found out about the upcoming execution, and he concocted a plan to rescue Marcel. You see, he had been having some difficulty with the sector commander, a French general, and he thought that such a move would put him in good with the French. He selected my lieutenant to lead the rescue patrol, and my lieutenant selected my sergeant to choose the men for the patrol. I was one of the men selected."

"What did you think about that?" Charles asked.

Thurman laughed softly. "Son, I was a private. I wasn't paid to think," he said. "Actually," he went on, "I had no idea what the patrol was all about. We were sent out on frequent patrols anyway, and in a strange way, we almost welcomed them as a way to get out of those trenches. We were beginning to think we were going to spend the rest of our lives in the trenches, and, of course, several men did." Thurman was quiet for a moment, thinking about those friends of his who had died in the trenches of France during the 1917–1918 War.

"Did you rescue Marcel?" Charles asked.

Thurman smiled. "Oh, yes, we rescued him all

right," he said. "It actually turned out to be quite an easy show. You see, our patrol discovered two German soldiers who were being sent to the temporary jail where Marcel was being held. They were carrying written orders to escort him back to the place he was to be executed. We discovered that fact when we went through their papers. I speak German, of course, so I was given the tunic of the sergeant, and another fellow was dressed as the private, and the two of us walked right into the jail and took Marcel away, as slick as a whistle." Thurman laughed. "The Germans who were guarding him never thought to question the authority of the orders we showed them. As it turned out, Marcel's father owned a restaurant very near, so we just dropped Marcel off there. He and his father were so pleased that they gave us each a bottle of the special brandy they had, leaving them with only one. Henri's grandfather had bottled the brandy especially for Napoleon, you see, when he had visited the village in 1792, and the family had saved the remaining bottles for over a century."

"Whatever happened to Marcel?" Charles asked.

Thurman chuckled. "I wrote a review of Ernest Hemingway's *The Sun Also Rises* when it was published some time ago, and in reading about the book, I saw that Hemingway claimed to have done some of the writing at the café of his friend, Marcel Garneau. That's quite a common French name, of course, but nevertheless, on impulse, I wrote to Marcel Garneau to see if it could be the same person, and it was. We exchanged a few letters, and we promised to get together at some future date, but, of course, we never have. With Paris under German control now, I've no idea what has become of Marcel, or even if he is still alive. It makes me sad, and angry with myself that I never went to France during the intervening years when I had the chance."

"That's a good story, Dad," Charles said. "That's a wonderful story. Why haven't you ever told it before?"

"The time had never been right before," Thurman said. "But I think it's right now. Just as I think it is right to drink some of this brandy now." He touched his goblet to Charles' goblet, and they both drank. Charles could taste the fire he had seen in the bottle earlier, like the controlled fire of the sun on the fruit which made the brandy.

"What are you going to do now?" Thurman asked. "Now that you can't go into the service?"

"I don't know," Charles said. He ran his hand through his hair. "I never really thought I would be that useful in the service anyway, not like Martin, I mean. But I hoped I would be able to do something."

"Would you mind a suggestion from your father?"

"I don't mind at all," Charles said.

"They've adjusted the curriculum at school. If you take the right classes this fall and summer, you can get your degree before school starts next fall."

"And then what?"

"America is going to need scientists and physicists," Thurman said. "Our industries are going to have to develop new airplanes and ships, more effective gunpowder, more efficient fuels, artificial rubbers, new metal alloys, and hundreds of other things that I don't even have the technical knowledge to think of. Charles, this war will be different from any war man has ever fought before. Cities are being bombed from the air . . . not military bases, mind you, but cities, full of civilians. It is a total war, even beyond the prior definition of the term. Everyone will be involved, whether they are in uniform or not, and it is only by marshaling all our military, technological, scientific, and moral strength, that we can entertain any hope of winning. You can be a part of that, Charles. You can contribute more than you ever dreamed, more than Martin, even, though, God help us, Martin might well give his last full measure. You do understand that, don't you?"

"Maybe I do," Charles said. "Maybe I do at that."

That conversation had taken place almost a month ago, and Charles had given a great deal of consideration to what his father told him. He had been granted permission to self-study for credit for many of his classes, and had enrolled in others, so that before the fall semester, he would have his B.S. degree. His post-graduate work would have to wait until after the war. He was anxious to begin work in a defense factory as soon as he could, and he had already prepared several resumés to be sent off when the time came.

Charles had one major paper to write, then little more than a series of exams to complete the adjusted curriculum which would lead to his graduation. His paper was for physics, and he had chosen as his subject *Gaseous Diffusion and Uranium Enrichment*. In the paper, he discussed the theory of explosive energy from nuclear fission.

> *Ever since Einstein's Special Theory of Relativity, published in 1905, which stated in the formula $E = MC^2$ that a small amount of mass could be changed into a tremendous amount of*

energy, scientists have been intrigued by the possibility of unleashing this energy. In accordance with the theory, and with no outside factors acting upon it, one pound of matter would release as much energy as ten thousand tons of TNT. Of course, such a complete transference of mass to energy is not possible in any case, and only partially possible, if the theory is proven, in certain materials, called fissionable materials.

Of these fissionable materials, the material deemed most promising is U235, one of the two isotopes of uranium. Unfortunately, U235 makes up only .7 of one percent of the natural state of uranium, and is so rare as to be impractical for use in fission energy. However, it may be possible to produce this material from the more readily accessible U238, through a system of gaseous diffusion.

Charles' paper went on to explain the method of changing uranium into gas, then forcing it through a series of filters which would be designed to trap the heavier U238 atoms of gas while allowing the lighter U235 atoms to pass on through and be collected.

Charles finished reading his paper, then closed the folder over it and set it on his desk by the clock. The clock said 1:30 A.M. He hadn't realized that it was so late, though he did know that the house had been quiet for some time. Now that he thought about it, his back and neck hurt a little from the strain of working so long.

Charles turned the lamp off, then looked out over the darkened town. He could see the river from here, though this was the only place in the house where one could see the river. It winked back at him, gathering the moonlight and scattering its silver through the night. Crickets were singing outside the window, and by the no longer used goldfish pond in the back corner of the yard, a frog called. Somewhere a dog barked, and way off in the distance he could hear a train.

"Excellent paper, Charles," Dr. Nunlee said as he handed it back to him. "An absolutely brilliant paper. I took the liberty of having it copied, and, with your permission, I should like to submit it for publication."

"No, I don't mind at all," Charles said. "In fact, I would like that very much."

"I'm going to try and have it published in the *American Journal of Physical Arts and Sciences*," Dr. Nunlee went on. "It will be quite a feather in the cap of old Standhope College if it is accepted. We've never had a paper published in such a prestigious journal."

"Well," Charles joked. "It's not quite like running for a touchdown against the University of Alabama, is it? But I'll do what I can for the old Orange and Black."

"I'll say it's not like running for a touchdown against Alabama. It's much, much better," Dr. Nunlee said. "You do realize the prestige of such an event, don't you?"

"Yes," Charles said. "I was only joking about the football thing. I would be thrilled if my paper were selected for publication. And I would be heartened to share that honor with Standhope College."

"Have you sent away any of your resumés?" Dr. Nunlee asked. "I know you were preparing them."

"Yes," Charles said. "I've sent a few out, though I haven't had any responses as yet."

"Charles, how would you feel about staying here?" Dr. Nunlee asked.

"Staying where, in Mount Eagle?" Charles asked. "Dr. Nunlee, the only two places I would be able to use any of my education here would be the condensed milk plant and the fertilizer factory. Besides, if I stayed here I would feel bound to continue to work on the newspaper, especially as Martin has gone into the Army now. And though I readily admit the necessity of a free pass, I don't see it as vital to the defense effort."

"I meant stay at Standhope College," Dr. Nunlee said. "Go on with your education, get a Masters and a Ph.D., and, while you are working toward that, help me in the science department."

"Dr. Nunlee," Charles said. He sat down, and let out a grunt which was half way between a sigh and an ironic laugh. "If it weren't for the war, I could think of no greater privilege than to stay here just under those circumstances. I consider it an honor even to be asked. But I feel that I must make a direct contribution in some way. I just must. I hope you understand that."

Dr. Nunlee nodded. "Yes," he admitted. "I can understand. I hoped I could convince you that training our young is a contribution, a very significant contribution."

"It is a significant contribution," Charles said. "And one that I readily recognize. But I want to have a more direct input into the war effort. That's why I must go."

"All I can say," Dr. Nunlee said, smiling, "is that some defense plant is going to get one fine man."

"Thanks," Charles said. "Thanks for your vote of confidence, and"—he smiled broadly and held up his paper—"thanks for the A."

"You earned both," Dr. Nunlee said.

Charles looked at his watch. "I've got to get back home," he said. "Dottie is graduating from high school tonight, and I'm sure she and Mom have a dozen things for me to do."

"Will Dottie be coming to school here next year?" Dr. Nunlee asked.

"I'm sure she will," Charles said. He laughed. "After all, this school has had Mom and Dad and Martin and me. It's a Holt family tradition by now. But the truth is, I think the family has breathed a collective sigh of relief that Dottie is graduating from high school."

"Oh?" Dr. Nunlee asked with raised eyebrows.

"Oh, don't misunderstand me," Charles said. "Dottie made outstanding grades, and never had a moment's trouble, it's just that she is such a vivacious girl, and eager to get on with life. Dottie moves to a different clock than the rest of us mere mortals. She makes 24 hours do the work of 30. I've never known anyone with such boundless energy, or such limited patience."

"I think all young people are like that today," Dr. Nunlee said.

Charles laughed. "I'm not exactly what you would call an 'old' people."

"Yes, you are," Dr. Nunlee said. "Now, don't get me wrong, I mean that as a compliment. You have the maturity, the depth of concentration, the judgement and the analytical acumen of someone much older. In the brains department, Charles, I would say that you went from 19 to 40. You aren't at all like your brother."

"I know," Charles said. "Lord knows, I've been told enough."

"Well this time, you are being told in a way

which leaves your brother wanting," Dr. Nunlee said. "And that's saying a lot, because Martin was a fine student, and a good, solid boy. But he was a boy, given to boys' games. Oh, I don't mean just his football skills and athletic prowess, I mean in student society. I got the impression that Martin never really thought beyond the next day. He was a good student and an asset to Standhope, because the outer reaches of his environment did not go beyond the campus gates. You, on the other hand, have always been aware of the world beyond. I hope you are not embarrassed by all this."

"A little," Charles admitted. He laughed self-consciously. "I'm not really used to such accolades. That's always been Martin's department."

"Get used to them, Charles. For Martin, they ended with last Thanksgiving day's football game. For you, the praises are just starting."

7

My father would *kill* me if he knew what I was using the car for," Liz said. "I mean, he would actually *kill* me."

"He doesn't ever have to find out," Dottie said. "Here, help me get this closed, will you?"

"You've got too much stuff in it." Liz said. "How are you going to ever get it closed?"

"Sit on it," Dottie said. "If you'll sit on it, I can get the snaps closed."

Liz sat on the suitcase, which was on Dottie's bed, and Dottie, after making certain that nothing was hanging out, managed to get the snaps shut.

"There," Dottie said. "Now all we have to do is get it in the back of your car, and then down to the ticket booth at Shaky Jake."

"Are you sure it will be safe there?" Liz asked.

"Sure I'm sure," Dottie said. "Who goes into the ticket booth in the summer time? Besides, there's a cabinet over in the corner that's big enough to hold it, I measured it. I'll hide it there until I'm ready for it."

"Won't your parents miss all your clothes?"

"No," Dottie said. She laughed. "Daddy wouldn't

know if every stitch was gone. He never pays attention to clothes. You could probably take half of *his* clothes, and he'd never know. And Mom is too caught up in my graduation tonight. Honestly, you'd think she was graduating from high school instead of me."

"I know, my mom's the same way," Liz said. "And Dad is just as bad. And he's going to *kill* me when he finds out."

"How is he going to find out?" Dottie asked.

"Dottie, by this time tomorrow, *everyone* is going to know. There's no way I can keep it from Dad."

"Well, he doesn't have to know that you helped me," Dottie said.

Liz laughed. "I guess you're right," she said. "Oh, but Dottie, you must promise you will never tell a soul that I helped you."

"I promise," Dottie said. "Now, let's get this down to the car. Oh, wait, let me make certain that no one is home."

Dottie opened the door of her bedroom, and stepped out into the upstairs hallway. The doors to what had been Martin's room, as well as the two empty bedrooms, were closed, but the doors to Charles' room and her parents room were standing open, the better to let the breeze circulate and cool. Dottie walked down the rose patterned carpet to Charles' room and looked in.

"Charles?" she called lightly.

There was no answer, then she walked down to her parents' bedroom, and stood with her hand on the doorjamb and looked inside. It too was empty. At least, it was empty of people. It did hold a lot of memories, though, and they all came pouring back to her right now, as she contemplated what she was about to do. She knew she would not be in this room again for a long time, if ever.

The bed was a big, four-poster, dark, mahogany, with a carved headboard of some floral design. The bed was covered with a light blue bedspread, contrasting with the dark blue of the carpet. The wall paper was white, with a large print design of baskets of flowers, all in blue. Against the wall sat a big dresser with an oval mirror, and on the dresser top was her mother's silver comb and brush set.

When Dottie was younger, it was a treat to lie in her parents' bed at night, before bedtime, and watch her mother brush her hair with that silver brush. Sometimes Dottie would close her eyes and pretend she was asleep, hoping they would leave her in bed so she could spend the night with them. The trick never worked; they always made her go to her own bed.

Dottie smiled. She had not realized when she was a little girl what went on in the beds of husbands and wives at night. When she did find out, not from her mother, but from some girl friends in the sixth grade who had started their periods, she knew why she was always banished to her own bedroom at night. Since then, she had spent considerable time wondering if it really went on between her mother and father. Oh, the fact that there were three children was proof that it had, but there had been no children since she was born. Besides, try though she may, Dottie couldn't really imagine her mother and father making love.

Dottie's mother was such a prude that Dottie knew she could never talk to her about such things. When her own body began to change she started experiencing feelings she had never experienced before. She would have liked to have discussed those feelings with someone, not a friend, but someone closer, like a sister, or a mother. But she had no sister, and she couldn't discuss it with her mother.

Once she thought of discussing it with Charles. If anyone in her family could help her cope with things which troubled her, it would be Charles. Instinctively, she knew that Charles would help her, but she never got around to discussing it. Then, three months ago, just before Jim went into the Army, while she was petting with him, she was unable to keep the raw hunger dammed up any longer. As his hands and fingers explored her body, she gave in to the tumult which was sweeping over her. Jim expected her to give the usual protests, apply the usual brakes, but she didn't, and almost before either of them realized what they were doing, they were answering the urgent demands of their bodies.

After that, it was too late to talk to Charles, or her mother, or anyone.

"Is the coast clear?" Liz called quietly.

"Oh," Dottie answered, jerked back to the present by the urgency of Liz's call. "Uh, yes, the coast is clear. Come on."

The suitcase was so heavy that it required both girls to carry it downstairs, through the house, and out the back door. Liz raised the trunk deck of her father's car and they put the suitcase inside, then got it closed as they saw Charles walking up the street toward the house.

"Oh," Liz said. "You don't think he saw, do you?"

"No," Dottie said. "I'm certain he didn't see."

"Well, hello, ladies," Charles said as he walked up the driveway. "Where are you two going?"

"We've got some last minute things to do," Dottie said. "You know, women's things for graduation."

"Is there anything I can do?" Charles asked.

"Well, I can't think of anything, but I'm sure Mom can," Dottie said. "You know how she is."

"Yes," Charles laughed. "By the way, what time is Jim supposed to get in?"

"He's supposed to be home by four o'clock this afternoon," Dottie said. "He promised me he would be."

"I figured you would know," Charles said. Then an expression of sudden understanding crossed his face. "Dottie, don't tell me that Jim got a leave just for your graduation?"

"Yes, he did," Dottie said.

"Well, I'll be darned," Charles said. "I have to admit, sis, that after ole Jim boy went into the Army, I was fairly certain it would be all over between the two of you."

"Why would you think a thing like that?" Dottie asked.

"Because Jim was there and you were here," Charles said. "And there are so many other boys who are still here."

"That's just it," Dottie said. "The boys who are still here are still boys. Come on, Liz, we must go."

Dottie got into the car, and as Liz backed out of the driveway, Charles waved goodbye to them.

"Oh, I hope he doesn't figure out what's going on," Liz said, as they drove away.

"He won't," Dottie said. "Don't worry about it."

*   *   *

The Mount Eagle High School gym was festooned in streamers of blue and white. The high windows were raised, and the big, double doors were propped open, and a couple of large fans, sitting on tall stands, stood just beside the doors, helping to circulate the breeze. Dozens of handheld fans moved back and forth gently as men and women in the audience fanned themselves in an effort to keep cool.

There was a constant drone as the people in the audience talked among themselves, then that drone changed in intensity, and finally quieted as the principal, Noah Graves, a tall, thin man with glasses and a moustache, stepped up to the microphone. He blew into the microphone a couple of times, and the rush of air came back through the speakers. He cleared his throat.

"Ladies and gentlemen, the Mount Eagle High School band. Notice, if you will, that as they take their seats, there will be several empty chairs among them. Those chairs are the chairs of the graduating seniors, who will be filing in with the class. It is the band's way of honoring their own, who are graduating here tonight."

The band filed in then, to the applause of those present, and the band members took their seats. There were several empty seats within the band, and a red rose was on some of the chairs, while a white carnation was on the others. The program explained that the rose was for a graduating girl and the carnation for a graduating boy. Those mothers who had a son or daughter band member graduating wiped away the first tears of the evening.

The band director tapped his baton against the stand and raised it, then the band broke into the stately processional tune of *Pomp and Circumstance*. At the playing of the music, the class began filing in.

The speakers droned on constantly, talking of the glorious opportunity which lay before them, of the challenge they faced in a world at war.

". . . and so we say to those who shall come behind us, take up this torch we pass to you. Hold it high, and ever let the flame give off the light of freedom!" Emma Rittenhouse said at the conclusion of her address. It was met with thunderous applause. Then Mr. Graves returned to the microphone and began calling out the seniors, name by name, handing them a rolled diploma tied in a blue and white ribbon, as they walked across the stage.

Immediately after graduation there was a party for all the graduating seniors and their families and guests, at the Mount Eagle Country Club swimming pool. Nancy had suggested it, and though some wanted to restrict the party so that it included only those seniors whose families were members of the club, the membership voted to allow *all* to attend on that special night. That was a victory for Nancy, who had proposed the party in the first place for everyone. Nancy was able to hold sway with the others, because she had greatly strengthened her social position with the successful dogwood festival.

The pool was decorated with hanging paper lanterns, and an orchestra sat in a rock garden which was lighted with colored lights, and played soft music. There was one bar set up for the adults, and another, dispensing soft drinks and ice cream sodas, set up for the younger set. Most of the men and boys were wearing white dinner jackets, while the girls wore dresses of silk or taffeta.

Not all the boys were in white dinner jackets. Here and there, one could spot an army or navy uniform. One of those uniforms was being worn by Jim Anderson.

"You look so handsome in your uniform," Emma was saying to Jim.

"You can look, Emma," Dottie said. "But you can't touch." She smiled sweetly as she said it, and the others around them laughed, but Dottie took Jim's hand possessively, and the others knew that there was an element of truth in Dottie's joking remark. "Come on, Jim. It looks like the only way I'm going to have you for myself is to walk with you."

"It's a nice party," Jim said, as they strolled around the pool deck. Dottie unabashedly hung onto Jim's arm. "I hear tell your mom is responsible for it."

"Mom has become the social *grande dame* of Mount Eagle," Dottie said with a little laugh.

"I don't suppose she knows?" Jim asked. "About us, I mean?"

"No," Dottie said. "No one knows except Liz, and that's only because she helped me get my suitcase out of the house."

"Dottie, are you sure you want to go through with this?"

"I've never been surer of anything in my life." Dottie said. "Oh, Jim, you aren't having second thoughts, are you?"

"No," Jim said. "I've thought about nothing else since I went into the Army. The long marches, the bivouacks, the hours of guard duty in the middle of the night, even the long, hot days on K.P., I've had you constantly in my mind. That's the only thing that has kept me going."

"How long will we have together before you have to ship out?"

"I'm going to Camp Rucker, Alabama, and from there I'll be going on to the ETO. My Sergeant tells me we should have at least three months before we ship out. Three months isn't very long. I feel guilty about asking you to marry me, only to see me leave in three months."

"Don't be silly," Dottie said. She squeezed Jim's arm. "We'll put more into those three months than most people can put into three years."

"That's just it," Jim said. "Honey, I'll be at camp most of the time. There will be other wives there too, but I don't know how often any of us will be able to get off the base to see our families."

"If it's only one hour per night, we'll make the most of it," Dottie said.

"I bought a car," Jim said with a shy grin.

"You did?" Dottie asked excitedly. "You mean we won't have to go in a train, we can go in our own car."

"Don't get too excited," Jim said. "It's not much of a car. I bought Frank's '35 Chevy. But it's good on gas, and with the rationing we'll need that. Also the tires are in pretty good shape."

"Oh, I hadn't even thought of such things as gas rationing. Will we have enough to get to Alabama?"

"Yes," Jim said. "All the soldiers can get a special issue when they are transferred from one camp to another."

"Well, here are you two walking arm in arm, engaged in deep, philosophical conversation," Charles said. "What weighty things have you to discuss on such a night? Hello, Jim, you're looking fit."

"Hello, Charles," Jim said, taking the hand Charles offered him. "I heard about your physics paper. Congratulations."

"You heard? How did you hear?"

"Well, Dottie wrote me about it, of course, but I also happened across Dr. Nunlee this afternoon. He's very high on it, and he says it will be published."

"We hope it will be published," Charles said. "We don't know whether it will be or not. Listen, are you going to take any extension courses while you are in the Army? You know, Standhope is offering to graduate those who qualify. In fact Martin graduated today."

"That's right, this is graduation day, isn't it? It must seem strange, not having commencement ceremonies," Jim said.

"Well, there were so many who are graduating who weren't here, like Martin. And then there are others who will be graduating this summer, like me. The student body voted not to have the ceremony, but, listen, they are getting together over at Beartracks. Why don't you come along? All our friends'll be there."

"Beartracks!" Jim said. "God, how I missed that place. I wonder if my beer mug is still on the wall?"

Charles laughed. "Not only is it on the wall, but it is occupying a place of honor. Beartracks has designated one whole section of the wall to those who are, and I quote, 'serving with honor and distinction in our Nation's armed forces'. Your mug is hanging there with Martin's and a dozen others. Those of us who only serve by standing and waiting salute it nightly."

"I heard about your 4F deferment," Jim said. "And I heard how upset you were by it, but Charles, don't let it bother you."

"Yes, well, I try not to think about it," Charles said. "So, listen, shall we be off to Beartracks, then? I have the panel truck."

"I'd like to, really," Jim said. "But I probably shouldn't."

"Why, because of Dottie?" Charles said. He smiled at his sister. "Dottie, come on, let us guys have him for one night. You have him for the rest of his leave."

"But you'll be too tired to . . ." Dottie started, then she stopped. "That is . . ."

"Don't worry about me," Jim said. "Listen, I've just spent 12 weeks of staying up 24 hours a day. I'm used to it now, really I am. I'll be all right."

"Okay," Dottie said. "Jim, you won't—"

"Don't worry," Jim said, patting her hand reassuringly. "I promise you, everything will be okay."

"I parked the truck out front," Charles said as they were walking away from the pool. Behind them the party and the pool glowed, while to the side, the golf course lay quietly under the moon. Across the rolling greens and fairways, the black shadows of trees moved gracefully under the night breeze.

"I've got a car," Jim said. "I'll follow you."

"Oh, well, why don't I just tell Dad to take the panel truck back and I'll ride with you?" Charles offered.

"No," Jim said quickly. "That is, I'm really pretty beat, I don't know how long I can hold up. I may want to leave early and that would spoil your fun. Why don't we just meet there?"

"Okay," Charles said. "Sure, that'll be all right."

Beartracks was *the* college hangout in Mount Eagle. It was a beer and sandwich tavern which occasionally had live music. Most of the time, though, it depended on the entertainment of the gaily colored jukebox which sat on a raised platform at one end of the long, narrow building, and the conversation and horseplay of its patrons. It was owned by Carl Sawyer, a football player of some note during the twenties, who earned the nickname 'Beartracks' by supposedly leaving his footprints all over the backs of opposing players. He first tried to call his establishment Sawyer's Bar, but it was so universally called Beartracks that even he gave in and changed the name officially.

Every fraternity on campus rented a section of wall from Beartracks, and each student bought his own beer mug. Part of the ordeal of the fraternity pledge was to design a personal coat of arms. Those who belonged to a family with an existing coat of arms could not use the family emblem, but had to come up with one of their own. The coat of arms was then submitted to a 'Board of Validation', consisting of upper classmen, and when the coat of arms was approved, it would be painstakingly painted on the mug, then the mug would be hung from a nail within the square belonging to that particular fraternity.

Charles and Jim parked side by side at Beartracks, and they could hear the music and the laughter and the boisterous conversation from out front, even before they went inside.

"I see the lack of full commencement ceremony hasn't dampened anyone's spirits," Jim teased.

"Speaking of spirits and things damp," Charles said, "let's go inside and imbibe, shall we?"

"After you, friend," Jim said, bowing and sweeping his arm out grandly.

A thick cloud of smoke hung just beneath the ceiling of Beartracks, oddly, above the whirling ceiling fans which moved the lower, humid air around, but did nothing to cool the place. A Benny Goodman record was on the jukebox, though it could barely be heard above the clinking glasses and the laughter and the buzz of conversation.

"Hold it, hold it!" someone shouted, seeing Charles and Jim come in. "Behold, fellow graduates and students of Standhope! One of those to whom we have dedicated this night of revelry hath made an appearance. Hail, the conquering warrior!" The one who shouted out, raised his hand and held it stretched before him in a salute.

"That's a Nazi salute," someone scolded.

"Sir, before it was a Nazi salute, it was the salute rendered to Caesar's Legions," the saluting graduate said. "And I'll be damned if I'll let some Bavarian corporal usurp my prerogative to render honor in the style of Caesar."

"Hail, Caesar!" someone else shouted, laughing, and soon everyone in Beartracks was on their feet, rendering what to anyone else might look like a Nazi salute, but to them, was honor to Caesar's legions.

After the initial fanfare of their entrance, things quieted back to the normal dull roar, and Jim and Charles found a booth and a beer and a few old friends. Three beers later, Charles excused himself to go to the restroom.

As usual, the urinals were busy, so Charles went into one of the toilet stalls. As it happened, the two who were standing at the urinals had their backs to the door, so they didn't see Charles when he came in.

"I thought you said he was getting married," one of them said to the other.

"He is getting married. Hell, he got a special leave just for that purpose, and he bought a car so he could take her with him to the next camp he's going to."

"It's supposed to be secret, isn't it?"

"Yes. The only reason I know is because my sister told me. Liz helped with the packing."

"Well, do you think the girl's family knows? I mean, her brother is here with him."

"I don't know. Maybe he knows, maybe he doesn't. I think we'd be smart not to say anything though, just in case."

"Yeah, I guess so. You really don't know how to handle something like this do you? You don't know if you should butt in or stay out of it."

"Yeah, I know what you mean." He laughed, a short, lusty, laugh. "I'll tell you one thing though. I sure wouldn't mind trading places with old Jim about 24 hours from now. Damned if I don't think Dottie is about the sexiest woman I have ever seen."

"She's still in high school."

"Not any more she isn't. And she's about to be married."

The sound of flushing water covered up the next comment, but it didn't cover up the lascivious laugh of the two as they left the restroom.

Charles was alone in the stall, and he stood there feeling a queasiness in the pit of his stomach.

8

Charles stood at the corner of the bar, looking through the smoke and the crowd at the booth where Jim was sitting with the others. Jim was somewhat slimmer now than he had been when he left for the Army. There was a more self-confident air about Jim than Charles had remembered.

Jim was exactly Charles' age. They had played together as children and been friends through high school and into college. Jim had worked for the newspaper nearly as long as Charles had, starting with a paper route, just as Charles did, and moving up to the composition and press room. He was nearly as good with the presses as Martin, and could lay out the paper even better than Charles could.

Charles had always liked Jim. He was a generous person, both with his possessions and his time. He was intelligent and serious-minded, and in the days when Charles had considered his little sister nothing but a pest, Jim had been amazingly tolerant of her. If Charles had to pick a brother-in-law, he could think of no one he would rather have than Jim.

But not now. Not yet, anyway. Dottie was too young. She just turned eighteen in March.

"Charles, over here!" Jim called, laughing. "What's the matter, did you get lost?"

Charles' first inclination was to go over to Jim and sound him out, right now, right in front of everyone. He would persuade him to give up this crazy idea if he could; embarrass him, if necessary. Whatever it took to stop this insane marriage, Charles would do it. He took a deep breath, as if about to plunge into an icy stream, then started back toward the table.

"We were just talking about your paper," Jim said when Charles returned. "You're going to be a celebrity, my good man. And, we're all going to say we knew you when."

"Listen, Jim, I've got something I want to say to you," Charles said, blurting it out before he lost his courage.

"Sure, what's on your mind?" Jim asked innocently.

Charles checked himself. If he blurted it out now, it might not do any good at all. And as far as embarrassment is concerned, the people who would suffer the most embarrassment would be his own family. No, this wasn't the time, or the place. He sighed.

"I'm going to have to leave early," he said. "I just thought of something I had promised Dad I would take care of down at the newspaper office."

"Then my advice to you, friend, is to get it done. I haven't forgotten what it's like to work for your old man. You don't tell him you are going to do something, and then not do it."

"You don't even do that to him if you are in his class!" one of the others said, and they all laughed.

Charles left Beartracks, but he didn't go to the newspaper office. Instead, he went just a block away, then parked off the street so he could see Jim's car without himself being seen. Then he waited.

It was almost two hours before Jim came out, alone, got into his car and drove away. Charles followed, staying about a block behind, driving in the dark, keeping Jim in sight only by his tail lights, and staying on the road only by the dim lights of the occasional street lamps.

Jim drove straight to the Holt house, passed by once in front of the house slowly, then turned around to come back by. When Charles saw him turning around, he was afraid he was going to be seen, and he turned off the street and drove right across someone's front yard, stopping behind a hedgerow, praying that the owner of the house wouldn't see him.

When Jim came back by the house a second time, he turned his lights off and pulled into the driveway. Charles got out of the truck and walked through the shaded yards, moving silently from tree to porch and from porch to tree again, until he was standing under the huge old elm tree which was in his own front yard, less than 20 yards away from Jim.

Jim picked up a piece of gravel and tossed it lightly up against the window screen of Dottie's bedroom. Charles could hear it thump quietly against the screen.

"Dottie!" Jim called, whispering loudly. Jim tossed another piece of gravel. The window screen swung open.

"I wasn't sure you would be here," Dottie called down.

"Are your folks asleep?"

"Yes. Let's hurry before they wake up."

Jim looked around. "Do you have a ladder?"

"I don't need one," Dottie said. She climbed out of her window, then inched along the ledge until she reached the roof of the side porch. She walked across the roof to the trellis work and climbed down it as easily as if she were coming down a ladder. "I've been coming down this way since I was ten-years-old," she said.

"Practicing, huh?" Jim teased. Jim met her on the ground, and they went into each other's arms with a long, deep kiss.

"Come on, if we leave now, we can have breakfast in Piggott, get married, and be on our way before noon," Jim said, starting for the car.

Charles darted out of the shadow of the tree, raced to the car and grabbed the keys before Jim and Dottie could reach it.

"Charles!" Dottie gasped. "Charles, what are you doing?"

"It seems to me that the wrong person is asking that question." Charles hissed angrily. "Shouldn't I be asking you what *you* are doing?"

"How long have you known?" Jim asked quietly.

"I found out tonight at Beartracks," Charles said.

"That's why you left early?"

"Yes," Charles said. "I wanted to get here in time to stop you."

"You can't stop us," Dottie said resolutely.

"I have already stopped you," Charles said, holding up the key. "All I have to do is throw this key far enough, and you won't find it before morning. By then it'll be too late."

"Charles, you've always been one of my closest

friends," Jim said. "What if I told you that if you throw that key I'll beat the living hell out of you?"

"It would be painful, but it wouldn't stop me," Charles said. "And you know it won't stop me. That's why I don't think you'll really do it."

"Charles, please," Dottie said desperately. "What are you trying to do? Why are you trying to ruin my life?"

"Ruin your life? Can't you see I'm trying to save it?" Charles said. "Dottie, think what you are doing, girl."

"I know what I am doing," Dottie said. "I'm going to be with the man I love. I'm going to marry him."

"Not tonight, you aren't," Charles said.

"Yes, tonight."

"Like this?" Charles said. "Sneaking away in the middle of the night? You remember what Mother and Dad thought about Corabeth, how shocked they were. Don't you think they'll be far more shocked and hurt by what you're trying to do?"

"I remember what they said about Corabeth, yes," Dottie said. "But, Charles, I also remember what you said. Do you remember? You said that if they were really in love, who were you to say they had no right. You said no one could say that they have no right to get married. Do you remember that?"

"Yes," Charles said. "I remember. But this is different."

"How is it different?"

"Corabeth isn't my sister," Charles said. "You are."

"I see," Dottie said. "In other words, you can talk about tolerance, but you can't show it. Is that it?"

"Perhaps," Charles agreed.

"Charles, please, if you have any love for me as your sister, if you care one ounce about my happiness, you'll give Jim the keys and get out of our way. Please."

"I can't, Dottie," Charles said. He sighed. "I just can't."

"But you must!" Dottie said. "Oh, Charles, you blind fool, don't you see you must?"

"Why must I?" Charles demanded. "You just give me one good reason why."

"Because!" Dottie said. And now a sob escaped from her throat to accompany the tears which were rolling down her cheek. "Because I'm pregnant. I'm going to have Jim's baby."

"What?" Charles asked, staggered by his sister's words. "What did you say?"

And now Charles saw that Jim was looking at Dottie with as shocked an expression as his own.

"Dottie . . . are you . . . serious?" Jim asked. "Are you really going to have my baby?"

"Yes," Dottie said quietly. "Oh, Jim, I didn't want to tell you. I wanted to know that you were marrying me because you loved me, not because you had to."

"You silly goose, of course I'm marrying you because I love you," Jim said, taking her in his arms and holding her tightly. He kissed her on the forehead and on the eyes. "And I'm glad about the baby. I'm very glad."

"I . . . I didn't want to have to tell you like this," Dottie said. "I wanted the time to be right, I wanted—"

"There, hush," Jim said quietly. "Darling, good news is good news, no matter how you get it."

Suddenly the window screen to Thurman and

Nancy's room was swung open. As Jim heard the screen open, he pushed Dottie quickly back toward the house, and she crouched under a wisteria bush.

"What's going on down there?" Thurman called in a rather gruff voice. "What's all the racket?"

Charles looked at the panic in his sister's face, and at the determination in Jim's. Then he stepped away from the car and called up to his father.

"It's just Jim and me, Dad," he said. "We're getting back from Beartracks, and we've been talking about old times."

"Well, for heaven's sake, can't you do that in the morning?" Thurman said. "You're making enough racket to wake the dead."

"I'm sorry, Dad," Charles said. "We'll be quiet."

"Good night, Professor Holt," Jim called up.

"Good night, Jim," Thurman replied. "It's good to have you home." Thurman pulled the screen shut again, and for several seconds after that the three figures in the driveway formed a tableaux, with Charles looking up at the screen, and Jim and the crouched Dottie looking at Charles.

"It's in your hands now, Charles," Jim said quietly.

"You have no right to put me in this position," Charles said. "Neither of you have the right."

"You put yourself in this position," Dottie said. "First by coming out here to try and stop us, and then by not telling Daddy what was really going on. Don't blame us for your involvement."

Charles looked at the keys in his hand, tossed them up and caught them a couple of times, then, with an audible sigh, he tossed them to Jim. "Here," he said.

Jim went to him quickly and took his hand, then

embraced him. "Thanks," he said. "Thanks for caring, and for understanding."

"I'm not sure that I do understand," Charles said. "But I care. God knows I care." Charles walked over to his sister and embraced her, pulling her tightly against him. "Take care of yourself, Dottie. Please take care of yourself."

"I will," Dottie said.

"We'd better go," Jim hissed. "I don't want your father coming to the window again."

Dottie and Charles let go of each other, and Dottie started toward the car. She stopped just before she got in, and looked back at her brother who was just standing there, looking on helplessly. Dottie's eyes glistened with tears, and they reflected the light of the moon.

"I'll never forget you for this, Charles," she said quietly. "You've always been something special to me . . . and now, you'll be more special than ever. I think the reason I love Jim is because he was always your friend, and he reminds me so much of you in so many ways." She smiled. "I suppose a psychologist might try and make something of that."

"Good-bye, Dottie," Charles said quietly and sadly. "I'll do what I can with Mom and Dad, but I don't promise much."

Jim got in, then scooted across and Dottie got into the car right behind him. That way, only one door would slam, and thus avert any curiosity on the part of Dottie's father as to why two doors would slam, when only Jim was supposed to be leaving. He started the car, then backed slowly out of the driveway. His headlights flashed across Charles, just standing there, as he backed onto the street. Then, as he put it in gear and drove away, Charles faded into the shadows behind him.

"Are you sure this is the place?" Dottie asked.

Jim looked at the piece of paper in his pocket. "191 Orr Street," he said. "That's what it says. He's supposed to be able to issue the license and marry us, all at the same time."

"Knock on the door again," Dottie said. "Maybe he isn't awake yet."

"It's 0730 hours," Jim growled. "Who *wouldn't* be up at this time of day?"

"You're spoiled by the Army," Dottie giggled. "Believe me, if it weren't for the fact that I had something to do this morning, *I* wouldn't be up yet."

Jim laughed. "You mean that's what this is? Something to do?" He put his arms around her and pulled her to him for another kiss, and they were still kissing when they heard the door being opened.

"Yes, yes, what is it? What do you want?" A man asked. He was a short man, wearing a night shirt, and, Dottie noticed with astonishment, a nightcap. She had never seen anyone really wearing a nightcap, only pictures and drawings.

"We want to get married," Jim said. He looked at the sheet of paper in his hand. "You are Judge Head, aren't you? Judge Vernon Head?"

"That's me," the man said. "But you're too early. Come back at nine o'clock, that's when I open for business. You woke me from a sound sleep."

"Please, Judge, can't you open up earlier for us? We're in a hurry and—"

"Young folks are always in a hurry," the man in

the nightshirt said. "I could tell you are in a hurry by the way you were carrying on on my front porch. God knows how far it would have gone if I hadn't come to the door."

"It's just that I have orders, you see, sending me—"

"Overseas, right away," Dottie interrupted. "He has to leave tonight. And we want as much time together as we can have."

Judge Head looked at the two, then sighed, and stepped back as he pushed open the screen door.

"Come on in," he said. "Be quick, don't let the flies in. I've hung a piece of cotton on the screen door, they say that keeps the flies out. Scares 'em into thinkin' it's a white moth or somethin', I don't know. The only thing I know is, it don't work. I, uh, haven't even had m' breakfast yet. Would you kids like the woman to fix you breakfast? It'll only cost you a dollar extra, 'n it'll be a lot more satisfyin' than anythin' you can get in a restaurant."

"We just ate, thank you," Jim said.

"The only place you can eat this time of mornin' is the City Pig, 'n if you had their red eye gravy, you didn't have much, I'm tellin' you."

"Please, would you marry us now?" Dottie asked.

Judge Head looked over at her, and his eyes flashed with a deep light which Dottie started seeing in men's eyes at about the same time she began maturing into a woman. When she was younger, the look frightened her with its hint of something forbidden. Now, she sometimes took a secret pleasure in it. She knew that she possessed a certain power over any man who looked at her in such a way.

"You are anxious, aren't you?" Judge Head said.

Dottie looked down and forced herself to blush,

as if Judge Head's innuendo was embarrassing her. It wasn't, but she knew that he would realize a certain sexual thrill from thinking that it did, and she knew also that it would hasten him to do her bidding.

"All right," Judge Head said. He pointed toward the living room. "You two jes' wait in there. I'll go 'n get dressed 'n—"

"You don't have to get dressed on our account," Jim said quickly.

"It ain't gonna cost you no time," Judge Head said. "No time a'tall. The wife'll be down directly to fill out the marriage license, 'n while she's doin' that, I'll be gettin' dressed. They's got to be some dignity to a marriage, no matter how much a hurry a body gets in, 'n as long as I'm duly empowered to perform weddin's, they's gonna be performed with dignity."

"I was raised on the Mississippi River," Dottie said. "And here, I'm about to spend my wedding night in sight of it."

"There's a difference though," Jim said from the room behind her. "This is the fabulous Hotel Peabody in Memphis, Tennessee, home of the famous rooftop restaurant and orchestra, coming to you over WREC."

"You sound just like a radio announcer," Dottie said, giggling.

"Wah-wah-wah-wah-waaaah-wah-wah-wah," Jim said, cupping his hand over his mouth and doing an imitation of a muted trumpet. "Yes, ladies and gentlemen," he went on. "Only the most elegant and the most dignified people of society are here tonight, in the rooftop restaurant of the fabulous Hotel Peabody. Hold it, I think I see over there, yes, could it be the well-known military genius, Private First Class Jim Anderson, and his lovely young bride, fresh from a wedding which was performed with dignity?"

"You're a nut," Dottie said.

"You mean because I'm happy?" Jim replied.

"No," Dottie said, unbuttoning her blouse. "I mean because here you are playing silly games, when we could be in bed."

Dottie slipped out of her dress, then stepped easily out of her bra and panties, until she stood naked before him. She could feel a gentle breeze kiss her naked skin as softly as a touch of silk, and she could see the light in his eyes she had seen in other men's eyes, only this time it was her husband's eyes she was seeing.

Quickly, and without taking his eyes off her, Jim removed his own clothes, then, hungrily, he pulled Dottie's naked body against his own. Dottie felt the soft hair on his chest, the muscles of his thighs, and the impatient thrusting of his manhood as she leaned into him. They were all new sensations to her. Her one previous experience had been the groping, fevered session with him in the seat of a car, and it had left her aching with the desire for more ... but pregnant with its results.

They moved to the bed then, and Jim's kisses travelled from her lips, down her throat, across her bare shoulders and on to her breasts. Jim's lips had been at her breasts many times before, always with an aching urgency which promised what couldn't be delivered. But now it promised pleasure which could be fulfilled, and under Jim's tender, loving caresses, Dottie felt a need in her body, growing in intensity, igniting fires within, until she stood poised on the brink of some utterly new cataclysmic event.

All the nerve endings in Dottie's body were geared for the ecstasy of lovemaking and she gave herself to Jim completely, moving to facilitate the entry, touching him with her fingers, guiding him when necessary, following his lead when needed, giving and taking and glorying in that which had long held the promise of ecstasy, and was now being fulfilled in ways even more wonderful than her most erotic fantasies. Then, quite unexpectedly, it happened. It felt like the long drop from the high diving board at the Country Club pool, a dizzying expectation, then an explosion of sensation, bursting within and spreading throughout her body in concentric waves of rapture. After that there was another, and still another, and yet another. Dottie rode with the pleasures of the experience until the flaming meteor's blaze was a glowing cinder, still warm, but no long burning.

Only then did Dottie realize that Jim had shared the same experience with her, and was now moving off her body to lie gasping and panting beside her.

"It was wonderful," he said. "I never knew how wonderful it could be."

"More wonderful than it was in the car, the night before you left for basic training?" Dottie asked.

"Yes," Jim said. "More wonderful even than that."

Jim slid his hand across the bed and took Dottie's and squeezed it very tightly for a moment. "Everyone knows by now," he said.

"I know."

"I hope Charles is able to comfort your mother and father."

"He'll comfort them," Dottie said. "They may not forgive us, but they will listen to Charles. It's almost as if. . . ." and she laughed.

"Almost as if what?"

"You'll think I'm silly."

"No, go ahead."

"It's strange," Dottie said. "But Charles isn't like their son. I mean he *is* their son, but they listen to him, and they, they *respect* him, as if he were a wise, old uncle or something. It seems like it has been that way for as long as I can remember."

"I know," Jim said. "Charles has that effect on all his friends too. He's always been smaller, weaker, and slower . . . but, somehow none of that has ever mattered. He's always been the one whose approval we most wanted."

Dottie and Jim lay side by side for a long, silent, moment after that, looking up at the spinning paddles of the ceiling fan, feeling the breeze cool their dampened bodies.

It's a spinning wheel, Dottie thought. That fan is a spinning wheel, spinning my future. What sort of future is it spinning?

9

Second Lieutenant Martin Holt was looking through a *National Geographic* magazine. He found a picture of two handsome men and two beautiful women, cooking over an open campfire while their horses stood in the shadow of a giant saguaro cactus behind them.

Glowing desert and mystic mountains, unbelievable starlit nights, jingling spurs and lilting cowboy tunes—this is Arizona, beckoning you to solace and satisfaction. Add a warm, friendly certified climate—certified when the U.S. Army chose it as an aviation training center and you have Phoenix, in Arizona's famed Valley of the Sun.

To that glowing descriptive ad, a reader before Martin had added his own prose.

Scorpions in your boots, sand in your gas, sweat in your eyes and cactus in your a___.
That's Luke Field.

Martin smiled, then tossed the magazine to one side, stood up, and stretched. A ray of sun, stabbing through the high windows of Union Station, caught the gold bar on his collar and the silver wings on his chest, and flashed brilliantly for an instant. Martin had just completed bomber training, and was being assigned to his first duty after a delay-in-route which would allow him one week at home.

It was late September, and though some parts of the country were already beginning to feel the first, bracing effects of fall, it was still hot in Phoenix. Martin walked over to check the timetable, and saw that he still had an hour before the train, so he walked from the shade of the car shed, out into the bright Arizona sun. A couple of enlisted men were standing just outside, and they came to attention and saluted Martin, and Martin, still a little self-conscious over his lofty status, returned their salute.

An old Mexican woman was operating a taco stand right across the street from the station. She didn't have any teeth and she kept her mouth closed tightly so that her chin and nose nearly touched. A swarm of flies buzzed around the steaming kettles, drawn by the pungent aromas of meat and sauces. She worked with quick, deft fingers, rolling the spicy ingredients into tortillas, then wrapping them up in old newspaper as she handed them to her customers.

"Lieutenant," a woman's voice called softly. "Lieutenant?"

Martin turned toward the sound of the voice. The speaker was a beautiful woman in her early forties. She was cool and poised looking despite the heat, seeming somehow to rise above it. She was the kind of woman whose picture one might see in *Life Magazine* in a feature such as *Life goes to a party*.

"Yes, ma'am?" Martin replied. "Are you speaking to me?"

The woman smiled a cool smile. "Oh, please, don't say 'ma'am.' "

"I'm sorry," Martin said easily, returning her smile.

"I've seen you checking the timetable. Are you going east, by any chance?"

"Yes, I am," Martin said.

"Perhaps we can do each other a favor," the woman suggested. "My name is Linda Busby. You may have heard of my husband, Colonel Frank Busby?"

The name did have a familiar ring, then he remembered that Colonel Busby was with the Inspector General's office and on one inspection, had been responsible for Martin's entire wing being restricted to base for four weeks. He smiled.

"I see you have heard of him," Mrs. Busby said.

"I know the Colonel," Martin said. "I'm sure he doesn't know me. Tell me, Mrs. Busby, what can I do for you?"

"As I say, Lieutenant, it's what we can do for each other. I have a drawing room on the Delta Flyer, but as I am alone, and they allow the military and their dependents to board first, I will lose the drawing room, perhaps even lose my seat entirely. So I have a proposal. I would like to become your dependent—temporarily, of course," she added with a smile. "That way, I can preserve my space on the train, and you can share a drawing room with me, rather than having to fight for a seat. What do you say?"

"Well, I'm, I'm flabbergasted," Martin said. "I must confess, it would seem to me that I am getting the better deal. Why did you pick me? Surely there would be somone else nearer your—"

"Age?" Mrs. Busby asked, raising her eyebrows in a challenging smile.

"I was going to say rank," Martin said. "That is, your husband's rank."

"There are one or two officers more senior, but they have their dependents with them," Mrs. Busby said. "My choice seemed to be between you, and one of several enlisted men. I thought that you, being an officer and a gentleman, would be the most logical choice. However, if you feel it is improper, I shall relinquish my drawing room and take a chance on. . . ."

"No," Martin said quickly. "No, don't do that. I accept your offer. In fact, I accept it with thanks. You don't know how I've dreaded the thought of two nights and two days sitting straight up."

"Good," the woman said, and she took his arm in her hands and flashed a beautiful, radiant smile at him. "Now, since we are supposed to be married, I think we should be on a first name basis, don't you? Call me Linda. What can I call you besides Lieutenant?"

"Martin," Martin said.

"What was it Bogey said in *Casablanca*?" Linda asked. "Oh, yes. 'This is going to be the beginning of a beautiful relationship.'" Linda laughed, a low, throaty, cultured laugh, and she leaned against Martin so that he could feel the heavy warmth of her breasts through the cool blouse she wore.

"Would you be needing anything?" the porter asked from the door of the compartment. He had quickly appraised the age difference between the two, but had not yet made up his mind whether it was useful to him only as a curiosity, or in some more tangible way. He seemed to be studying them.

"Would you bring us a pitcher of martinis?" Linda asked.

"Yes, ma'am," the porter said, touching his forehead in sort of a salute, then disappearing on his errand.

Linda closed the door, then settled into the seat by the window, across from Martin. "Oh, doesn't the air-conditioning feel good in here," she said, fanning herself with her hand. "I am so thankful that you agreed to our little arrangement. Those poor people out there. I feel so sorry for them."

"At least they have seats," Martin said. "I've watched three trains pull out today with passengers left behind."

"I know," Linda said. "Isn't it awful what the war is doing? Travel on a plane is absolutely impossible, travel on trains is nearly as bad, and, of course, I simply refuse to travel by bus. But it's the same with everything; you have to wait as much as an hour to get a long distance call through, you can't buy the meat you want or the coffee or the sugar."

Martin wanted to say that it was probably worse in England or France, where the Germans already occupied the country, but he held his tongue in check.

Linda suddenly laughed. "Thank you," she said.

"For this? I told you, it is I who should be thanking you."

"No, I don't mean this. I mean thank you for not telling me how good we actually have it, and how it is our patriotic duty to undergo some hardship. Frank is always telling me that, and I'm sure that he is right. But you didn't say anything, and for that, I thank you. Did you just complete your Q course?"

Q course meant qualification course. It was not a term with which civilians were generally familiar, and for a moment it surprised Martin to hear her ask the question. Then he recalled that her husband was Colonel Busby; of course she would know.

"Yes," Martin said. "I qualified in B-17s. I would have rather—" he stopped, and smiled sheepishly.

"Let me complete your sentence for you in 25 words or less," Linda said, using the line used in so many radio and magazine contests. "You would rather become a fighter pilot, right?"

"Yes," Martin said. "How did you know?"

"Oh, my dear, all the young aviators want to be fighter pilots. You see, they are the true gladiators of the sky. A fighter pilot is a little like a knight in the days of old, you and your machine against the other fellow and his machine. It's the last individual element of warfare, where skill, daring and courage still count for something. A bomber is nothing more than a killing factory. You go to work on the assembly line, each bomber does its part, and each person in the bomber does his part, so that it all becomes a series of small parts to gain one whole, and no one person can feel a sense of accomplishment."

"That's right," Martin said, amazed at Linda's perceptiveness.

"What none of you young gladiators seem to realize is what a tremendous accomplishment it is just to stay alive," she said.

Suddenly, and strangely, tears flashed in the eyes which but moments before had been cool, confident, and laughing. "You don't know what you are getting into," she added. "You have no idea what it's really like."

"No, I don't," Martin said. "But I'm anxious to find out."

"Oh, yes," she said. "You are all anxious."

There was a light tap on the door.

"That'll be our martinis," Linda said, and she gave Martin a ten dollar bill.

"I should pay my—"

"Nonsense," Linda said in a tone of voice that brooked no further response from Martin.

The whistle blew, there was the sound of brakes being released, then the cars jerked as the train began to move. They were still under the shed, and Martin looked through the window to see the platform sliding by slowly. Just on the other side of the long, narrow platform another train sat, and he could see the people through the windows, getting settled for their own journey.

Linda took out a book and began to read, while Martin leaned his head back and closed his eyes, grateful that at long last he was on his way back home . . . back to Yolinda and the wedding.

The ringing bells of a railroad crossing started low, grew loud, and then low again as the train flashed by. The sudden intrusion of the bells penetrated Martin's dream, and he thought it was the bail-out bell, the warning bell sounded on a crippled multi-engined aircraft when it is necessary for everyone to bail out. He sat up with a jerk. "What?" he said aloud.

Linda was still sitting across from him, still reading her book. She had turned on the reading lamp because it was now quite dark, and when Martin looked toward the windows he could see nothing but pitch black, and their own reflection, brought on by Linda's reading light. He felt the gentle rocking of the car, and he could hear the wheels clicking rhythmically over the railjoints.

"My," Linda said. She folded the book closed and put it to one side. "Did you have a bad dream?"

"No," Martin said. "That is, I don't know if I was dreaming or not." He pinched the bridge of his nose. "What time is it?"

"It's ten o'clock, or 2200 hours, if you prefer."

"I didn't realize I was that tired."

"You were sleeping so soundly that I didn't want to wake you for dinner," Linda said. "So I got a sandwich for you. It was supposed to be sliced turkey, but I think it is bologna. I hope that's all right."

"Yes, that's fine," Martin said, as he took the sandwich from her. "Thank you."

"There's ice in the bucket, and Coke on the table there," Linda pointed out.

"Do you want one?"

"No, I'm doing quite well with these, thank you," Linda said, holding up her martini glass.

"Good book?" Martin asked as he began eating his sandwich.

"What? Oh, it's *Anna Karenina*."

"Tolstoy is good to read on trains," Martin said. "It gives you time to get to know his characters."

"Do you know the book *Anna Karenina*?"

"Oh, yes, it's required reading in my father's class."

"Your father's class?"

"He's an English professor at Standhope College," Martin said. "And he also owns the Mount Eagle *Crier*."

Linda laughed. "The Mount Eagle *Crier*? Why do I get a picture of some man, dressed in eighteenth century costume yelling, 'all is well'?"

Martin laughed with her. "You're not too far wrong. For a circulation promotion once, my mother suggested that all the paperboys should dress that way."

"I'd like to hear about your family and your home town," Linda said.

"Well, there's my dad, of course, I already told you about him," Martin said, then he went on to describe his father's personality to her, then his mother's personality, and he almost felt guilty because he found things about his mother he could exaggerate so that Linda laughed until she cried. He told her about Charles, too, about his quiet, unassuming strength, and then he told her about Dottie, and how she had broken his parents' hearts by running away to get married.

"How do you feel about that?" Linda asked.

"I don't know," Martin said. "I think if she wanted to get married, she could have done what I am doing. I'm going home to get married, you know."

"Really? No, I didn't know," Linda replied. "That's odd, I would never have guessed it."

"Oh? Why not?"

"Because generally a young man who is going home to get married talks about the young woman he is to marry almost to the exclusion of anyone or anything else. You've told me about your family, your hometown, your college, even the fact that you would rather be a fighter pilot than a bomber pilot. But you've said nothing about the young lady. What is her name?"

"Yolinda," Martin said. "Yolinda Semmes."

"Well, then," Linda said, holding up her martini glass. "Here is to the wedding of Lieutenant Martin Holt and Yolinda Semmes."

The train swept around a curve at that moment, and Linda, in order to keep from spilling the drink, had to shift her weight. When she did, she lost her balance, and nearly fell out of seat, and Martin reached across quickly and grabbed her.

Linda looked up at him, then smiled. "Oh," she said. "This is nice. Yes, I would say this is very nice." She reached up and pulled his face down to her. He could smell and taste the gin as he kissed her, not an unpleasant taste, but one which seemed clean, and antiseptic. Her mouth opened, and her tongue met his.

After a moment of dizzying sensation, Martin pulled away. "I'm sorry," he said. "I'm sorry, I had no right to do that."

Linda laughed, again her low, throaty laugh. "You didn't do it, I did," she said.

"It isn't right," Martin said. "You're married, and I'm engaged and—"

"We're alone together, two people seeking to comfort each other in a time of need," Linda said, pausing before the last word. She kissed him again, and this time Martin didn't back away from it, but let it carry him as far as it could.

Linda was not one of the young and innocent girls of Martin's experience, but an older, sophisticated woman. Despite the fact that she was much older than the girls Martin knew, he discovered that in his arms she was every bit as exciting. In fact, even more so, for her sophistication and easy acceptance of her own womanliness eliminated the awkwardness, the fear, and the guilt.

When she stood up and pulled the bed down, then began to get undressed, she did it as naturally as if she was pouring a cup of coffee. She had no false modesty about her body, and in fact even seemed proud of the flat stomach and firm breasts which were soon exposed to Martin's view. She lay back on the bed then, and smiled up at him as she stretched, arching her back hungrily, proudly, ready to receive him.

Martin undressed quickly, then got into bed with her, kissing her once more and placing his hand on her breast. The skin of her breast seemed incredibly hot, and as he moved his hand from her breast, down her body, it was as if he were passing it through a lake of fire. Finally his hand stopped at the junction of her thighs, cushioned by a luxurious growth of silken hair, and dampened by the copious flowing of her desire.

Martin's blood was hot, and he felt a hollowness in the pit of his stomach and a throbbing, pounding need in his groin. His entire body was trembling with urgent anticipation.

Martin moved over her, and Linda took him in her hands and guided him into her. She thrust her hips up as Martin pushed forward, and they came together so closely that his hairs tangled with hers.

They began to move with each other then, pushing, rotating, seeking their own pleasure but trying to give it as well. Martin felt himself penetrating her deeply, then he felt the tiny tingling which began deep inside and went pinwheeling out, spinning faster and faster until every cell in his body was caught up in the gigantic vortex of the sexual centrifuge.

Afterward, they lay there in the dark, with the motion of the train gently rocking them, and the clicking of the wheels providing them with a soothing rhythm, and Linda moved her hand over to take his.

"We have two nights and two days, my young darling," she said. "I'll teach you how to be slower, how to prolong the sensations, how to help a woman achieve all that she can achieve at such a time. For men it happens only once, but for a woman it can happen many times if her lover is patient and skilled. My wedding gift to Yolinda will be to teach you that patience and skill."

10

You look nice in your uniform," Charles said. He was sitting in an old arm chair in the corner of Martin's bedroom, while Martin was standing in front of his dresser, combing his hair.

"Thanks," Martin said.

"Then of course you always did look nice in uniform," Charles said. "Baseball uniform, basketball uniform, football uniform, army uniform. . . ." He laughed. "Does it seem to you as if you have spent a great deal of your life in a uniform of one kind or another?"

"Well, if you put it that way, I suppose it does," Martin said, laughing with him. "I missed you, Charley. How's it been?"

"Quiet," Charles said. "Enrollment is way down for the new class at Standhope. Dad isn't even going to teach this year."

"He isn't?"

"There aren't enough students to justify doubling the English schedule, and since Dr. Parish has to depend on his teaching job, Dad withdrew and is running the paper full time. I was lucky that Dr. Nunlee could find a spot for me as his assistant."

"You're going to teach at the college then? Gee, that's great!"

"It's only temporary," Charles said. "Now that I have my degree, I've applied for several defense jobs, and as soon as I get an interesting offer I'm going to take it. In the meantime, I'm helping Dr. Nunlee and I'm taking some post-graduate courses."

"What about your paper, what was it? Something about atoms?"

"*Gaseous Diffusion and Uranium Enrichment*," Charles said. "It's funny, but since Dr. Nunlee sent it off, we haven't heard another thing about it. We don't know if it was accepted or rejected. You'd think they would have made up their mind by now, wouldn't you?"

"Maybe it's a good sign that you haven't heard anything," Martin suggested. "Maybe if they were going to reject it, you would have heard by now."

"That's what Dad keeps saying. You know he's had dozens and dozens of articles published in national publications, and he says they are awfully slow. But I don't know, it's been such a long time."

"Have you heard from Dottie?"

"Yes," Charles said. "She writes to me at least once a week. She's still at Camp Rucker with Jim. Actually, she's living in a little town called Ozark, Alabama. It's about the size of Mount Eagle, she says."

"What do Mom and Dad think about her? Have they gotten over it yet?"

Charles sighed and pulled his leg up to wrap his arms around his knee. "No," he said. "Not really. I don't know. I thought I would eventually be able to talk them into coming around, but they were both terribly hurt by it. And, of course, I hurt them too, because I was a party to it. But Martin, I had no choice. You know she was pregnant? What else could I have done but let them go?"

"Dottie and Jim had no right to put you in that position," Martin said.

"I sort of thrust myself into it," Charles said. "Anyway, I've had time to think about it, and I really do think this was the best thing under the circumstances. I think Mom and Dad are wrong in being so obdurate. Dottie needs their love and their support now more than ever. She has their love, of course, no matter how upset Mom and Dad are with her I know they still love her. A couple of weeks ago I caught Dad looking at her picture. He was sitting behind his desk in his office and he was looking at those desk photographs of us, but as I watched, I realized he wasn't looking at all of us, just at Dottie. I backed up a few paces, then made some noise as I approached his office, and when I got there he had put the pictures down and was busy working on the advertising log. But I knew."

"Have you ever tried to talk to Dad? Alone I mean?" Martin asked. "Maybe you could bring him around first, then work on Mom."

"I've tried that," Charles said. "I've tried Dad alone, and Mom alone, and both of them together. I guess it's just going to take time."

"In the meantime, Dottie has you, brother," Martin said. "And Jim."

"What little she gets to see of him," Charles said. "I understand that he is on the base for the entire week, and manages to get out only on weekends. Dottie keeps herself busy though, because she's doing volunteer work with the Red Cross, in family services." Charles laughed. "She's helping other people over personal crises. Can you imagine that? Someone actually going to our sister when they're in a pinch?"

Both brothers were laughing at the thought, when there was a knock on the door.

"Martin? Martin, are you about ready?"

"That's Dad, getting nervous," Martin said, walking over to open the door. Thurman stood on the other side, wearing a tux and a big smile.

"Hey, who's getting married today anyway?" Martin said. "Me or you?"

"Does it surprise you that your old man can still look good when he's dressed up?" Thurman asked.

"Not at all, Dad," Martin replied easily. "After all, where do you think I get my good looks from?"

"Thanks a lot," Charles teased. "And what about me? Did I come from under a cabbage leaf or something? Why didn't I get any of those handsome features?"

"Charles, I wish you wouldn't put yourself down so," Nancy said then, appearing in the hallway just behind Thurman. "You are a very handsome boy. Now come along, all of you. We surely don't want to be late."

Nancy led the way down the hall, moving quickly as if by so doing she could convey a sense of urgency to the others. Thurman was right behind her, while Martin and Charles brought up the rear.

"You are *very, very* handsome," Martin teased in a low whisper to Charles, and they both laughed.

St. Paul's was in the northeast section of town, just off highway 51. It was a small, white church, set in a well-tended lawn beneath great oak and redbud trees. The leaves of the trees had already changed color, and they formed a golden arch over the roof of the church. A couple of maple trees added a splash of red to the scene as their leaves glowed in fiery crimson. Behind the church the hills were a painter's palette of fall color beneath a bright, blue sky. It was a scene from a Rockwell *Saturday Evening Post* cover come to life.

There were already several cars parked around the church, and to one side of the church children laughed and kicked through the fallen leaves. Father Percy greeted Martin and his family as they got out of the car.

"Are the Semmes here yet?" Nancy asked.

"Not yet," Father Percy said. "You two can go right on in, the usher will show you to your seat. Martin, you can come around the side of the church and use the back door to my office. Charles, you're the best man, right?"

"Yes," Charles said. "And before anyone asks me for the one hundredth time, I have the ring," he said, putting his hand over his breast pocket. He, like his father, was wearing a tuxedo. "Somewhere," he said, slapping his breast pocket. "I know I have it." He made a big show of slapping all his pockets. "It's here, I know it is. It must be."

"Charles!" Nancy gasped. "Charles, have you *lost* it?"

Charles smiled, and produced the ring, holding it up for his mother to see.

"Oh, Charles, don't tease me so," Nancy said. "You're making me a nervous wreck."

"Hey, Charley, what do you say," Martin said. "Do you want to go fishing?"

"Sure, why not?" Charles replied.

"Get around there where you are supposed to be," Nancy said impatiently, and Charles, Martin, Thurman, and even Father Percy laughed.

Once inside Father Percy's office, Martin and

Charles sat on the red covered chairs alongside the wall and waited for the ceremony to begin. Martin studied the walls. Behind Father Percy's desk there was a Crucifix, and beside the Crucifix, a picture of a lamb above the words *Agnus Dei* in stylized lettering. There was a church calendar with all the holy days and seasons of the church marked in the liturgical colors, and there was a bulletin board, filled with papers. Prominent on the bulletin board was a paper saying, "Holt wedding, October 5th."

"Are you nervous?" Charles asked quietly.

"A little," Martin admitted. "It's a big change, you know."

"I know," Charles said. He laughed. "I wonder if Yolinda has had time to get nervous yet?"

"What do you mean?"

"You wouldn't think there would be that many things a girl would have to do to get ready for a wedding," Charles said. "But I swear, the last two months, every time I looked up, I saw Mom and Yolinda driving down to Cairo, or over to Cape Girardeau, or up to St. Louis to get something. I didn't know if they were planning a wedding or a Broadway opening."

"Have Mom and Yolinda been getting along well?"

"Are you kidding? They have become as close as—"Charles stopped in mid-sentence.

"What?"

"I was going to say as close as mother and daughter, but under the circumstances with Dottie, that may not be such a good analogy."

"Do you think Mom is using Yolinda as a surrogate?"

"Yeah," Charles said quietly. "Don't get me

wrong, Martin, Mom and Yolinda get along very well, and even if Dottie were still here I know it would be just the same. But, to tell the truth, I do sometimes think that Mom is trying to use Yolinda to cover the pain. She has insisted that Yolinda live with us when you leave, and Yolinda has agreed."

Martin heard organ music then, and the clear, sweet notes of a young woman singing *Oh Promise Me*.

"It's Mary Tulley," Charles explained to Martin's questioning glance. "Yolinda wanted her to sing."

Martin laughed. "I thought Father Percy wouldn't let anyone sing anything that wasn't in the hymnal. Remember the big flap when Julie Robbins got married? Her mother wanted to sing *Because*, or something."

Charles laughed quietly. "Yes, I remember. But wasn't part of the problem the fact that Mrs. Robbins couldn't carry a tune?"

"I think the way Dad put it was, she couldn't sing *Come To Jesus* in whole notes," Martin said.

After the song, Father Percy opened the door and stuck his head in. "All right," he said.

"Into the breach," Martin said under his breath, and he and Charles walked out into the nave to stand between the lectern and the pulpit and await Yolinda's entrance.

The organ began playing the *Wedding March*, and there was Yolinda, carrying a spray of flowers, and accompanied by half a dozen bridesmaids, and a trainbearer and a flowergirl.

Martin caught his breath. He had never seen a more beautiful woman in his life than the vision of loveliness gliding down the aisle toward him.

*   *   *

Martin parked his father's Buick in front of the cabin at Big Springs, Missouri, then turned the engine off and leaned back in his seat. "This is it," he said. "Our honeymoon cabana."

"It was nice of your father to rent it for us," Yolinda said. She was wearing the lime green linen dress, very correct for the wedding trip, into which she had changed immediately after the Country Club reception. There had been literally hundreds of people at the reception, including many people that Martin had never even heard of before. He had heard several people comment on the fact that his and Yolinda's wedding was "*the social event*" of the season, and it had irritated him because he didn't want to be part of a show. But Yolinda was obviously pleased by it, and she had talked about it for the most of the one hundred and fifty-mile drive from Mount Eagle to Big Springs, so Martin never commented on his own feelings about the wedding.

Martin's father had given him the keys to the Buick, along with enough gas coupons to ensure that they would have enough gas to drive to Big Springs and back. Big Springs was a natural spring in the Ozark mountains of southern Missouri. It was a huge, natural fountain which poured out millions of gallons of water per day with a roar which could be heard from miles away. The water was clear and swift and cold, and it became Current River, winding through some of the most beautiful and primitive scenery in the Nation. There were trails around the spring, where crystalline rock formations dazzled the hiker with their diamond-like clusters, and there were boats and canoes available for river rides, and there were cabins along the river's edge.

Martin carried the suitcases into the cabin, then closed the door behind them and grabbed Yolinda, pulling her to him, smothering her with kisses.

"Uhmmm, wait a minute, hold it," Yolinda struggling to free herself. "Martin, what are you doing?"

"What am I doing?" Martin asked in a surprised tone of voice. "What do you mean, what am I doing? I'm kissing you. I want to make love." He started unbuttoning his shirt.

"Oh, Martin," Yolinda said. "You haven't changed a bit, have you? You are just as grabby as you ever were."

"My God, Yolinda, we're married," Martin said.

"I know," Yolinda said. Then she smiled, sweetly, and put her hand out to touch Martin's face. "That means we have time, darling. We don't have to rush things like two kids in a parked car."

Martin laughed. "Yeah," he said sheepishly. "I guess we've had our share of that, haven't we?"

"Let's walk around, unwind from the trip, and see some of the sights," Yolinda said. "Then, tonight, when we go to bed, it will be as it is supposed to be."

"All right," Martin agreed, taking her hand and kissing her fingers.

"It'll be ever so much nicer," Yolinda said. "You'll see. I know you'll agree with me."

Martin and Yolinda walked all through the park, hand in hand, exclaiming over the crystal rocks, gazing in wonder at the multi-colored hills of fall foliage, and standing on the edge of the spring beholding all its fury and power. They were the perfect couple, she, beautiful in her hiking slacks, also bought just for the occasion, and he in his khaki Air Corps uniform.

As the sun was setting they went into a rustic, log-cabin type building which was the only restaurant in the area. Martin had wanted a steak, but he was told, apologetically, that they had run out of their rationed quota, but they did have fresh venison, supplied by local hunters. Martin and Yolinda both ordered the venison which had been marinated in wine before roasting, and both agreed that it was as good as any steak would have been.

When they finished dinner and went back to the cabin, Martin put his arm around Yolinda and he felt her tense and stiffen.

"Are you afraid?" he asked.

"Of our future?"

"Of tonight?"

"No," Yolinda said quickly, perhaps too quickly. "Why should I be afraid?"

"Exactly," Martin said. "Why should you be afraid? Just think of it as the most wonderful moment two people can share, an ecstasy beyond your wildest imagining. Darling, I want to make you happy, and I want to make you feel everything a woman can feel."

"You talk as if you have had experience in this," Yolinda said.

"What makes you say something like that?"

"The most wonderful moment two people can share, and ecstasy beyond my wildest imaginings," Yolinda said. "Do you have experience?"

"Darling, what is it?" Martin asked. "Why are you asking me this? What difference does it make? Isn't now what's important?"

Yolinda started to cry. "That's just it," Yolinda said. "Now is important. Only I was naive enough to think that it was something that we would do together, experience together."

"I'm sorry," Martin said softly. "Believe me, darling, the last thing I would want to do in this world is hurt you in some way."

"Did you love her?" Yolinda asked.

"I . . . I thought I did. It was a long time ago. A very long time ago," Martin lied.

"Is it someone I know?"

"No," Martin said. "It happened the summer our family spent in Colorado. She was the daughter of the lodge operator."

There had been a summer in Colorado when Martin was in high school, and he had had a brief, unconsummated affair with the lodge operator's daughter. He had been teased about the girl when he returned to Mount Eagle, and Yolinda heard about her after he and Yolinda started going together. Because of that, it was believable enough for her to accept the story, which Martin knew would hurt her much less than the truth would. The truth was his experience on the train with Linda Busby had been his very first.

"I . . . I'm sorry," Yolinda said. She laughed a small laugh, through her tears. "I guess I'm just nervous."

"It's natural enough," Martin said. He grinned at her. "I'm as nervous as you are, I assure you. It's just that . . . I love you, Yolinda, and I want you. And that love and desire is stronger than my nervousness."

"I . . . I want you too," Yolinda said, and she leaned into him and kissed him, and this time when Martin deepened the kiss, she didn't back away. Then, after a moment, she did break off the kiss.

"Wait," she said. "Let me go into the bathroom and get ready for you."

"Okay," Martin said. "But don't take long. I've waited long enough for you, I don't want to wait anymore."

While Yolinda was in the bathroom, Martin slipped out of his clothes and turned back the covers of the bed, then climbed in. The night air was already cool enough that the sheet felt comfortable over him, and its texture felt good against his naked skin. He waited for several moments, then Yolinda came out of the bathroom. She was wearing a long, silk nightgown, and over that, a dressing gown, like everything else she had worn on this day "correct" and selected for the occasion. She took off her dressing gown, then, shyly, slipped into bed. Martin moved to her.

"Martin!" she gasped. "You don't even have on any pajamas!"

"They're a waste of time," Martin laughed. "Just like this thing is," and he began pulling at the nightgown.

"Don't you like it?" Yolinda pouted. "I bought it just for you."

"The present is wrapped very pretty," Martin teased. "But when I was a kid, I always tore through the wrapping to get to what's inside."

"All right," Yolinda said. She giggled. "I guess you're still just like a little boy at Christmas. Here's your Christmas present."

The light in the bathroom was still on, and it illuminated the bed so that Martin could see Yolinda as she undressed for him. He saw then, for the first time, that which he had only felt before, groping in the car, or on the front porch, or in the parlor of her house after everyone was asleep.

"My God," Martin said reverently. "You are beautiful. You are absolutely beautiful."

"Do you think so?" Yolinda asked. "Do you really think so?"

"I'll show you what I think," Martin said, and he went to her again and they made love.

It was a satisfying experience for Martin, he felt the tenderness, the pleasures, the quick, hot rush of orgasm, then the total relaxation afterward. And Yolinda seemed to enjoy it as well. She didn't embrace it with the uninhibited enthusiasm shown by Linda Busby, but she did seem to attain some pleasure, if not total fulfillment.

Martin passed it off as being a normal reaction for the first time, and he vowed privately that he would lift her to the stars, and have her writhing with pleasure and screaming for more before their four-day stay was concluded.

But, though he used every technique he had learned at the skilled fingers of his first woman, and though he showed Yolinda all the tenderness and patience of which he was capable, it never seemed to be more to her than a mildly pleasant experience. And this from a woman whose petting had kept him tied in knots for the last three years.

11

The last flies of summer," Mrs. Holman said. "They are always the fattest and the peskiest." She brushed her hand impatiently across her face, disturbing, but only momentarily, the fly which had been buzzing around.

Mrs. Holman was Dottie's landlady. She told Dottie that she was 28, but she looked to be of an indeterminate age. She could have been nineteen, or fifty-nine. She wore gray, colorless dresses which hung as a shapeless covering from her thin frame. Her hair had the color and texture of sunburned grass. Her skin was weathered and wrinkled, and her bosom was flat.

"You bein' your way 'n all, it must be terrible bad for you."

Dottie was ironing clothes. She had only her own clothes to wash and iron, Jim's uniforms were done by the base laundry. Even so, it was a chore which left her exhausted, because of the heat, and the fact that she was now six months pregnant.

"I don't know which is worse," Dottie said, brushing her hair away from her sweat-dampened face. "The flies or the heat."

"Oh law, child, it's the flies what's worse," Mrs. Holman said. "Why the heat is pert' nigh over now. Hit'll be comin' up a frost here one mornin' afore you know it. Have you heard how much longer your husban's gonna stay here?"

"Colonel Bidwell promised me he'd keep Jim here until the baby was born," Dottie said. "He said Jim was going to be promoted to corporal, and he would be in the cadre for the next training group. They always select some men from one training group and keep them back for the next, then they send them on and replace them with a new cadre."

"That's real lucky for you all, ain't it?"

Dottie smiled. "It isn't all luck," she said. "My working with the Red Cross has its advantages. But don't ever tell Jim. I don't know how he would take it if he thought I was trying to pull strings behind his back."

"Ain't that the truth though?" Mrs. Holman said. "Oh, speakin' o' not tellin' your man, I went ahead 'n tole the plumber to pipe you some water down here so's you don' have to go up the stairs 'n tote a bucket down from the back porch. I jes' up 'n done it on my own, 'n I didn' tell Dale nothin' about it. By the time he finds out it'll already be done 'n it'll be too late for him to do anythin' about it."

"Thank you, Mrs. Holman," Dottie said. "That will be a big help."

"Well, I don' think you ought to tote water like that, bein' as you're gonna have a young'un come January." Mrs. Holman looked around the basement which had been converted into an apartment, of sorts, for Dottie. "I got to say, you've done heaps with this ole' basement. When Dale first said we ought to rent it out 'n get some o' that war money, why I wondered who'd rent such a place. But you've got it lookin' near 'bout pretty."

"I found some colored muslin on sale at the dime store," Dottie said. "And those blue flowers are just stick-on paper flowers, but I thought they really brightened up the walls."

"It looks plumb pretty," Mrs. Holman said. "I jes' wishin' we could afford a linoleum rug to put on the floor down here, 'stead of the concrete. Then it would really look bright 'n pretty."

"It's a place I can be with my husband on the weekends," Dottie said. "It's pretty enough for me and I'm glad to have it."

"I hear Dale's ole' truck a'comin'," Mrs. Holman said. "He's been out cuttin' wood most o' day. I swear, here lately I don' see no more of him than you do o' your'n." Mrs. Holman laughed. "Course, in my case, that don' bother me none too much ... it'd be differ'nt iffen I had me a man as pretty as your'n is, though."

Mrs. Holman was still laughing as she climbed the stairs out of the basement, then walked across the back porch and into her own house.

When Dottie and Jim arrived in Ozark, Jim had two more days before he had to report. Dottie had foolishly thought they would find a place quickly, then have the rest of the time together, but that wasn't to be the case. They spent two whole days looking, sleeping the night in the car. There was either nothing available, or that which was available was just too expensive. When they found the basement, it was the first thing they had found which was anywhere near what they thought they could afford, and even it was high enough to cause them some concern. There was no running water in the basement, and there was only one electrical outlet, a naked lightbulb which hung on a frayed cord down from the maze of pipes and boards which was the underneath floor for the house. A screw-in receptacle between the bulb and the wire gave Dottie a place to plug in a hotplate, and that was all she had to cook on. She was now using that outlet to plug in her iron.

The apartment was "furnished" with an old ironframe bed, an unpainted table with two rickety chairs, a sofa, covered with a bedspread to hide the tears and stains, and a large old dresser which Dottie actually liked. The walls and floor were concrete, though the walls had been painted white. The stairs leading up to the door were also painted white. There were eight small windows, located at the top of the walls, around the basement.

Dottie had hung curtains, and applied blue flower stickers to the walls, and cleaned and arranged, so that within a month the basement began to take on a home quality. Besides, she reminded herself often, it was her first home, and no matter what it was like, she would always remember it with warmth and love.

Things improved when Dottie got a job. It was nice to be able to get out of the apartment every day, and it was nice to have the extra money coming in. Her job had started as volunteer work with the Red Cross. Then, a paid worker's husband was transferred, and that left an opening. Dottie asked for the job, and she got it. She was paid one hundred dollars a month, which was nine dollars more than Jim was making. As an added bonus, Dottie was able to see Jim for a few moments even during the week, and this week Jim had proposed that they go down to Panama City,

Florida, with a friend of his, Mel Berg, and his wife, Bonnie. They were going to leave right after Saturday morning inspection, and they would be at the beach by early afternoon.

"Just think," Jim said. "All Saturday afternoon, all night and all day Sunday. We'll come back Sunday night."

"Where will we sleep?" Dottie had asked.

"Where will we sleep? Why, we'll sleep on the beach," Jim said enthusiastically. "It'll be great fun!"

It was Saturday now, and the fact that Mr. Holman had come back from the woods indicated that it was probably pretty close to twelve. Jim had said that he would be home by twelve.

Dottie unplugged the iron, and took the clothes over to the dresser, then put them away. She had welcomed the ironing this morning, because it helped to pass the time while she was waiting for Jim. She had even welcomed the visit from Mrs. Holman, though Mrs. Holman's extreme drawl and corrupted use of the language grated on Dottie's nerves.

Dottie heard the *ooga* sound of a klaxon horn, and she squealed with delight and ran up the stairway, just in time to see Jim pulling in, honking wildly, and grinning from ear to ear. She ran out to the car and met him as he got out, hugging his neck and plastering him with kisses.

"Oof," Jim teased, as her belly pushed into him. "Listen, what are you trying to do, knock the breath out of me? That's a dangerous weapon you are carrying around there." He patted her stomach.

"What? How dare you call our baby a dangerous weapon!" Dottie said.

There was another honk, and a '41 Ford pulled

in behind Jim's old Chevrolet. Mel and Bonnie got out, smiling and waving, and Mel slapped the fender of the car, then pointed at Dottie. "What are you standing around here putting on a big front for?" he teased. "How come you aren't ready to go?"

"I am ready," Dottie said. "Oh, and I fried some chicken. In fact, I fried three chickens. I worked that little old hot plate to death."

"Well, it couldn't have died a more noble death," Mel said. "Now go get the chicken, then pile into the back, or, would the girls rather ride in the back and us men in front?" he teased.

"Are you kidding? I haven't seen you in a week," Bonnie said.

"I know, I know," Mel said. "But you 'n me, we got enough maturity to handle a week's separation without doin' somethin' shockin'. These two kids, though, I mean, if we let them alone in the back seat there's no tellin' what they might do. Only thing I've got to say is, remember that you are with child, and you should be awfully careful about sexual things when you are with child."

"Mel!" Bonnie said. "Will you hush up?" She laughed. "Will you listen to him? He is an absolute nut sometimes."

"Yeah, well, I got a right to be. Me 'n the young lover boy here got news, right, Jim? Or should I say, right, Corporal?"

"That's right, Corporal," Jim replied.

"Corporal?" Bonnie said. "You two have been promoted to Corporal?"

"That's right," Mel said. "And that isn't all the good news. You tell them the rest, Corporal Anderson."

"Right, Corporal Berg," Jim said. He looked at

Dottie and smiled. "Honey, I'm going to be here when the baby is born. I got the word this morning. I'm staying on as cadre for the next cycle. That'll take me until the last week in January before I have to go overseas."

"Oh, Jim," Dottie said. "That's wonderful!" She hugged and kissed him again, and breathed a prayer of thanks for Colonel Bidwell's helping hand. He had even managed to extend Mel's stay on her request, for no reason other than that Jim and Mel had become good friends during their training cycle.

"Boy, are we going to whip some lard asses into shape in this next cycle," Mel said. "They are going to learn what it's like to be *in-fan-try soldiers,*" he added, dragging the words out.

"Infantry, Queen of Battle!" Jim said, and he and Mel let out a cheer, then laughed out loud.

It was about a three hour drive over the crushed shell and macadam roads, until they crested a little hill and suddenly saw the sparkling blue Gulf before them.

"Oh, look at that!" Bonnie said. "Have you ever seen anything more beautiful in your life?"

"There it is," Mel said. "The Father of All Waters."

Dottie laughed. "That's the Mississippi, silly."

"What?"

"The Father of All Waters. That's what the word Mississippi means, in some Indian language."

"Well, what's that thing in front of us?"

"It's the Gulf of Mexico," Jim said.

"Is that the truth? You mean a puny-assed river has a grand name like Father of All Waters, and the Gulf is just called the Gulf?"

"No one has ever named it anything else," Jim said.

"That's crazy," Mel said.

After they came down the little hill, the road made a "T", then ran east and west along the beach. A sign pointed east, toward Panama City, but Mel turned to the right, away from the city.

"Where are you going?" Dottie asked. "I thought we were going to Panama City."

"I've got a surprise for you," Mel said. "Tell 'em, Bonnie."

Bonnie turned around in her seat, then smiled and held up a key. "Mr. Parker, our landlord, has a cabin on the beach. He's letting us use it."

"What?" Dottie said. "You mean we actually have a cabin?"

"That's a fact," Mel said.

"What's he charging us?" Jim asked.

"Nothing," Bonnie said. "It's absolutely free."

"I never knew a banker with a heart before," Jim said.

Mel laughed. "Well, it's not all out of the goodness of his heart. It seems there is a large banker in New York named Berg, who has some say-so in the credit extension of Parker's bank here."

"Berg? You mean someone in your family?"

"No," Mel laughed. "But you know hów these southern folks are. They think all us Jews are kin anyway, and when the name's the same, they just know it."

"And Mel didn't discourage him any when he found out," Bonnie added laughing.

"Anyway, Parker gave me the key," Mel went on. "And he said"—Mel did a perfect imitation of Tom Parker's southern drawl—" 'lissen, why'nt you 'n the little lady there take that other nice couple on down to the beach 'n stay in my cabin? Ya'll have a nice time down there, you heah? 'N then you can write your kinfolk up in N'Yawk 'n tell 'im 'bout how nice us gentiles been'a treatin' our joosh guests.' "

Everyone in the car broke up at Mel's impersonation, then Bonnie let out a squeal. "There it is," she said. "Mar Vista, see?"

Mel turned off the road and parked the car in the sand in front of the cabin. It was a white clapboard house, with a screened porch and a red roof. There was no lawn at all, only sand and brush, between the house and the road, and only sand between the house and the Gulf itself.

"This place is really fine," Jim said. "You know, I could stay here for the duration."

"Let's check it out," Mel suggested.

The four got out of the car and walked across the sand to the house. Mel slid the key in the door, twisted it, then pushed the door open. Inside, the house smelled a little musty, like any house which had been closed up for a while, but the predominant smell was the pleasant scent of the sea and salt air. The house consisted of a living room and kitchen, and two bedrooms. Both bedrooms were on the back of the house, and when Mel and Jim started raising the windows to let in some air, they could hear the crashing thunder of the surf.

"Listen," Dottie said. "I love this place, and it's a thrill to think that we won't have to sleep outside tonight, but, could we eat on the beach tonight, like a picnic?"

"Sure we can," Jim said.

"And, could we gather some driftwood and make a fire on the beach?"

"Oh, yes," Bonnie said. "Oh, Mel, let's do that."

"I don't know about the fire," Mel said. "The Coast Guard has a ban on building fires on the beach. They act as signal beacons to the German subs."

"German subs?" Dottie said. She looked through the window toward the water, blue and dancing with a million sun jewels. "Do you mean to tell me that under that beautiful Gulf there are German submarines?"

"Yeah," Mel said, and for the moment the gaiety of their vacation was interrupted. "The bastards are out there, all right."

"Then of course we won't build a fire," Dottie said.

Mel had three cases of beer in the trunk of the car, and he and Jim brought the beer in while the girls brought in the food. They loaded the beer into the refrigerator. "What I wouldn't give to have one of these back in Ozark. All I have is an icebox."

Mel had walked down to the surf. It was a dark night, and the line between the sea and the sky couldn't be seen. Only the frothing surf gave tint or texture to the blackness of the sea, while the white sand of the beach showed clearly the line of separation between sea and land.

Dottie and Jim were lying back on their elbows, looking out toward the sea, while a few feet away, Bonnie was sitting quietly, drinking a beer. Mel had stood a few moments before to walk down to the sea's edge, and his shadow was barely discernible from where the picnic had been.

"What's Mel doing down there?" Dottie asked.

"Just looking, I guess," Jim said. He kissed Dottie.

"We don't get too many quiet moments. It's nice to take advantage of the ones we do get. I guess that's what he's doing."

"I am so happy you are staying until the baby is born," Dottie said.

"Tell Colonel Bidwell thanks," Jim said easily.

"What?"

Jim laughed. "Honey, when the Captain called me in and gave me my orders, he asked who did I know in high places? It seems that he had already chosen his cadre and he was overruled. I figured that could only come from Colonel Bidwell, and if it came from Colonel Bidwell, that means it came from you and the Red Cross."

"You aren't angry?"

"No," Jim said. "I want to see this baby before I leave. I'll stay any way I can."

"What about your captain? Will he be hard on you and Mel?"

"No, I don't think so," Jim said. "I don't think it really matters that much to him. He'll be going out with the next cycle, just like us."

"I don't want to think about that," Dottie said, and she shivered, though there was no chill in the air.

Jim put his arms around her. "You have to think about it, darling," he said quietly. "And there's something else you have to think of as well. Honey, if I, that is if something should happen to me that—"

"No," Dottie said, kissing him on the lips to seal off his talk. "No, I don't want you to say it. I don't even want you to think it."

"But, we have to consider the possibility," Jim said.

"I refuse to consider the possibility," Dottie said.

"Nothing is going to happen to you, Jim Anderson. You are going to come back to me. I promise you that."

Jim laughed. "Well, all right," he said. "I'll hold you to that promise. Now, what are you going to do while I'm gone?"

"What do you mean? I'm going to wait for you, of course."

"I know that, darling," Jim said. "But the question is, where? Now, I've been thinking. I know how you feel about your folks and all now, but I think you should go back to Mount Eagle anyway."

"I'm not going back to Mount Eagle until you can go with me," Dottie said.

"But, where will you stay? What will you do?"

"I've already spoken to Colonel Bidwell about that, too," Dottie said. "I'm going to New York. That way, I'll have Bonnie as a friend, and I'm going to work with the Red Cross in a military hospital there."

"New York?" Jim said. He gave a small, puzzled laugh. "What? Why would you want to go there? You're a small town girl, New York is so big."

"I know. But, when you come back to the States, that's where you'll come, and I want to be there," Dottie said. "As long as I'm there, I'll feel like I'm as close to you as I can possibly get."

"But what about the baby?"

"What about the baby?" Dottie asked. "Bonnie is going to help me find a nurse during the day, and I'll take care of it at night."

"Dottie, don't you think it would be better if you—"

"I'm going to New York," Dottie said. "My mind is made up."

Jim laughed in surrender, then kissed her again. "I'm glad you're on our side, Dottie."

Mel came walking back then, and he settled down on the blanket next to Bonnie. "Well, I named it," he said.

"You named it? You named what?" Jim asked.

"The Gulf," Mel explained. "I told you it needed a better name than Gulf. It needed something at least as good as Father of All Waters. So, I named it."

"What did you name it?" Jim asked.

"I named it the Prince of Puddles."

Dottie laughed. "That's a pretty good name, but you ought to mark it in some way, you know, have some kind of a ceremony."

"I did," Mel said. He burped. "I pissed in it."

12

Left scanner to pilot, left gear down and locked."

"Roger."

"Right scanner to pilot, right gear down and locked."

"Roger, main gear down and locked."

"We're over the threshold," Martin said to the man sitting on his left. Martin was flying as the co-pilot on the *Truculent Turtle,* a B-17 belonging to the 605th Bomb Group. Pilot in command was Captain Leo Greenly, the bombardier was Second Lieutenant Gregg Harris, and the navigator was Second-Lieutenant Manny Byrd. They were on final approach to runway 27 at Nesbitt Field, Long Island, New York.

"Chop the power," Leo Greenly said, and Martin pulled all four throttle levers back. The airplane settled onto the runway with a protesting chirp from the tires, then slowed to taxi speed as they took the first turn. Behind them another B-17 was landing, touching down even before Martin's plane was clear of the runway, and still in the air behind that one was a third, while others were on the base and downwind legs. In all there were twelve airplanes in the group, twelve bombers which had been flying practice missions for over two months; learning how to form a combat box, wherein the guns of all planes form an umbrella of machine gun fire through which enemy fighters could not penetrate. At least, that was the theory.

"God rest ye merry gentlemen, let nothing you dismay. . . ." Leo sang as the B-17 lumbered down the taxi-way toward the parking apron. Already there was a follow-me jeep in front of them, leading them to their particular spot. "Are you ready for Christmas, Marty?" Leo asked.

"I guess so," Martin said. "I never thought I'd still be in the States this Christmas."

"Oh, I see. You thought you'd be somewhere over Germany, bombing the Reich into submission, did you?"

"Or the Pacific," Martin said.

"Yes, well, we'll be there soon enough, my friend. We'll be there soon enough. For my ticket, I'm glad enough to have this Christmas with the wife and boy. I'd think you would be too, what with that pretty wife of yours. But no children? Are you fallin' down on the job?"

"Yolinda doesn't want any children yet," Martin said. "She'd rather wait."

"Wait? Wait for what? For the war to be endin'? Listen, I don't want to be gloomy, but there is something we may as well face. Our chances of coming back from this little fracas are about 60-40 at best. Now with that kind of odds, it'd be good to leave something behind, if you know what I mean. I don't know if you are a religious man or not, but one thing is true 'n certain, and that's that children are a type of immortality. We may go down in flame over some Kraut city somewhere, but as long as we leave a kid behind, there's a little part of us that goes on."

Martin had thought of that, and he had also wondered why Yolinda would not want to have his baby to remind her of him. But she had been almost paranoid about getting pregnant, insisting always that he 'wear some protection'. She watched the calendar and the onset of her periods so closely that Martin once laughed, and said she reminded him of a co-ed who was loose and nervous.

"That's easy enough for you to say," Yolinda said. "You aren't the one who'll have to carry the baby."

"No, I would think that would be a little hard, don't you? I don't think they make maternity flight gear." Martin tried to joke about it, but a little of the hurt came through, even in the joke.

The ground guide held both arms up, then moved one finger across his throat in a chopping action, and Martin pulled the engines into idle cutoff. They stopped after just a few spins of the prop, and then all was quiet, except for the hum of the gyros as they spun down. He turned the fuel off.

"All switches off?" Leo asked.

Martin ran his hand over all the switches, on the panel, and overhead. The last switch he turned off was the master switch and then the airplane was completely dead.

"I hope we never have to drop bombs on Boston," Leo said, as he filled out the log book. "But if we do, I damn sure know how to get there. We must have flown a dozen bombing runs over Beantown in the last two weeks."

"Only eleven," Martin said. "But who is counting?"

"I'm counting," Manny Byrd said. "Only nine days to Christmas. What do you think of that?"

"Are you expecting something from Santa Claus?" Leo teased.

Gregg came back from his bombardier's spot in the nose. "He's expecting a map," he said. "Did you fellas say we've been flying to Boston? He's been looking for Baltimore."

"Well, hell, I gave you three choices the last time," Manny said. "I told you we were either at Boston, Baltimore, or Topeka."

"Is there ocean by Topeka?"

"Hey, you guys up there," someone called from the ground. "There's a meeting of all officers at 1900 hours."

"Oh, no," Gregg said. "Tonight is my wife's birthday. I promised her we'd go out."

"What time is it now?" Leo asked.

"1745."

"Well, if we hurry, we can get home for some chow. You wanna ride, Marty?"

"Yes, if you don't mind," Martin said.

The air crew climbed down from the plane just as the ground crew took over. They started refueling, and checking it out for the next flight. Parachutes and flight gear were pitched into the back of a 3/4 truck known as the alert vehicle, and then the crew was free until the next formation for the enlisted men, and the officers until the officers' meeting at seven that evening.

Each crew of officers was furnished with one jeep, but Leo had his own car on the base, so he let Manny and Gregg have the jeep, while he shared his car with Martin. Martin, Leo, and Gregg were married, so they had been provided with quarters on the base. The married officers quarters consisted of a quonset hut, divided by a wall across the middle, so that each end became a private home. They were modest quarters, but they were clean. They included a living room, kitchen, dining area, two bedrooms and a bathroom. They also came with an enlisted man who took care of the lawn and all repair work. The housework for anyone whose rank was below colonel had to be done by the housewife. There were some officers who wanted to hire a maid for their wife, but base security was extremely strict, and maids were not allowed.

"When are you going to put up your Christmas tree?" Leo asked as he let Martin off in front of his quarters.

"Christmas eve, of course," Martin said. "You aren't supposed to put up a Christmas tree during Advent."

"Who said so?"

"Well, that's just the way it is," Martin said. "I'm Episcopalian, you see, and at home we'd always put up the tree on Christmas eve, then we left it up all through the Christmas season." He laughed. "That's the way we would sing Christmas carols, too. We always seemed a little out of synch with everyone else; sometimes it seemed like it was Christmas until almost Easter."

"That's nonsense," Leo said. "You're in New York now, and Christmas begins when Macy's says it does, and that's anytime after Thanksgiving that you *want* it to begin."

"You may be right," Martin said. "Anyway, maybe a Christmas tree will brighten things up. Lord knows I need something," he added, almost offhandedly.

"Beg your pardon?"

"Oh, nothing," Martin said. "I was just thinking out loud, I guess. About Yolinda. This is going to be her first Christmas away from home and I guess she's taking it pretty hard."

"Well, tell her to cheer up. At least she has you." Leo waved, then drove on to his own quarters, which were only about three houses down the street. Martin walked up the sidewalk then pushed the door open.

"Hello," he called. "Honey, I'm home."

Martin didn't get an answer, and he looked in the kitchen. She wasn't there, and it didn't look as if she had even been there. The stove was cold, and there was no smell of cooked food.

"Yolinda?"

Martin heard a sob coming from the bedroom, and he turned and moved quickly toward the sound. He saw Yolinda lying across the bed. Several tissues had been wadded and tossed aside, and she was crying.

"Yolinda, darling, what is it?" Martin asked, moving quickly to her. He sat on the bed and put his hands on her shoulder. "Sweetheart, what is it?"

"Don't touch me!" Yolinda said, sobbing again.

"What?" Martin asked, taking his hands away quickly, as if they had been burned. "What do you mean? Honey, what is it? Why are you crying?"

"I went to the doctor today," Yolinda said.

"The doctor? Honey, are you sick?"

"No," Yolinda said. "That is, yes, yes I'm sick, in the worst way. I'm pregnant. Oh, Martin, I'm going to have a baby."

"A baby? Why, darling, that's wonderful!"

"Wonderful?" Yolinda screamed. "What's wonderful about it? Martin, I'm not ready for a baby yet . . . not with you . . . with you gone. Don't you understand? I did not want to get pregnant yet."

"I know you didn't, darling, but you did and now we may as well make the best of it," Martin said.

"I'm miserable," Yolinda said. "Oh, I thought you were going to be careful."

"I was," Martin said. "I was as careful as I could be. Those things aren't one hundred percent perfect, you know, sometimes they leak, or split, or . . ."

"Oh, how horrid! I don't even want to hear about the nasty things. Just quit talking about them."

"Honey, I've got news for you. If it weren't for the fact that the Army has those in the supply system, we wouldn't be able to use them at all. They are made of rubber, you know, and civilians can't even buy them anymore."

"Well, a lot of good they did us," Yolinda said. She began to cry again, and Martin tried to comfort her, though she couldn't be consoled. Finally, she quit crying, from exhaustion more than anything else.

Martin looked at his watch. If it weren't for the fact that it had a luminous dial, he wouldn't have been able to see it, because it had grown dark now and there were no lights on in the house. It was six-fifteen. Martin could hear the radio playing loudly in the house at the other end of the quonset hut, and he could smell pork chops cooking. It reminded him that he was hungry.

"Did you eat?" Martin asked.

"No. I'm not hungry."

"I flew for five hours," Martin said. "And I *am* hungry, and I have to get back for an officers' meeting at nineteen hundred."

"You know I don't know what time that is," Yolinda said in irritation.

"I'm sorry," Martin said. "I mean seven o'clock. Listen, is there anything to eat? Something left over from lunch, maybe?"

"I ate a salad for lunch," Yolinda said. "I thought I was putting on weight and a salad would help. Ha," she said disgustedly. "Nothing will help now. I'm going to get as fat as an old cow."

"You won't be fat, darling, you'll be pregnant. There's a difference."

"What difference? I don't see how any woman can stand herself when she is that way."

"Dottie is pregnant, and she's always been very aware of how she looks. I'll bet she—"

"Don't compare me with your sister!" Yolinda spat. "*I* didn't get pregnant before I got married. *I* didn't run off in the middle of the night to—"

"That's enough!" Martin snapped. "What Dottie did and is doing is her own business, and you'll not belittle her for it. Do you understand me?"

Yolinda grew silent.

"I'm sorry," Martin said a moment later. "I didn't mean to yell at you. It's just that, well, Dottie must be going through her own kind of hell about now, and I don't want to add any to it. It'll soon be Christmas and she'll be away from home for the first time. Not like you, you've still got your parents' support and letters and telephone calls. Dottie has nothing. It's going to be hard for her."

"I'm going home," Yolinda said quietly.

"What?"

"I said I'm going home," Yolinda said again. "I have a plane ticket to St. Louis, and a train ticket from St. Louis to Mount Eagle."

"When?"

"Tomorrow," Yolinda said. "My plane leaves New York at one tomorrow afternoon. Mrs. Greenly is going to take me there."

"I see," Martin said. "And when did all this come about?"

"Oh, Martin, I've been wanting to go home for a long time now," Yolinda said. "I, I can't stand it here. I don't like these tin houses ... you can hear everything your neighbor is doing. I don't like the fact that you are gone most of the day and I only get to see you late in the evening."

"If you go back home you won't get to see me at all," Martin interrupted.

"That will be easier to take," Yolinda said. "Believe me, it will be easier to adjust to not seeing you at all, than having to wait hour upon hour, never knowing when you'll be home. And now I'm pregnant, and I don't want to be away from home while I'm pregnant."

"Couldn't you at least wait until after Christmas?" Martin asked. "Couldn't you at least spend Christmas here with me?"

"No," Yolinda said. "No, that's the worst part of all. I do not want to spend Christmas living like a ... like a sharecropper in a tarpaper shack."

"All right," Martin said quietly. "If you feel that you must."

"Oh, Martin," Yolinda said, and she began crying again. "Oh, Martin, I love you, I do love you. But darling, please understand that seeing you like this is harder than not seeing you at all. Oh, I do pray that this war will be over quickly so we can get back to living a normal, decent, ordinary life."

"Yes," Martin said. "Don't we all."

It was Christmas eve, and, as if on cue, requisitioned by the U.S. Air Corps, a heavy, luxurious, white snow fell on Nesbitt Field. Martin had moved out of the family quarters, partly to make room for another married officer and his wife, and partly because nothing was more lonely than family quarters for one person.

Martin was living in a B.O.Q. room now, just a short walk from the flight line, and it suited him fine. His room was decorated for Christmas, to a degree, with a wreath and a red candle in a sprig of holly. There were also half a dozen Christmas cards taped to the wall; one from his parents, one from Charles, and one from Dottie and Jim:

> "... the stork beat Santa. Your niece, Cynthia Holt Anderdon, arrived at 0530 hours, 19 December, weighing in at five pounds, three ounces."

There was also a card from Yolinda. It was a large, red card, with gilt script saying *"To my husband on this Christmas Day, may all be joyous."* Yolinda had penned a note inside the card.

> "Well, I suppose you have heard by now that you are an Uncle. It's a girl, and they named it Cynthia Holt. I suppose the Holt is some attempt to make up in some way to your mother and father for all the hurt Dottie has caused them. She didn't even come home to have the baby. She had it in the military hospital at Camp Rucker, Alabama, and, get this. She wrote to Charles and told him she is going to move to New York after Jim goes overseas. Can you imagine that?"

There was a knock on the door, and Martin

went over to answer it. Leo, Manny and Gregg were standing on the other side, each holding a bottle, and all smiling broadly.

"We three Kings of Orient are. . . ." they started to sing.

"Listen, if you guys are carolling, you'd better get into another business," Martin laughed. "You sound terrible."

"Come with us," Leo said.

"Where, to your house? No, thanks, your Christmas eve celebration will be a lot more pleasant if you don't have an odd man out."

"Yeah, it probably would be," Leo said. "But we aren't going to my house. We're going to the O club for a special party given by the Group Commander."

"Colonel Prescott? That's even worse."

"Huh-uh," Leo said. He flashed a broad smile. "Prescott was just our training commander. We got our operational commander today."

"Operational commander? You mean . . . Leo, are we operational?"

"Lieutenant, the 605th Bomb Group is now part of the Fifth Air Force. We are flying to England within the next thirty days, exact time of departure to be kept secret."

"Hey, that's great!" Martin said. "That's really great!"

"Come on, let's go meet our new commander," Leo said.

The four officers piled into Leo's car, then drove, singing and laughing through the snow, until they reached the Officers' Club. The Officers' Club was decorated with a string of colored lights which followed the roof line, another string on a big tree under the portico. They parked the car, then trudged through the snow toward the sound of music and laughter.

"What ho!" Greg said. "Would there, perchance, be a party within?"

"Yeah, but right now it's without," Manny said.

"Without?"

"Without us," he laughed. There was a crash of glass and a loud burst of laughter from inside the club.

"Come on," Leo said. "That place sounds dead to me. Let's liven it up!"

The master of arms let the four in with only a cursory glance, and after they hung their coats on hooks in the foyer, they moved on inside. An orchestra was playing up on the stage, but, even though it was a full orchestra, the music could barely be heard over the noise.

"Maybe it's subdued because it's Christmas eve," Leo said. "Christmas eve has a tendency to quiet a fella down. Oh, there's our new commander, over there. Come on, Marty, meet the guy who's taking us to England."

Martin walked over to a group of officers and ladies, and stood quietly until a tall Colonel turned at Leo's summons.

"Colonel Busby, sir," Leo said. "This is the co-pilot of the *Truculent Turtle*, Lieutenant Martin Holt."

"It's good to meet you, Lieutenant," Colonel Busby said, extending his hand and giving Martin a warm, firm handshake.

"Colonel Busby," Martin said. "You were the Inspector General for Cadet Training."

Colonel Busby laughed. "That I was, Lieutenant, that I was," he said. "But I certainly hope you don't hold that against me now. You'll find that the relationship between a pilot in an operational wing and his commander is considerably different from the relationship between an aviation cadet and a full colonel who is the Inspector General. I hope you'll find the difference to your liking."

"I'm sure I will, sir," Martin said, not knowing what else to say.

"Oh, and Lieutenant, may I introduce my wife? Linda, this is Lieutenant Martin Holt, one of the pilots of the 605th."

Martin looked into the cool, composed eyes of the beautiful woman Colonel Busby was introducing to him. She looked at him in the same amused way she had looked at him on the train. Her eyes spoke volumes, but her lips formed an easy smile.

"Lieutenant Holt, how delighted I am to meet you," she said.

"The pleasure is all mine, Mrs. Busby," Martin replied.

13

And so as you can see, in theory at least, energy could be produced at the expense of mass. I believe that the time will one day be here, when all the attendant problems of releasing this limitless energy will be solved, and fossil fuels will be replaced by fission energy."

The bell rang, and Charles dusted his hands together, then put the chalk on the tray. "We'll continue this discussion Monday," he said as the class stood and filed out of the room.

Charles erased the blackboard, then walked over to the desk to gather his papers together. He was still assisting Dr. Nunlee, and had been ever since his own graduation in the fall of '42. It was now March of 1943, and as yet he had received no offer challenging enough to interest him.

"Whereas your academic credits are exceptionally meritorious, your age and lack of experience preclude us from placing you in any defense-critical research position. We would certainly be interested in employing you in a monitoring capacity, however."

There were more than a dozen replies similar to that reply from Montgomery Industries, and

Charles had come to the reluctant conclusion that he was slated to spend the entire war at home, teaching at Standhope College.

Charles sat down and leaned back in his chair, then looked through the window at the Standhope campus. The tree limbs were still bare so he could see through them all the way to Shackleford Jackson Stadium. Charles laughed. Shackleford Jackson? Had he actually thought of it as Shackleford Jackson, and not Shaky Jake? Did that mean that he had, subconsciously, accepted the fact that he was a permanent part of the faculty now?

"No," Charles said. He pointed to the stadium. "That place is Shaky Jake, and I'm going to get out of here," he said aloud.

Charles saw the letter from Martin, and though he had read it before, he opened it and read it again.

Charley, my boy,

So you've joined the other side and are now dishing it out in the classrooms instead of taking it. My kid brother a professor. . . . I know, you aren't a full professor, but you are close enough to being one that they probably took your beer mug down at Beartracks. What with you and the old man teaching, it may well be that even my membership at Beartracks is threatened. Seriously, I'm proud of you. I always knew you had more brains than the average bear, and this just proves it.

I told you in the one quick letter I was able to write before, that I saw Dottie before I left (THIS WORD CENSORED) didn't I? I couldn't believe it, there we were, at 0330, it was pitch black outside, cold as a well-digger's you know what and suddenly in comes an army of Red Cross girls, carrying coffee, doughnuts, pencils and paper for last minute letters, anything and everything you could think of, and who do you think was in charge of them? In charge, now, mind you, not just one of the chorus line. None other than our own, dear, bobby-sox sister, only she wasn't in bobby sox, she was in a Red Cross uniform, and she was an absolute knockout. Of course, I went immediately into the big brother protector routine. . . . in fact, you would have thought it was the old days at Shaky Jake when Dottie was still in high school, and I had to keep the college guys away from her.

But, now, for the best part. I saw Holt. Yes, that's what Dottie is calling her. Her name is Cynthia Holt, and she is the cutest little thing you ever saw. Of course, she was sleeping when I saw her. Dottie explained that the woman who cares for her during the day doesn't come in until 0700, so Dottie just wrapped her up warm and brought her down to the (THIS WORD CENSORED.) It is such a shame Mom and Dad haven't seen little Holt. I know that if they saw her just once, everything would be all right again. I tried to talk Dottie into going home, at least long enough for the folks to see their granddaughter, but she wouldn't do it. She said there was too much hurt between them right now, and she didn't know if she had it in her heart to forgive them. That's what she said, forgive them. I hadn't thought of it like that before, but I'm sure Dottie has a side to this too, and I'm sure she was hurt and is hurt. It's a difficult position for you and me to be in, Charley. We love both of them, of course, and we don't want to see anyone hurt. I'm *sure it's beyond my poor powers to do anything about it though, especially as I* (THIS PARAGRAPH CENSORED.)

I saw (THIS WORD CENSORED) *and* (THIS WORD CENSORED) *but they have been* (SEVERAL SENTENCES CENSORED) *Thanksgiving Day Game. I told him I owe him several cracks in the ribs, but he just laughed. It turns out he's a pretty nice guy after all, even if he did play for* (THIS WORD CENSORED.)

I hear from Yolinda at least two or three times a week. She's been very good about writing, though she never says anything about how she is getting along . . . the pregnancy, I mean. I guess no news is good news, but this expectant fatherhood can get to a fella after a while. Let me hear from you, Charley, my boy, and if (THIS SENTENCE AND THE REMAINDER OF THE PARAGRAPH CENSORED.)

Martin

Charles folded the letter and put it in the envelope. It was like Yolinda to say nothing about her pregnancy. She was seven months pregnant, and had made absolutely no plans. She was living in the house with the Holt family, using Martin's old room. She said it made her feel closer to Martin. Thurman had suggested that they cut a hole in the wall between Martin's room and the empty bedroom next door, so they could convert it into a nursery. Nancy thought it was a fine idea, and she bought several magazines for Yolinda to look through, so she could pick the style and color of the new wall paper and curtains, but Yolinda had done nothing about it yet. The door was still uncut.

Dottie had sent Charles pictures of Holt, and he left them on the dining room table once, in full view of his parents. He learned later that they had looked at the pictures, one at a time, but they still weren't receptive to any suggestions of reconciliation. Yolinda didn't help things any. She did little things to keep the wounds fresh. They were so subtle that even Charles didn't realize what she was doing for a long time. And when he did realize, he knew that he would never be able to tell his mother or father about it, because their own hurt was still fresh enough that they wouldn't be able to see around it.

Yolinda did everything she could do to become the perfect daughter-in-law. She even excused away her lack of movement on the nursery by saying that it would be a "shame to cut through a wall in this lovely house." Thurman and Nancy were convinced that she just didn't want to impose on them, but Charles suspected that she just didn't want to face up to being a mother.

"Professor Holt?" a voice asked from the door.

Charles looked up to see two men standing there. The men were wearing dark blue suits and grey hats. Charles didn't know how he knew, but somehow he sensed that they were connected in some way with the government.

"Are you looking for me?"

"Are you Professor Holt?"

"Actually, no," Charles said. "My father is a professor. I'm an assistant."

"We are looking for Charles M. Holt," the spokesman said. The other man had yet to say a word, and his silent though penetrating gaze was somewhat unsettling.

"I'm Charles M. Holt. What can I do for you gentlemen?" Charles stood up and the two men came into the room without being invited. As one, they reached into their inside jacket pockets, and pulled out a leather billfold, then flashed it toward him.

"I'm Agent Craig, this is Agent Taylor. We are with the FBI."

"The FBI? What does the FBI want with me?" Charles asked. Then he smiled. "Lord, you don't think I've dodged the draft do you? I wanted to go, in fact, I'd give anything if I *could* go. But I'm 4F fellas, honest."

"This has nothing to do with the draft," Agent Craig said. "We have a man here who wants to ask you a few questions."

"Who?" Charles asked. "Look here, what is this about?"

"Would you come with us, please?"

"Come with you? Come where? Listen, I have a class in a few minutes. I can't just leave without—"

"That's been taken care of," Agent Craig said.

"Taken care of? How? Who took care of it?"

"Please, Mr. Holt, would you not make any trouble?"

"I'm not taking a step until I know what this is about," Charles said resolutely.

Agent Craig sighed. "Mr. Holt, you can come with us willingly and quietly, or you can come with us unwillingly, and cause yourself some discomfort and embarrassment. But one way or the other, you are coming with us."

Charles looked at the two men, and then at the hall outside the door. There were several students moving between the classes, and he knew that within a few moments, the students for his next class would be coming in here.

"May I see your identification again, please?" he asked.

Both men raised their badge and card a second time, and Charles studied them, comparing the pictures to the men. He was familiar enough with printing to know that the cards were either genuine, or someone had gone to a great deal of trouble with the most minute detail. One of the cards even bore the age mark from prolonged contact with the badge, proving that it wasn't put together just for this . . . whatever this might be.

"All right, gentlemen, I'll come with you," Charles said.

Charles followed the men through the hall of the Physics building, down the concrete steps which had been polished by thousands of student footsteps over the years, and across the sidewalk to a black Packard which sat next to the curb. Agent Taylor, the silent one, opened the door.

"Please, Mr. Holt, get in," the man in the back seat said, smiling up at Charles.

Charles looked at him, and took in an audible gasp of breath. "You are Professor J. Robert Oppenheimer."

"Yes," Professor Oppenheimer said. "Have we met? Have you attended one of my classes or lectures?"

Charles slid into the seat enthusiastically now, and closed the door behind him. He reached out to shake Oppenheimer's hand.

"We've never met, Professor, but I've read all of your papers, and I've long admired your work."

Oppenheimer smiled, and signaled for the driver

to drive on. "Well, my young friend, you and I have something in common," he said.

"Oh?"

"You've read my papers, I've read yours."

"You've read my papers?" Charles asked, surprised by the statement.

"Let us say I have read one, in particular," Oppenheimer said. "It's title was, I believe, *Gaseous Diffusion and Uranium Enrichment.*"

"*You* read that? But how? I mean, it's never been published, in fact, I haven't heard another word about it since I submitted it."

"It's a brilliant paper, young man. An absolutely brilliant paper."

"Then it's going to be published?" Charles asked excitedly.

"Uh, no," Oppenheimer said. "No, I'm afraid it won't be published."

"But, why? I mean, you said you liked it, didn't you?"

"I said it was brilliant," Oppenheimer said. "That's considerably greater than merely liking it. Tell me, young man. How old are you?"

"I'm 23," Charles said. "I'll be 24 in July."

Oppenheimer smiled. "That means you were 22 when you wrote the paper. That's interesting. You know, Newton was 22 when he developed his three laws of motion, and Professor Einstein was only 22 when he first began toying with the theory of relativity, though he did have the decency to wait until he was 26 before he made it public. I guess you are not too young at that."

"Professor Oppenheimer, what is all this about?" Charles asked. "Don't get me wrong, I am flattered—more than flattered, I am absolutely flabbergasted—that you have called on me personally to talk about my paper. But if it isn't going to be published, then why are you here?"

"I want you to come to work for me, Charles."

"You want me to come to California to teach?"

"I'm not at Cal Tech anymore," Professor Oppenheimer said. He smiled sadly. "I wish I were, God, how I wish I were. Maybe someday I can go back to teaching, and studying and. . . ." Oppenheimer sighed. "Ah, but one must accept what one must accept. I'm working for the U.S. Government now."

"What are you doing?"

"I'm a physicist, doing what a physicist does. I'm looking at things, exploring, examining possibilities for—"

"My God!" Charles said. "My God, you don't mean it? Professor, you aren't, I mean the government isn't trying to . . . to—"

"To what, Charles?" Oppenheimer asked.

"To develop some method of unleashing the energy of atoms for a weapon," Charles said quietly. "To build an atom bomb?"

"Yes, Charles, that is exactly what we are trying to do."

"But the potential destructive force of such a weapon . . . Dr. Oppenheimer, in theory such a device could set off a chain reaction which could *destroy the world*."

"There is a billion to one chance that could happen, yes."

"A billion to one? In physics, a billion is no more than a handful. The odds are too great."

"Charles, the Germans have forbade the export of uranium. That can only mean that they are also working on such a device," Oppenheimer said. "And right now I'm afraid they are ahead of us."

"Are you serious?" Charles asked. "Could you see something like that in Hitler's hands? He's a madman."

"Precisely," Oppenheimer said. "And in the hands of someone like Hitler, I think the chance of destroying the world would be considerably greater. It wouldn't be just the crap-shoot of a possible chain reaction, it would be the result of demonic design. Charles, we must have the device before Hitler does."

"What have we done about it?"

"We are involved in something called the Manhattan Project. Top scientists and physicists from all over the country are working on it," Oppenheimer said. "We have absolute priority over everything, any source of supply, any conflict of scheduling, any type of transportation. Say the magic word and you have everything you need. There has never been a project like the Manhattan Project. Never in the history of mankind."

"That has a rather ominous ring to it, doesn't it?" Charles asked. "When you say the history of mankind in that way, it is as if we were writing the final chapter."

"It could also be the first chapter of a new era," Oppenheimer said. "We must hold on to that hope. Now, how about it? Will you work with us?"

"Dr. Oppenheimer, I'm flattered beyond words that you would ask me. But, in the company of such men as you describe, what could I possibly contribute?"

"Gaseous diffusion for one thing," Oppenheimer said. "If this device is going to work, we are going to have to have about ten to twenty times more U-235 than the known supply in the entire world. That means we are going to have to find some way to create it, and I think you can get it for us."

"But my paper is just a theory," Charles said. "I didn't have the material to work with and nothing is proven. It is all hypothesis and conjecture."

"Your hypothesis and conjecture was right on the money with a couple of experiments we have already done," Oppenheimer said. "We had the material to work with, you had only your imagination. Think how effective you would be with your imagination *and* the material. You'll have everything you need except time. You have no time, Charles. You are going to have to work night and day, seven days a week, 52 weeks a year. And I don't have to tell you how important secrecy is. As of this moment there are fewer than 15 people who realize all the implications of what we are doing. You are now one of those fifteen. The President knows, of course, and so does the Secretary of War. But no one else in the President's cabinet knows, and neither does the Vice-President. We are asking scientists and engineers all across the country to make contributions, and they don't even know to what they are contributing. There are thousands working on the project, and they don't know what the project is all about."

"The FBI men who came by?" Charles asked.

"They are like the thousands of others who are working with the project. They know it involves a secret, but they don't know the secret."

Charles pointed to the driver of the car and Oppenheimer smiled. "I see that you are concerned about our driver."

"Well, yes," Charles said. "I mean, if this is as big a secret as you suggest."

"He isn't just a driver," Oppenheimer interrupted. "He is one of the Trinity 15."

"How do you do, Mr. Holt?" the driver asked. "My name is Hans Werfel."

"Hans Werfel? The German physicist, who developed the theory of energy conversion by isotope enhancement?"

"I'm flattered," Hans said. He had large, brown eyes with the suggestion of a drop in the lids which gave him an almost Oriental look. "But if you know that, you must know that I am also Jewish, and being German and Jewish is not compatible in these days."

"So you've come to America?"

"I came over in 1939," Hans said. "I left much later than most of my other colleagues, but I had escaped the personal mistreatment which had befallen so many others, and I was so engrossed with my work that I paid little attention to what was going on around me. Then I discovered that I had been spared, because Hitler was interested in the results of my experiments ... he wanted to build an atomic weapon. I knew then it was time to leave. Dr. Franck, Dr. Fermi, and of course, Dr. Einstein had left long before I saw what was happening. Now, I thank God every day that we left Germany before our research advanced far enough to be put to such use by Hitler. If I thought I had contributed in the slightest way to that monster, I couldn't live with myself."

"You will be working with Dr. Werfel," Dr. Oppenheimer said. "There is a team at Chicago University, working with Dr. Fermi, on the acquisition of fissionable material, but Dr. Werfel has the theoretical development testing division at Los Alamos, where the weapon will actually be assembled, and I would rather you work there, if you don't mind."

"I would be honored to work with Dr. Werfel," Charles said, still somewhat stunned by it all.

"I've read all your resumés, Charles. I may call you Charles?" At a nod from Charles, Hans smiled, and went on. "In all your resumés, you have stated that you wish a defense research job. This is the biggest defense research job in history. It's what you said you wanted, and it is what you're going to get."

Charles laughed. "Well, I'm glad someone came through. I was beginning to think that nobody wanted me."

"Oh, there were several who wanted you," Dr. Oppenheimer chuckled. "But I had them back away. I didn't want anyone getting you before we got you."

"I must say you took your time about it," Charles said. "I was afraid I was going to spend the entire war in the classroom."

"You may wish you had done just that before this is all over," Hans said. "I want you to understand fully the magnitude of what we are doing."

"I, I think I do understand," Charles said quietly.

"I'm sorry it took us so long, but we've been checking you out." Dr. Oppenheimer said, explaining the delay. "We've checked you down to the birthmark on the little toe of your left foot."

"I take it I'm clean," Charles said easily.

"Almost too clean," Dr. Oppenheimer said with a chuckle. "I think some of the FBI types didn't quite want to believe what they found."

"When does all this start?"

"I want you in Los Alamos on Monday," Hans said. "We have people there, and in Chicago, as I said. We also have people in Oak Ridge, Tennessee, but Los Alamos is where it will all come together."

Charles laughed. "This may sound like a dumb question, but, where *is* Los Alamos?"

"It's in New Mexico."

"New Mexico? Why, that's three days by train, even if I can get the ticket."

"Don't forget, you are now one of the Trinity 15," Oppenheimer said, handing a piece of paper to Charles. "Call this number, and when they answer, tell them it is a Trinity-priority request. Then ask to have a military transport plane at the local airport on Monday."

"What?" Charles asked, astounded at Dr. Oppenheimer's words. "You mean to tell me that the Army will send a transport plane all the way to Mount Eagle, just for me?"

"If the Army won't, the Navy will," Hans said.

"But, what would keep just anyone from doing this?"

Hans chuckled. "In the first place, there aren't very many people who know of Trinity-priority. And in the second place, only those people whose names appear on this Trinity-priority list will have the request granted."

"Will you have my name on the list by Monday?"

"Your name has been on the list for two weeks now," Hans said. "You'll also find your quarters set up for you at Los Alamos, complete with your favorite books, magazines, and even a record player."

"With a generous supply of Benny Goodman and Bach," Oppenheimer added, laughing. "Your two favorites, I believe."

The car stopped, and when Charles looked out

the window he saw that they had returned to the Physics Lab Building. He had been so absorbed by the conversation that he didn't even realize they had returned.

"Oh," Hans said, as Charles started to get out of the car. "Your cover story will be that you are working on a means of increasing the efficiency of gasoline. There have already been a few stories 'leaked' which imply that, and one working document was conveniently 'lost', to support it. But you will say only that you are engaged in classified defense work and nothing else. If you hear anything about the fuel project, deny it vigorously."

"Right," Charles said, grinning. "I'll deny it vigorously."

The two FBI men had been standing on the steps of the Physic's Lab building, and now they returned to the car. Charles waved at the two scientists as the car drove away, then turned to go back into the building. He was bubbling over with the excitement of being selected for the most important defense research project in America, and yet, he couldn't shake the terrible sense of foreboding about where such research would lead. He didn't know whether to laugh or cry.

${}_{\text{F}}$igs?"

"Yes, figs."

"You mean like you eat? Is this where figs come from?"

Jim laughed. "Where did you think they came from?"

"I always got them at the delicatessen," Mel said.

Staff Sergeant Jim Anderson, and Sergeant Mel Berg of A Company, 1st Batallion, 35th Infantry, were standing in the courtyard of a bombed-out opera house in Palermo, along with several hundred other soldiers. They had been gathered there by orders from headquarters, though they had no idea why. Jim had noticed the fig trees, and invited Mel to walk over and pick a few with him.

Mel picked one of the figs and tasted it. "You know, you shouldn't be telling me about figs, I should be telling you. They raise figs around Jerusalem you know, and that's my home town."

"I thought New York was your home town."

"Jerusalem is every Jew's home town," Mel said. "Or is it dates?"

"What?"

"Maybe it's dates they grow there. Or olives. Who the hell knows? Who the hell cares? Hey, why are we at this opera house, anyway? Is Kate Smith going to sing for us?"

"I don't know," Jim said. "How should I know? I didn't hear about it any sooner than you did."

"Yeah, but you are the one with the rocker. I'm just a lousy three striper. I figure you high-rankin' sons-of-bitches get the poop straight from group."

"Sergeant Anderson," a captain called. "Can I see you a minute?"

Jim walked easily over to the captain and handed him a fig. The captain took a bite before he started to talk. "Uhn, what is this thing? I thought it was a pear."

"It's a fig," Jim explained patiently.

"Oh, a fig, right. Listen, I just got word that only one platoon from each company has to stay, so you're selected."

"Stay for what?"

"Beats the hell out of me," the captain said. "Anyway, you take charge of your platoon, find out what the hell is going on here, then bring the men back down to our bivouack. The word is we'll be movin' out in a few days."

"Where are we going?"

"The mainland," the captain said. He reached down and took two more figs from Jim's helmet. "You know, these things aren't half bad."

Jim watched the captain walk over and speak to the first sergeant, then the entire company, except for the 1st platoon, marched away, joining dozens of other units which were leaving the grounds. He looked around and saw his men in various stages of rest, some sitting, some lying down, a few even sleeping. They had marched 100 miles in three days during the rush to capture Palermo, and though enemy resistance had been light, the fact that the men had moved so quickly over mountainous terrain, blown bridges and destroyed roads, spoke well for them.

Someone started blowing a whistle, then the orders were shouted to form by companies.

"Company A, right here," Jim called out.

"They ain' no A Company left, Sarge," one of the soldiers said, looking around, noticing for the first time that everyone else seemed to be gone.

"We're it," Jim said. "Fall in."

When his platoon was formed, Jim did a sharp about face, then waited to render the report. The reports rippled along the formation, each report exactly the same with the exception of the identification of the unit. Finally it came Jim's time, and he brought his hand up in a sharp salute, and sounded off as loud as he could.

"A Company all present and accounted for, *SIR!*"

The reporting continued until the last unit, then there was silence. Ahead of them they could see a balcony hanging out from the remains of the opera house, and an American flag rippling in the breeze. It wasn't until that moment that Jim noticed a microphone on the balcony, and a full colonel stepped up to the microphone and looked out over the troops.

"Officers and men of the American Forces, our Commanding General."

"It's General Patton," someone whispered, and his words were picked up by others until a buzz of excitement permeated the entire courtyard. Finally everyone grew silent as they waited expectantly.

General Patton strolled up to the microphone. He was wearing a uniform which seemed to be of his own design, khaki riding breeches tucked into highly polished boots, an olive drab tunic ablaze with medals and sashes, and a glossy, buffed helmet liner. He was carrying a riding crop and wearing a pair of ivory-handled pistols. He stood there in silence for several seconds ... for so long that a buzz of curiosity began to move through the ranks. Finally Patton spoke.

"I thought I'd stand up here and let you fellows see if I am as big a son of a bitch as you think I am."

The soldiers were shocked by his remark, and there was a beat of silence, then one man could no longer hold in his laughter, and his laughter was a signal to the others, so that the entire formation of several hundred men broke out into uproarious laughter.

"I have been ordered to apologize to all of you," Patton said after the laughter subsided. "It is an odious thing for me to do, but I am a soldier, and I will obey my orders. As you may have heard by now, I recently struck two soldiers, men who had cowered from battle and were disgracing the brave wounded, and you brave men, by their very existence. I felt that in striking them I was doing them a favor. I tried to rouse them and restore to them their self-respect. After each incident, I confided to those officers who were with me that I believed I had probably saved an immortal soul."

Patton turned abruptly then, and left the balcony to the thunderous cheers and applause of the assembled soldiers. After the cheering died the colonel gave the order that the formation was dismissed, and the individual units could return to their bivouacks.

"Jim, answer something for me," Mel said a few moments later.

"What?"

"Was that an apology?"

Jim laughed. "That's probably the closest to an apology old Blood and Guts has ever come, or ever will come."

Company A was bivouacked about a mile from the opera theater, and by the time Jim took his platoon back, there were letters waiting for them. The mail had been backed up during their drive on Palermo, and Jim and his men let out a cheer as they saw the mail. Jim got seven letters from Dottie.

Dottie opened the door to her apartment, then took off her hat and tossed it onto the scarred, blond coffee table.

"Mrs. Aikens, I'm home," she called. She looked through the mail Mrs. Aikens had piled on the coffee table for her: a letter from Liz and a letter from Charles. There were no letters from Jim.

"Oh, hello, dear," Mrs. Aikens said, coming into the living room. She was wearing an apron, and she was carrying Holt. Holt recognized her mother and flashed her a wide grin. A line of spittle drooled down from her lips, and she started reaching for Dottie, anxious for Dottie to take her. "You're home early, aren't you?"

"Yes," Dottie said. "Bonnie wants Holt and me to come over to her parents' house for dinner tonight."

"That will be lovely," Mrs. Aikens said. "I'm sure Holt will enjoy getting out, won't you, Holt? Oh, look at her. She wants her mama."

Dottie took Holt and gave her a hug, and Holt babbled happily.

"Something's wrong," Dottie teased, feeling the baby's bottom. "She doesn't have wet diapers."

"She was just changed," Mrs. Aikens said. "She's all powdered and dry. . . . I do wish we had some real diapers for her, though. Those we made from a bed sheet can't be comfortable for the little dear."

"I know," Dottie said. "But according to an article I read last week, defense industry and the military have bought up all the diapers. There are only 40% of what we actually need on the market."

"Well, my word, what would the defense people and the Army be wanting with diapers?" Mrs. Aikens asked.

"They use them as wiping rags. I'll be going very close to your house when I go see Bonnie. Would you like to wait, and I can take you home?"

"No, thank you," Mrs. Aikens said. "If you don't mind, I'll go on now and get home a little early myself today. I can catch a bus right at the corner."

"Of course I don't mind," Dottie said. "You go right ahead."

Mrs. Aikens, a woman of 55, took her hat down from the top shelf of the closet and pinned it to her grey hair with a long, pearl tipped hat pin. She was very proud of her hat pin, and she had shown it to Dottie on the first day she came to work for her. Her son had given her that pin, sent it all the way from Hawaii, where he was stationed in the Navy. He had been a Chief Petty Officer on the battleship *Arizona*, in charge of the powder magazine, and he had been killed on the 7th of December, 1941.

As Dottie watched Mrs. Aikens get ready to leave, she impulsively rushed over to give her a hug. "I can't tell you how grateful I am for you," she said. "You have been wonderful to little Holt and me."

"Oh, heavens, dear, it isn't you who should be grateful to me. I should be grateful to you. This gives me something to do with my days, and it stretches the budget a bit. And I look on Holt as the grandchild I'll never have."

"No child ever had a more loving grandmother," Dottie said.

Later, with Holt bouncing happily in her swinging canvas chair which Dottie had moved into the bathroom, Dottie took a bath and thought of what she had told Mrs. Aikens. No child had ever had a more loving grandmother. In the case of Holt, Mrs. Aikens was the *only* grandmother Holt had yet known. Jim's mother was out in California, Dottie had only heard from her once, and her own mother had yet to acknowledge that Holt even existed. It's funny, she thought. She had once been too embarrassed to sit in the same box seat with them at a football game, and now, she would give anything in the world if she could. It's very funny, she thought. So why wasn't she laughing?

Dottie didn't really have much of a problem getting gasoline. Because of her job with the Red Cross hospital and family services, she had an extra ration. Not only did she have to drive to work every day, she also had to make frequent visits to the homes of wives and servicemen. Emergency leaves for all servicemen could only be granted if the emergency condition was verified by the Red Cross, and that was one of Dottie's jobs. Gasoline wasn't a problem, but tires were, and when Dottie stopped the old '35 Chevrolet in front of Bonnie's apartment, she got out and looked apprehensively at the right front tire. It had a large, oval-shaped spot exactly in the middle. Tread was a thing of the past.

"It doesn't look good, does it, miss?" a man's voice said behind her.

Dottie turned and saw a young man standing on the sidewalk looking at the tire. He was about 26, tall, with dark curly hair and light blue eyes. The left sleeve of his shirt was rolled up and tied off, just beneath the elbow, because he had only one arm.

"No," Dottie said. "No, it doesn't look good at all."

"You'd probably be better off putting the spare on and just using that tire in emergencies," the young man said.

Dottie laughed a short, helpless, laugh. "This *is* the spare," she said. "Or rather, it was the spare. I have no spare at all now. The tire that I had on here is completely gone."

"Oh, well, you shouldn't be driving without a spare, miss. This tire could go at any time, and then you could find yourself in a terrible situation, stranded out on the highway, or in a bad neighborhood, or anything."

"I know," Dottie said. "I know what you are saying is right, but I really have no choice." Dottie opened the car door and reached in to take Holt out of her baby seat.

"Let me guess," the man said. "You must be Dottie Anderson, and that must be Holt."

Dottie looked around in surprise. "Yes," she said. "Yes, but how could you know?"

"I'm psychic," the young man said with a laugh.

"And besides that, Bonnie told me. My name is Kenny Satterfield. I'm Bonnie's brother."

"Kenny Satterfield! Why, you're the baseball player! Didn't you used to play for the Dodgers? Yes, I know you did! I saw you in Sportsman's Park when you came to St. Louis to play against the Cardinals. You got three home runs."

"You saw that game?" Kenny said. He laughed. "I hit all three of them off Murry Dickson. I sent him a telegram the next day, telling him to go out and have a steak dinner on me. The next time we played the Cardinals, Dickson pitched again, and that time he struck me out four times, so he returned the steak dinner."

"I never knew you were Bonnie's brother. She never said anything about it."

"Well, one-armed ball players aren't that great a conversation piece," he said bitterly, holding up his short arm. "There's only room for one Pete Gray in major league baseball."

"Pete Gray?"

"He's the one—armed ball player for the St. Louis Browns."

The front door of the apartment building opened and Bonnie came out onto the porch. "Oh, you met out here. I didn't want you to meet until you were in the apartment. Come on up. Here, let me hold the baby. My, how she's growing!"

Bonnie's parents had lived in the same apartment since before Bonnie was born. Her father was the foreman of a longshoreman gang, and though he had always made good money, his earnings were even greater now, with the many hours of overtime brought on by the war. Consequently the apartment was large, nearly as large, she realized, as her parents' house back in Mount Eagle.

There was a huge living room, a very large dining room, a parlor, a kitchen, three big bedrooms and two bathrooms. It was comfortably furnished with pre-war furniture, and though Dottie had thought an apartment could never really be anything more than a long-term hotel room, she immediately perceived the home-like atmosphere of this apartment.

"Put the baby on the floor and let her crawl around," Mrs. Satterfield said. "There's not a thing that a baby can get into; if there was, Kenny or Bonnie would have gotten into it a long time ago. Oh, Bonnie, isn't she the sweetest thing, though?"

"She sure is, mama," Bonnie said. "I just wish," she started, then she let her voice trail off. Dottie knew what she was thinking, Bonnie had confided to her while they were still in Alabama that she and Mel were trying desperately to have a baby, but they hadn't been successful.

"Your time will come," Mrs. Satterfield said, patting her daughter's hand reassuringly. "Just as soon as this war is over."

"I got a letter from Jim yesterday," Dottie said, "but nothing today. How about you? Did you get one from Mel?"

"No, I didn't get one yesterday or today."

"Well, you'll get one soon. Jim said that he and Mel were both writing letters home. Yours probably just got held up. He told the funniest story about General Patton."

"Patton," Mrs. Satterfield interrupted. "Isn't that the General that slapped those two soldiers?"

"Yes," Dottie said.

"He's a disgrace. They should bring him home."

"Jim says he is a very good general," Dottie said. "He says the men really like him and want him to stay with them."

"Well, all I know is if I were that poor soldier's mama, I would—"

"You would do the same thing those soldiers' mamas did," Kenny interrupted. "You wouldn't say one word, and hope that this whole silly mess blows over."

"I don't think it's silly," Mrs. Satterfield said.

"It's about as silly as getting your throwing arm blown off by a German .88," Kenny said bitterly.

Tears welled in Mrs. Satterfield's eyes, and she raised the hem of her apron to dab at them. "I wish you wouldn't say things like that, Kenny," she said quietly.

"I'm sorry, mama," Kenny said, and he walked over to his mother and put his good arm around her, leaving his stump hanging pointedly by his side.

The front door of the apartment opened then and Mr. Satterfield came in, just returning from work. He was carrying a lunchbucket and a hard hat, and he put them both on the top of the big radio. "I'm sorry I'm late, mama," he said. "We had a shipment to get out." He walked over to kiss his wife, then he gave Bonnie a buss, then he looked down at the baby crawling around on the floor. "And look at this little thing," he said. Holt babbled back at him, and clapped her hands together.

"Uhmm, do I smell a roast beef?" Mr. Satterfield asked, sniffing the air appreciatively.

"That you do," Mrs. Satterfield said. "And I'll have you know it cost me 37 points, so you had better enjoy it."

"Thirty-seven points," Mr. Satterfield said, sighing. "Red stamps, blue stamps, red tokens, blue tokens, whatever happened to just plain old green money?"

"Believe me, with the war inflation, it takes plenty of that too," Mrs. Satterfield said. "Now, come, let us sit down to the table."

Mr. Satterfield bowed his head:

"Lord, we thank Thee for this food and the blessings we enjoy. We ask you to watch over Dottie's husband, Jim, and Bonnie's husband, Mel, reminding You that even though he is Jewish, the Jews are Your chosen people, and our Savior was a Jew. Amen."

Bonnie laughed, then explained to Dottie. "Daddy worries a lot about the fact that Mel is a Jew."

"Of course I do," Mr. Satterfield said. "They never accepted our Lord, you know. Would you pass the beans, please?"

Mrs. Satterfield had been busily cutting Kenny's meat into bite-sized pieces, and now she sat his plate before him. Dottie tried not to look, then she was afraid that her avoiding would be even more obvious. She was glad that Kenny said nothing about it, but seemed, temporarily, at least, to be over his state of depression.

Kenny left shortly after dinner, and Dottie and Bonnie offered to do the dishes, if Mrs. Satterfield would watch the baby.

"Could I take her up to Maria's apartment?" Mrs. Satterfield asked. "I know she would love to see her."

"Sure," Dottie agreed.

Mr. Satterfield went into the living room and sat in the chair near the radio, listening to the evening news.

"You want to wash or dry?" Bonnie asked after the dishes were all stacked beside the sink.

"I'd better wash," Dottie said. "You know where to put things when you dry them."

"I guess you were surprised to see Kenny here tonight, huh?" Bonnie asked.

"Yes," Dottie said. "I was surprised to hear that he was your brother. I knew you had a brother, and I knew his name was Kenny. But I didn't know about the arm, and I never made the connection with the baseball player. He was a very good baseball player, wasn't he?"

"Yes," Bonnie said. "And that's why I never talk about it. He's very sensitive about the arm, and would really prefer that people don't know who he is. He must have been surprised when you realized who he was."

"Well, Martin is a good athlete too, so I sort of kept up with things like that. Martin was a very good football player."

"At least Martin wasn't making a living at it," Bonnie said. "That was all Kenny ever wanted to do. Then, when he lost his arm in North Africa . . . he . . . he lost something else as well. He lost his will to live."

"What does he do now?"

"Nothing," Bonnie said. "The Dodgers have offered him a job with their club as a coach, but he turned them down. He said if he can't play ball, he doesn't want to be anywhere around a ball team. He hasn't even seen a game since he was discharged. Mostly he just stays around his apartment and reads. He's also drinking a lot . . . quite a lot, and I'm afraid it's going to get worse." Bonnie took a deep breath. "I have to confess something, I invited him over tonight just so the two of you would meet. You've been working in family services with wounded veterans, and I thought, you know, there might be something you could do for him. He'd never go see you on his own, he doesn't want to admit that he needs any help. But he does need help, Dottie."

"Yes," Dottie said. "He does. But I don't know what I could do if he doesn't want it."

"I don't know either," Bonnie said. "I guess I was just making a desperate grab for a straw. Anyway, now you know what the family is going through."

"Perhaps if he would get a job of some sort," Dottie suggested.

"We've suggested it to him many times, but he has a disability pension coming from the army, and he had quite a bit of money saved from his playing days. He says he doesn't need to sell pencils or apples just yet."

"That's his problem," Dottie said. "He has a feeling of uselessness. If he could just get a job where he felt useful."

"I knew you would have an idea," Bonnie said enthusiastically.

"Whoa, now, hold it," Dottie said, laughing. "I don't have any idea what kind of job that may be. I just said that's the kind of job he needs."

"Well, at least you are thinking about it," Bonnie said. "We are all so close to it that we are no longer able to even try to think about it. Oh, Dottie, will you think very hard and try and come up with something?"

"I'll try," Dottie said.

Sometime later, after the dishes were completed, and Mrs. Satterfield had returned with the baby, Dottie made her good-byes, then left to go home. Bonnie walked down to the street with her. Dottie noticed her car the moment she was on the front steps.

"My car!" she said.

"What is it? Dottie, is something wrong with your car?"

"The right front tire, look at it," Dottie said. "It's a white sidewall. I didn't have a white sidewall tire. Bonnie, that's a new tire!"

There was a note under the wiper on the windshield, and Dottie hurried over to take the note out. She held it under a streetlamp to read.

"What is it?" Bonnie asked. "Who is the note from? What does it say?"

"It's from Kenny," Dottie said. She read aloud.

" 'I found a tire for you. I'm sorry it's white and the others are black, it may look a little funny on your car. But it's a safe tire, and safety is more important than looks. I put your spare on the spare mount, but remember, it is only for emergencies.' "

"Wasn't that sweet of him?" Dottie said, after she read the note.

"Yes," Bonnie said. "Oh, Dottie, I hope it is a good sign. This is the first indication he has ever given that he cares about anything since he returned from Africa."

15

Thurman straightened up when he reached the end of the row, and he leaned on his hoe as he looked back at his garden. The garden featured a healthy growth of tomatoes, squash, beans, cabbage, lettuce, potatoes, peas, and peppers. This was his victory garden, his answer to Secretary of Agriculture Wickard's appeal that Americans should grow their own vegetables, thus allowing the farmers to concentrate all their efforts on food for the military.

Actually, Thurman enjoyed working in the garden. When he came out here every evening after leaving the newspaper office, he found that the weeding, pruning, raking and hoeing was therapeutic, and he really enjoyed the quiet time. He also took a measured amount of pride in growing things. There was a definite sense of accomplishment in breaking the ground, planting, watering, tending, and then seeing the food actually grow from little packets of seeds.

The back door closed and Nancy walked across the lawn toward the edge of the garden. She was dressed to go out, and Thurman wondered which project she was heading for. She was on the War Rationing Board, the Nursery Board for Working Mothers, and she was now serving a term as President of the Mount Eagle Garden Ladies' Club.

The war had been kind to Nancy. Thurman knew that was probably a strange thing to think, but he could express it in no other way. Before the war Nancy had been little more than a woman who oiled the workings of the household occasionally, living her life as a shadow. Now she was involved and alive, and proud of her two sons, the one a bomber pilot in Europe, the other working on some secret defense project in New Mexico. The only shadow now was the shadow of Dottie. Thurman's heart hurt for Dottie, and he wanted her home. He wanted to hold her, to tell her he loved her and he forgave her, but he couldn't talk about it with Nancy, because Nancy's hurt was different from his. He hurt because Dottie was gone, Nancy hurt because she believed with all her heart that she had been betrayed by Dottie.

"Dear," Nancy said, going through her purse to find the car keys. "I'm attending a meeting of the Twentieth Century Club tonight."

"The Twentieth Century Club?" Thurman asked, raising his eyebrows to show that he was impressed. The Twentieth Century Club was the most exclusive club in town. Candidates for membership had to be proposed by at least three members, then submitted to an arduous screening board. After that they were voted upon at three successive meetings, and the vote had to be unanimous all three times for their acceptance. Nancy had never really mentioned that she would like to be a member of the club, but Thurman had known for a long time that she did.

"I've been proposed for membership," Nancy said, smiling. "And tonight they are giving a tea. I've been invited to pour." That was, of course, the supreme compliment.

"Well, I wish you luck," Thurman said.

"Thanks. Oh, Yolinda is with little Dennis now, but she has a meeting of the Civil Defense Air Raid Ladies' organization, so she is going to have to be gone from seven until nine. Will you watch Dennis then?"

"I was going to go down to the office and write tomorrow's editorial while it was quiet," Thurman said. "Couldn't she miss just this one meeting? I doubt that Mount Eagle will be bombed tonight."

"Don't be sarcastic, dear. You know how important it is to Yolinda. I guess she feels that with Martin flying bombers over Europe, she has an obligation to contribute in some way here. Besides, if Mount Eagle ever *did* get bombed, we would be awfully thankful that Yolinda and the other ladies have taken these first aid lessons."

"I doubt that we'll ever need her first aid lessons," Thurman said. He sighed. "But I can see where keeping busy does help her with the waiting. After all, each of us has to have something to do. With you it's your club, with me it's my garden." He looked at his garden. "I've no right to belittle Yolinda's way of passing the time, do I?"

"I knew you would understand," Nancy said. She smiled. "Charles gets it from you, you know."

"What? Charles gets what from me?"

"His wisdom," Nancy said. "His compassion, his understanding."

Nancy's candid, tender statement, surprised Thurman, and he didn't know what to say in answer. He just cleared his throat, then leaned over to kiss her on the forehead. "Go ahead," he said quietly. "I wouldn't want you to miss the opportunity to be inducted into the Twentieth Century Club."

"Oh, there's some tomato soup on the stove, and some pimiento cheese in the refrigerator. The bread is in the bread box."

"I'll make out all right," Thurman said. "Don't worry. You just have a nice time."

Nancy got into the Buick and backed it along the long driveway, past the old basketball goal with the netless hoop, and out into the street. Thurman picked up his hoe, shovel, trowel and other tools and carried them over to the garage, then he went into the house. Yolinda was in the kitchen, toasting sandwiches.

"I know how you like toasted pimiento cheese so I thought I would fix a couple for you," she said.

"Are you going to eat supper with me?"

"No, I'll be having a supper at the drill meeting tonight," Yolinda said. "Oh, and Dennis has been fed, and is already in bed. He should sleep until I get back. I don't plan to be too late."

"You mean he's already asleep?"

"Yes."

"Well, if I'm going to watch him, I ought to at least get the pleasure of playing with him."

"Don't wake him, Dad, he'll just get grouchy," Yolinda said.

"All right. I'll just read, and listen to the radio. Did you hear from Martin today?"

"No," Yolinda said. "Martin doesn't write very much."

Thurman put his hand on Yolinda's shoulder.

"I'm sorry about that. If it's any consolation, he doesn't write to us as much as he writes to you."

"He sure writes a lot of letters to Charles, though. Almost every letter we get from Charles, he's talking about a letter he just got from Martin. And he says Martin writes to Dottie, too."

"What can I say?" Thurman said. "The three of them were very close."

"I'm his wife. Wouldn't you think he would be closer to me?"

"Of course, and I'm sure he is." Thurman smiled. "It's just that when you are looking for mail, you never seem to get enough. A watched pot never boils, they say. Maybe a watched postman never runs."

"A watched postman never runs," Yolinda laughed. "I'll have to remember that. Oh, oh, darn!' Yolinda jerked open the oven door and reached in with a pot holder to pull out the cookie sheet. The two pimiento cheese sandwiches were very dark brown, nearly black on top. "Oh, I burned them," she said.

"Don't worry about them, I'll scrape them off," Thurman said. He slid open a drawer and took out a knife.

"Well at least let me do that," Yolinda said, and she started to pick up one of the sandwiches when a car horn honked out front. "Oh, that'll be Dr. Chambers. I'd better go. I'm sorry about the sandwiches."

"They'll be fine, really," Thurman said. "The cheese is all hot and melted and that's what I like."

Yolinda kissed him perfunctorily on the cheek, then darted out of the house. A bright red Chrysler convertible sat in front of the house by the curb, and Dr. Chambers sat behind the wheel, grinning as Yolinda approached the car.

Thurman watched through the window as Yolinda got into the convertible. Dr. Chambers said something to her, they both laughed, then the car pulled away with a roar of its engine and a squeal of its tires.

Carl Chambers was actually 46 years old, nearly as old as Thurman. But he was a divorced man, and his life-style was like that of men many years his junior. In fact, with the over-all shortage of eligible young men in town, Dr. Chambers had a field day with the single young women, and he would often show up at the country club with a girl young enough to be his daughter. He was able to carry it off because he was athletically slim, extremely handsome, with hair which was silvered at the temples but jet black everywhere else, and he had a great deal of money. There was as great a doctor shortage as there was a single, young men shortage, and Carl Chambers could command, and receive, generous fees for his services.

Carl Chambers missed the draft on three counts. He was too old, he was exempt by virtue of the fact that he was a doctor in a government-certified "doctor-depressed" area, and he had a bad knee, as the result of a college football injury. He didn't owe anyone an explanation as to why he wasn't in uniform. Nevertheless he had thrown himself whole-heartedly into Civil Defense work, and was the head of the Mount Eagle Civil Defense organization. He was the chief warden of all Air-Raid Wardens, and he was the chief and only medical officer for the Air-Raid ladies' organization, a group of women dedicated to learning first aid for use in the event of a bombing attack on the city.

Thurman left the window and turned the gas flame on under his soup, then went back to scraping the burned portion away from his sandwiches.

Dr. Hans Werfel climbed the little hill with two bottles of cold beer. Three-quarters of the way up the hill, Charles was sitting on a rock, looking down over the cluster of wooden barracks and houses which made up the research site. From here, Charles could see a big sign by the front gate of the high, chain-link fence which surrounded the settlement.

"*What you see here, what you hear here, when you leave here, leave here,*" the sign said.

"Hello," Hans said, when he reached Charles. He handed Charles a beer. "I brought you something."

"Thanks," Charles said. He took the bottle and drank several swallows, then let out an appreciative "*Ah,*" and wiped the back of his hand across his mouth.

Hans sat down beside him, and the two of them looked over the site in silence. Finally Hans broke the silence.

"We're going with you," he said.

Charles didn't say anything.

"Did you hear me? We've decided that gaseous diffusion is the way to go. We're putting everything into it."

"I heard you," Charles said.

"You show little enthusiasm."

"I know." Charles took another swallow. "Hans, if we are successful with this thing—"

"We will be," Hans interrupted.

"All right, *when* we are successful with this thing, and we drop it on a city somewhere, Berlin, for example—how many people do you think would be killed?"

"That's hard to say," Hans said.

"But surely you have an estimate," Charles said. "I know you've been party to the feasibility studies. Now what is the estimate?"

"Charles, it is not for us to worry about such things," Hans said. "It is for other people to do such worrying. All we have to do is enrich the uranium."

"Hans, *you* would say something like that? Isn't that exactly what's happening to the Jews in Europe now, because too many people are letting the *others* worry about it?"

Hans sighed and looked down for a long moment before he answered. "I am sorry," he said. "You are right, of course, such an answer does enable too many people to avoid the guilt, and the result is the mass murder of my people. But this weapon must be built, Charles. We must possess it before Hitler, or what he is doing to the Jews in Europe now, he will soon be doing to the entire world. You ask how many people would be killed if we dropped this bomb on Berlin. I have family and friends in Berlin, as well as a dozen other cities in Germany. Perhaps not so much family now, they have either left or have been killed, but friends, classmates and comrades I grew up with and students I taught. It pains me to think of dropping such a weapon on the head of my fellow Germans, and yet, I am prepared to do so if it will stop Hitler."

"How many will the bomb kill?" Charles asked again.

"Let me fill you in on some of the other possibilities before I tell you that," Hans said. "There is a very strong possibility, I would say at least three to one, that we won't get the device built at all. And if we do, one projection puts completion date as far away as 1970. There is also the possibility that we might get it built, but not be able to transport it anywhere. We'd have to let it sit here like a gigantic rat-trap in the desert and lure our victims into it. At any rate, it seems very unlikely that it could be carried by any airplane now flying, though the probability is that the B-29 will be operational soon. So you see, there are many and varied projections about the feasibility of the weapon, and they are all just conjecture, so we won't know until it is tested what the final results will be."

"All right," Charles said. "I'll buy that it is just conjecture. How many will it kill?"

"If Hitler beat us to the bomb and dropped it on New York or London, it could kill anywhere from one hundred thousand to one million people," Hans said.

"One *million*?" Charles gasped.

"Yes," Hans said quietly.

Charles hung his head for a long moment. "Hans, what sort of monster have we become, that the human race could conceive of such a thing?"

"We have not become a monster, but we have been exposed," Hans said. "We have a cancerous growth infecting the body of mankind. We must kill that cancerous growth, or surely mankind will die. Perhaps it will be enough merely to possess the bomb. Perhaps the mere fact that we have it will convince Hitler to surrender."

"Do you really believe that? You lived in Germany, you've seen Hitler up close. Would he surrender?"

"No," Hans admitted. "Hitler is crazed by the Wagnerian myth of a heroic, Teutonic society. He would rather perish in flames than abandon his perverted sense of purpose. That is why he is so dangerous, and that is why he must be stopped, at any cost."

"You are right, of course," Charles said. "It's just that. . . ."

"I know," Hans said. "I know what you are going to say, believe me. It isn't easy to live with the knowledge that what we are doing could result in the instantaneous death of one million human beings. I have the same nightmares as you."

"Will God let us do this thing?" Charles asked. "Will God let us build this bomb?"

"I'm Jewish, Charles, and you are Christian, and we share the same God. Perhaps my people have had a 3,000-year longer relationship with Him, but He is the same God. And I tell you now, that if the forces of evil which are loose in this world are not stopped, God will cease to exist. At least, He will cease to exist as far as man is concerned, for Earth will become a literal hell."

Charles finished the beer bottle and sat it on the ground beside him. He could hear music floating up from one of the buildings, playing a song that was popular in the summer of '41. He smiled and hummed along with it. "Do you remember that song?"

Hans smiled, self-consciously. "I have not learned too many American popular songs."

"I remember it," Charles said. "It was very big in that last summer before the war. That is, before we got into the war," he amended. "My sister had the record and she and all her friends would play it over and over and over. I remember one night I was trying to study and they must have played it ten times or more. I thought I would go crazy if I heard it again."

"I know what you did about it," Hans said with a smile.

"What?"

"You either got up and shut the door to your room, or you left the house."

Charles grinned. "I left the house," he said. "I took a walk, all the way down to the river. How did you know?"

"I have not known you long, Charles, but in this place, as close together as we are, you have become like my own brother. I know you better than I have known all but a handful of the people I have ever known, and I know that you could not be harsh with someone you love."

"Well, they did seem to be enjoying it," Charles said. "I don't think they were even aware there might be someone else in the house who would be bothered by it. I'm glad I didn't say or do anything. It was a happy moment for Dottie ... and I'm afraid she's not had too many of those over the last several months."

"Do you think your sister and your parents will ever reconcile their differences?" Hans asked. Charles had told Hans all about Dottie and Jim and the elopement.

"I'm sure they will," Charles said. "In fact, I'm sure they would have already done so if it weren't for this war. For the time being, I guess we'll just have to consider the entire episode a casualty of the war. It is a shame though, there are so many who are separated by things over which they have no control such as you, from your native land. To remain separated by your own doing is really a shame." He looked at Hans, then put his hand on Hans's shoulder. "When do we start, my friend?"

"You mean the diffusion?"

"Yes. You are right, we are doing what we must do. It is just that I cannot avoid the questions which strain and tear at my soul."

"When the questions stop, then you will no longer have a soul," Hans said.

"I'm glad you understand."

"It is good that we have talked," Hans said. "These are feelings we both share, and there are too few with whom we can discuss such things." Hans stood up and brushed off the back of his trousers. "You will start immediately as overall coordinator of the search. You are to take charge of the operation and quit conducting the experiments yourself, but assign the tasks to others, in order that your ideas may be developed. You have moved out of the laboratory, and into the directorship. This also means you shall have a new priority level."

"You mean instead of Trinity?"

"No, you still have Trinity. Now you also have Goldfire."

"What does Goldfire do?" Charles asked with a little laugh.

"It will cause President Roosevelt to break a dinner date to talk to you," Hans said easily.

16

It was quiet. Moments before the meeting room had been full of the buzz and laughter of a dozen women, dedicated to the proposition that a prepared corps of first aid workers would be able to take any air raid thrown at Mount Eagle, whether by the Germans or the Japanese. Now, the room sighed with the quiet whisper of oscillating fans, and the occasional bubble of the water cooler.

Yolinda moved through this quietness, checking drawers to see that they were closed, turning off fans, unplugging hotplates, and closing down the meeting room. The last thing she did was switch off the lights.

As the lights flickered off, the town outside the windows became visible for the first time. Yolinda moved through the dark protective blanket of the office and stood at the window, looking out over the city from the vantage point of being on the second floor of the hospital, which was itself on top of a hill at the end of Malone Boulevard, Mount Eagle's main street.

Lights winked at her from the ghostly shadows

of the town. She could see glowing red and white lights as cars moved up and down Malone, like grounded fireflys, seeking to run the maze of the evening traffic. Yolinda wondered about the people in the cars, and in the buildings out there. Did they know?

Sometimes, in a quiet moment such as she was having now, Yolinda would think about sin. That's what it all boiled down to. She was married to Martin Holt, but she was in love with Carl Chambers. That was a sin of the spirit. She was fornicating with him, and that was a sin of the flesh. She desperately wanted to divorce her husband, and that would have been the biggest sin of them all.

Yolinda had been attracted to Carl from the very first. She tried to resist the attraction she had for him, she knew it was wrong, but she couldn't control her feelings. They came from deep within, from some place beyond her control.

Yolinda had been riding to the meetings with Dr. Chambers to save gasoline, and it was a perfectly normal and acceptable thing to do. Carl was a doctor, and so had an unlimited gas ration allowance. Yolinda didn't have any allowance at all, because she didn't have a car. She sometimes used the Holts' car, but when she did she felt as if she was imposing on them. Riding to and from the meetings with Carl Chambers was the most logical thing to do.

Then, one night after the meeting, as they walked out to the car, Carl looked over at her and smiled. "Hey, what do you say I take you somewhere for a hamburger?"

"That sounds delicious," Yolinda agreed. She had not eaten supper before she came to the meeting and she was hungry. If she went home now and started messing around in the kitchen it would just disturb the Holts. Besides, Dennis had been really trying, all day long, and she wasn't anxious to go back to him yet.

They talked over dinner. Carl told Yolinda it had been a while since he had enjoyed an evening with a woman who wasn't straining to hear the sound of wedding bells. "In fact, I hate to see it end," he said.

"It doesn't have to end here, Carl," Yolinda whispered, scarcely believing her ears when she heard her own words.

"What?" Carl asked in surprise. "Look here, do you mean you would . . . Yolinda, you would go somewhere with me?"

"Yes," Yolinda answered. She could feel her heart pounding so hard that she was sure he could hear it. Her blood was racing.

"You aren't listening for the bells?" Carl said.

"I've heard them once," Yolinda said. "I don't care to hear them again."

"Where shall we go?" Carl asked.

"Oh, Carl, if you want to make love to me, the least you can do is find a place for us."

"Come on," Carl said. He didn't wait for the check, instead he just left a five dollar bill on the table. Yolinda walked slightly ahead of him and out into the street. She took a deep breath of air to try and keep her head from spinning, but nothing worked. Her head still spun and her blood still raced.

They drove south of town, almost all the way to Cairo, and they stopped at a tourist home, which consisted of several small cabins. Yolinda waited nervously in the car while Carl went in to register.

A couple walked by the front of the car. The little boy with them picked up a rock and threw it.

"Dennis," the mother said sharply. "Quit that."

Yolinda felt a sudden shock at the name. She almost decided to back out, and was verging on panic, when Carl returned.

"I've got us a place," Carl said. "It's the cabin in the rear."

Yolinda studied his face, his strong jaw line, the cleft in his chin, the silver at his temples. He was handsome, not in the All-American, boy-next-door way of Martin, but in the sophisticated way of a man who knew what he wanted and where he was going. It was that, more than anything, she believed, which attracted her to him. He was mature.

Carl drove the car around to the back, then stopped in front of the cabin that was to be theirs. "We're here," he said softly.

"Yes," Yolinda said. She was having trouble breathing.

They looked at each other for several seconds, then, slowly, gently, but very deliberately, Carl brought his hand up and traced his finger across her lips. He cupped her chin in his and pulled her to him. He kissed her on the mouth softly, then pulled away to look into her face. Her eyes were closed and her lips were slightly parted. They shone with the wetness of her tongue. Carl pulled her against him hard, crushing her lips to his. The kiss was long and demanding. After a while, they separated.

Yolinda quivered in his arms. "Let's go before I lose my nerve," she whispered, knowing at this point that it was impossible to back out.

Yolinda stood by nervously, listening to the frogs and the crickets in the nearby trees, watching the drive lest another car arrive while Carl was opening the door. Finally Carl got the door open and they stepped inside.

"Do you want the bathroom?" Carl asked.

Yolinda felt the thickness of her tongue and the dryness of her throat working against her. She tried to swallow. "If you don't mind."

Yolinda stepped into the bathroom, then undressed quickly. She wished she had a robe or a nightgown to put on. Finally she settled for wrapping herself in the towel.

Carl was in bed, his body covered by a sheet. He too, had developed some modesty, Yolinda thought. She walked to the bed and when Carl held the sheet up for her, she slipped beneath it. He pulled her to him, and she felt skin to skin contact along his naked body. His lips sought hers.

There had been times with Martin when she had approached the climax she had so ardently desired. And yet, despite Martin's patience and tenderness with her, the moment she was looking for had always slipped away. That first time, in the cabin at Big Springs, she told herself, it was because she was tired and nervous from the wedding. And yet, time after time the elusive rapture danced tantalizingly close, only to mock her as Martin left her unfulfilled. Then, she came to expect to be denied total satisfaction, and as she began to expect it, the goal slipped further and further away, until the last several weeks she was with Martin, sex was no more than the rote performance of her marital obligation. The bitterest irony of all was when she discovered herself to be pregnant, pregnant from an act that had left her frustrated and unfulfilled.

For a while, Yolinda was about ready to believe

herself to be through with sex altogether. It was convenient for Martin to be away, because she wasn't expected to be there when he needed her at night. And then she met Carl, and he awakened the feelings in her which had been stimulated in the days before her marriage, when the moments in the car promised more than Martin had been able to deliver. Those reawakened feelings grew stronger and stronger, until she knew that she had to try, once more, to attain the promised rapture which had thus far been just beyond her grasp.

Carl moved slowly and steadily with her now. His hands caressed her glistening curves. His tongue touched the nipple of her breast, and her body arched and quivered in delight. A soft moan escaped from her lips.

Yolinda's quick, shallow breathing filled the room as his tongue moved from nipple to nipple, and his hand slipped down to find the moist center of all her feeling. Then, wantonly, hungrily, she reached for him, and finding him ready, moved so that she was under him, and effected the connection with him.

"Yes," she said. She began to move then, thrusting up against him, meeting his thrusts, taking all of him into her, and then, suddenly, she knew that it was no longer an elusive dream but a definite reality as lightning flashed through her body, not once but two, three, four times. She screamed out the glory and the ecstasy of it, and then when it was over she cried, not from the shame, but from the pure joy of having known, if only for a moment, the rapture of the gods.

They had made love many times since then, and Carl often remarked of the wonderful relationship between them, a relationship free of society's compelling drive to marry every unattached man to every unattached woman. As she was already attached, there was no such pressure on them.

But Yolinda didn't want to maintain that relationship. Yolinda wanted to divorce Martin and marry Carl. She squeezed her eyelids tightly shut, and let the tears slide down her face. She could never do that. She would be condemned forever, for divorcing her husband while he was fighting in the war, and, it wouldn't get Carl for her. She was trapped.

". . . and so, as I say, perhaps it is not my place to write this letter to you, but, I feel someone should tell you. I know that what I am saying is true, because I am in the same Civil Defense organization as your wife and Dr. Chambers, and I have seen their carrying on with my own eyes. At first, I thought I was just being suspicious and nosy, but one night I followed them after the meeting broke up, and they went to the Moonlight Travel Court in Cairo, and went into one of the cabins. They were only there for a little over an hour, with all the lights off, so you can imagine what they were doing. I haven't told anyone else about this, but thought I would write straight to you, being as you are over there fighting the war and should have a right to know."

Martin folded the letter carefully and put it back in the envelope. There was no return address on the envelope, and the letter hadn't been signed. Ordinarily, that would have made him highly suspicious of the contents of the letter, but little things Yolinda had been saying in her own letters seemed to make more sense now in light of this information. She was having an affair with Dr. Chambers. Martin knew that she was. He closed his eyes and let his forearm rest on his forehead. Perhaps he should feel anger now, or betrayal, or sadness. It was odd, but he felt none of those things. He felt only a deep, deep, bone-weary tiredness, a tiredness which came from too many hours of breathing through an oxygen mask, and fighting the high-altitude cold, and the cramp of hours of sitting in one position, and the brief but fierce air-battles with the FW-190s and the ME-109s.

The 605th had lost three crews last week. When they first arrived, they began to think they were charmed . . . they flew seven missions over France and Belgium, and though they encountered fighters and flak, they did not lose a crew until the eighth mission. Now, with fifteen missions flown, and sixteen crews lost, they knew they weren't charmed, and the sense of false security had been stripped away, leaving everyone with the burning gut fear that they would be the next to go.

"Hey, Marty," Brad Phillips said, standing just in the door to his room. "There's a gooney bird going up to London. You wanna go?"

"You mean take the flight?" Martin asked.

"No, man, I mean go up on a 48-hour pass. The ole' man said he'd give out as many passes as the plane will take. Do you wanna go?"

Martin looked at the white envelope he had stuck between the board and the wall beside his bunk and he thought of what was in it. "Yeah," he said. "Yeah, I want to go."

"Well, move your ass," Brad said. "We've got to make sure we have two of the seats."

"Hey, don't worry about me moving my ass," Martin said. "You just better keep up, that's all. I know it's hard for a lineman, even an All-American lineman, but you can try."

"Yeah? Seems to me I didn't have a whole lot of trouble keeping up with you at the Thanksgiving game back in '41, pal. As a matter of fact, I thought about just giving you my jersey. You were wearing my number all afternoon."

Martin smiled. "You did stick me a few times," he said. "Come on, let's go."

Martin and Brad sprinted across the flight line, then climbed the steps to the C-47 which had already started one engine. Inside the airplane long, canvas benches were stretched down each side, and though they weren't able to find seats together, they did manage to find two. They settled in and buckled up, then grinned at each other as the door closed and the left engine wheezed and coughed into life.

"Have your fun, Yolinda," Martin said. "I intend to have mine."

"Beg your pardon?" the lieutenant next to Martin said. "Did you say something, Captain?"

"No," Martin replied.

It was raining when Martin stepped off the plane in London. It was a hard, drenching rain which blew across the runways and banged against the windows and made rivers out of the small drainage canals on the field. Martin and the others ran across the parking ramp through the downpour, to a large hangar where they would try to get transportation into the city.

The hangar was a large building with a tin roof, and the rain sounded like a drum roll as it banged down. The hangar was open at both ends, one end facing the airfield, and the other end facing a road, where olive-drab busses were loading up, then driving off. Martin started toward the buses, but he was met halfway by a cigar-chewing sergeant.

"Cap'n, if you ain't goin' to Edenhurst, you don't want to get on any of those busses."

"What? But all these people," Martin said, pointing to the ones getting on the bus.

"All these people are going to Edenhurst," the sergeant explained. "They're formin' up a new unit there."

"Thanks," Martin said. He started back across the hangar and saw Brad Phillips talking with a Navy lieutenant.

"Marty, the busses aren't going down town," Brad said.

"Yeah, I just found out."

"This is Terry Mason. We were in school together. We're gonna get drunk. You want to join us?"

"Come all the way to London just to get drunk?" Martin replied. "No, thank you."

"Well, what are you going to do?"

"I'm going downtown if I have to walk," Martin said resolutely. "And as for what I'm going to do down there, well, I don't have any idea. Try and get a hotel room I suppose and get one night's sleep away from the possibility of an alert."

"He a friend of yours?" the naval lieutenant asked Brad.

"Yeah," Brad said. "Hey, listen, you remember that Thanksgiving game where we went down to Standhope College and clobbered 'em good, don't you?"

"I remember it," Terry said. "I didn't get to see the game though."

"Well, this is Martin Holt. He was their All-American that year."

Terry smiled. "Oh, yes, Martin Holt. Sure, I remember hearing about you." He stuck out his hand. "Sorry about that Thanksgiving game, but don't take it out on me, I wasn't there."

"I wish I hadn't been there," Martin laughed.

"You really don't want to come with us and suck up some booze, huh?" Terry asked.

"No, thank you."

"All right, then I'll tell you what I'm going to do." Terry unbuttoned his jacket and stuck his hand into his inside pocket, then pulled out a small notebook. He scribbled something on a piece of paper, then tore it out and handed it to Martin. "Here, go to the Victoria Station U.S.O. and ask for this girl. Tell her I sent you. Terry Mason. You got that?"

"Who is she?" Martin asked.

"She's a friend of mine," Terry said. "She might be able to help you find a room for the night."

"I appreciate that, Terry," Martin said. "Now if I can just find a way to get there."

Martin stepped out into the rain to try for a taxi. He tried for an hour, but none were available without a transportation priority. *"There's a war on, mate."* Finally he managed to hitch a ride into town with a lorry driver. The rain had finally stopped, but the lorry had an open cab and Martin had to sit in the wet seat as the truck inched its way through the heavy traffic. For the whole trip the driver cursed and ground the gears together until Martin feared that the transmission would fall out.

"Stop here," Martin said, when he saw the Victoria Station U.S.O. He offered the driver some money, but the driver turned it down.

"Seein' as 'ow we are allies, I reckon the least I could do is give a Yank a ride," the driver said. "I would take a pack of American cigarettes though, if you've a mind to offer them."

Though Martin didn't smoke, he normally carried a couple of packs of American cigarettes with him, just for such a purpose. He handed the driver a pack.

"Thanks, guv," the driver said, as he stuck the pack in his pocket, then pulled away with a grinding and meshing of gears.

Inside the U.S.O., the air was heavy with the smell of wet, wool uniforms, coffee, and tobacco smoke. Near one wall a girl was playing a piano, surrounded by several men, and the strains of *Don't Sit Under the Appletree with Anyone Else But Me* floated through the noisy hall.

"Hello, captain," a pretty blonde said as she greeted Martin. "Won't you come in and have some coffee?"

"Yes, thank you," Martin said. "Oh, uh," he pulled out the paper. "Is there a girl here named Elaine Standridge?"

"I'm Elaine Standridge."

Martin grinned. "I'm Martin Holt. A friend, Terry Mason, asked me to look you up."

"Did he now?" Elaine said.

"He said you might help me find a place to stay tonight," Martin said. "I'm stationed down at Wimbleshoe, just in London for the night."

"Oh, are you a flier?" Elaine asked. "I really fancy fliers. We'll have to have a nice long chat." Elaine led him to a green settee, then drew two paper cups of coffee. She handed him one, then sat beside him. "I've come to appreciate coffee almost as much as the Yanks now," she said. "Though I do like my sugar and cream. So, you're looking for a place to stay, are you?"

"Yes," Martin said. "I would dearly love to be able to sleep the whole night through without fear of being awakened at 0430 for a mission. Could you recommend a hotel?"

Elaine laughed. "A hotel? In London on such short notice? Quite impossible without—"

"A priority, I know," Martin finished for her. He sighed. "I'm beginning to think that coming to London wasn't such a good idea after all."

"Let me see that piece of paper," Elaine said, taking the paper from Martin. She looked at it for a moment. "Yes, that's Terry's handwriting all right." She looked at Martin and smiled. "I suppose it will be all right."

"What?"

"Here," Elaine said, pulling a key out of her jacket pocket. "This is the key to my flat in the Cecil House. It's just two blocks north of here, you can't miss it. The flat number is right on the key. Mind, don't turn on any lights until the blackout curtains are all pulled."

"I don't understand," Martin said. "This is *your* place?"

"Yes," Elaine said. She saw the expression on Martin's face and laughed. "Oh, don't get the wrong idea, love. I won't be there with you. I'll be working here all night, and tomorrow I have to pop out into the country to see a friend."

"You're sure this is all right?" Martin asked, holding up the key.

"I'm positive. Now run along."

"Thanks," Martin said. "Thanks a lot."

The Cecil House was a narrow-fronted building with a big, black double door and a brass knocker right in the middle. A narrow stairway was tucked up against one wall, and covered with a worn carpet which may have been a maroon color at one time. Now it was gray and brown where some of the inner weave was showing through.

Once he was inside the flat, Martin checked the blackout curtains, then turned on the light. It was a single, bare bulb which hung from a frayed cord. There were cracks in the ceiling and spots on the wall, but there was a big double bed and that was all Martin really cared about.

There were a few other things in the flat, which was just one room. There was a small ice-box, a hot-plate, a table and three chairs, and a sofa. There was a sink, but Martin didn't see a bathroom. A bowl of wax fruit and a basket of flowers provided the only splash of color. Martin stripped down to his shorts and climbed into bed. He was asleep in just a few moments.

17

W ho are you, and what are you doing here?" The woman's angry and frightened voice barely cut through the noises of Martin's sleep: the formation of his dreams, with engines, radio-chatter, machine guns, men, screaming in fear and pain.

"Answer me," the woman said again. "Answer me at once, or I shall call the police!"

Now the roar of the engines subsided, and Martin opened his eyes to discover that he wasn't in the cockpit of a B-17, but in bed, and a young woman was talking to him. He looked at her, and saw someone with soft, wavy, chestnut hair, deep, deep blue eyes, and very pretty features, despite the expression of anger she wore.

"Who are you?" Martin asked.

"Who am I? I come home and find you in bed and you have the cheek to ask who I am? You're a Yank, aren't you? It would take a Yank to have this much gall. Now, shall I go to the police, or will you tell me who you are and what you are doing in my bed?"

"I'm Martin Holt, and the person who rents this

room told me I could stay here. See, she even gave me the key." Martin got out of bed then, and started toward the table where he had left his key, change, and billfold. As he was dressed only in his shorts, the woman turned her head away in quick embarrassment as he stood up.

"What are you doing?" she asked. "You're naked."

"What? Oh, no, I have on my skivvies," Martin answered distractedly. He shoved the coins around until he found the key, then he turned around and held it up triumphantly. "See, here it is right here."

"Where did you get that key?"

"From Elaine Standridge. I met her at the U.S.O. last night, and she told me she was going to be in the country, and I could use her room."

Now the anger on the girl's face fell away, to be replaced by amusement, and then she laughed out loud. "I might have known," she said. "Captain, did you bother to read the number on the key?"

Martin was puzzled by the girl's remark, and he looked at the key, then read the number aloud. "404," he said.

"This is 402."

"It is? But, I don't understand. The key fits."

"Half the keys fit half the doors," the girl said. "This is a very old hotel. I'm Allison Cairns, Elaine's neighbor."

"I'm Martin Holt," Martin said, starting toward Allison with his hand extended.

Allison looked away, this time with a bemused grin on her face. "I refuse to shake the hand of a naked stranger I've found in my bed," she said.

"I told you, I'm not naked," Martin said. He grinned broadly. "And now, I'm not a stranger."

"Please, do get dressed," Allison insisted.

"Okay. Say, I'm awfully sorry about all this," Martin said as he pulled on his pants. "Could I buy breakfast for you, to sort of apologize?"

It was still dark when the C.Q. shined his flashlight in Martin's face the next morning.

"Briefing at 0300, sir," the C.Q. said. "We've got a mission."

Martin groaned, then sat up and began pulling on his clothes. Then he thought of the day before, and he smiled. He had not only eaten breakfast with Allison, he had eaten lunch and dinner with her as well as they had spent the entire day together. She was a driver for the senior staff officers of the joint powers, and last night she had driven him to the airport to catch the flight back to Wimbleshoe.

Martin saw hundreds of shadows moving silently through the night as he walked to the briefing shack. The shack was full by the time Martin got there, and he searched the wooden benches looking for a seat, when he saw Doug Pyre waving at him and motioning him over. Leo Greenly, the first plane commander of the *Truculent Turtle*, had been promoted to Major, and now Leo had his own Wing. Martin had taken over the *Truculent Turtle*, and Doug Pyre was his new co-pilot. Gregg Harris was still bombardier and Manny Byrd was still his navigator.

When Martin sat down, Brad Phillips leaned forward from two benches back, and touched Martin on the shoulder. "Have a good time yesterday?"

"Yes," Martin said. "I had a very good time. Where were you when I came back last night?"

"I don't know," Brad answered. "Terry and I must have drunk up half of London. I think we hit every pub within a ten-mile radius. I woke up here this morning, but I don't know how, or when I got back."

"Did *you* have a good time?"

"I *must* have," Brad grinned. "I don't remember a thing. How was Elaine?"

"Who?"

"Elaine, the girl you spent the day with."

"Oh," Martin said, smiling. "I don't know, I only saw her for about five minutes."

"But I thought—"

Brad's words were cut off by the sight of a major stepping to the platform in front of the men. The room grew suddenly silent. A few people cleared their throat nervously as the major pulled aside a black curtain, disclosing a large map of Europe. A black ribbon stretched from Wimbleshoe east. Suddenly there were gasps of surprise from the men.

"That's right," the major said. "We're hitting Germany. Our target is Schweinfurt." The major pointed to the city with his pointer. "Schweinfurt is the city where the Germans make all their ball bearings. Everything in their war machine depends on those ball bearings, from their fighter planes, to their tanks, all the way down to the Fuhrer's desk chair."

"Well, by all means, let's take out Hitler's chair," someone shouted, and the others laughed nervously.

The lights went out and some slides were projected on a screen. "Here are our primary targets for today. The buildings of I.G.N. Kugelwerks. As you can see, they are in a large, triangular configuration, located about one mile south from this sports stadium. They will be well camouflaged and screened with smoke. In the target area there are more than three hundred known flak batteries, all 88 mm guns. We have routed you through the best possible channel so that only a minimum of their guns can come to bear at any given time."

"One .88 is enough," someone shouted, and his statement was greeted with nervous laughter.

The major stared coldly. "You'll pick up FW-190s and ME-109s on the way in and on the way out. They stay on station and are radar-vectored to you. You may get some of the twin engined ME-210s as well. They like to sneak up from a long way off, hide in the vapor trails, and fire rockets, so you tail-gunners must be on the lookout for them."

"What about fighter escort?" someone asked.

"We'll have P-47s at least halfway in. The rest you'll have to do by yourself. So keep your combat boxes tight. Now, if there are no questions, we'll get meteorology."

A small captain with a high-pitched voice gave them a weather briefing, and then an intelligence officer discussed the underground organizations in France, and how to contact them should they get shot down. Finally Colonel Busby gave a few words of encouragement, and the briefing ended.

Out on the flight line the airplanes loomed like ghostly shadows as the trucks began delivering the crews. The ground crews had been working on them since long before the air crews were even awake, and now all of them were full of fuel, bombs, machine-gun ammunition, coffee, sandwiches, and everything else it would take to make them ready to go. Martin and his crew climbed in, took their stations; then, the silence of the early morning English countryside was broken by the whine and cough of engines as one by one the airplanes started up.

* * *

Martin could taste the rubber as he breathed the oxygen through his mask. They were at 25,000 feet and just crossing the coast of France. The sky was a bright crystal blue, lined with the vapor trails which extended from each bomber. The airplanes were enveloped in an avalanche of sound from the pounding engines and beating propellers.

Far below the formation of bombers, the green and brown fields stretched from horizon to horizon. They seemed to lay serenely in the sun, totally belying the fact that there was a war on.

They had not yet reached the point of radio silence, and there was an incessant chatter over the air.

"Seven, tuck it in a little, you're too wide."

"This is seven. Who's calling me, the flight commander?"

"No, this is three, on your wing. You're too wide, tuck it in."

"This is ten, I'm going to check my guns now."

"Roger, this is flight commander. It's okay to check guns."

The guns on the *Truculent Turtle* exploded in staccato firing as they were cleared.

"Seven, you're still too wide."

"Where are the P-47s?"

"Seven, tuck it in a little more!"

"Three, I'm going to tuck it right into your ass if you don't get off my back!"

"All right, you guys, let's can the chatter," the flight commander said.

"Bogies, eight o'clock high!" someone called, and instantly all eyes looked in the direction indicated.

"They are friendlies," someone said with a sigh of relief. "They are the P-47s."

The P-47s stayed with them for a while, then, when their fuel ran out they zipped through the formation wagging their wings. They flew from the front of the formation to the rear, so that the combined speeds of the bombers and fighters made them pass at almost six hundred miles an hour. They were little more than a blink of the eye, then they were gone.

"They didn't do us much good, did they?" Doug asked Martin.

"We weren't jumped, were we?" Martin replied.

"No."

"Then they did us good. Now, get set. The fun begins soon."

Martin was right. Less than fifteen minutes later the word rang out that "bandits" had been spotted at two o'clock high. Martin looked toward the area indicated and he saw eight ME-109s flip over onto their backs and come roaring down a long, invisible track which led to the bomber formation.

"Here they come," someone said.

"Hey, there are some climbing on us from six o'clock low!"

"They're all over the place!"

All the guns opened up and the sky was suddenly filled with brightly glowing balls of fire. The first attack wave slammed through the formation, apparently with no hits scored by either side.

There was a rather macabre cooperation of sorts between the enemy fighters and the bombers, in order to avoid collisions. The fighter pilot was the only one who could maneuver his aircraft enough to avoid collision, so the B-17 pilots never took evasive action in order to let the German pilots slip through.

More fighters flashed through, and the guns

erupted with a roar again. Martin twisted around in his seat to follow one group and he saw the left wing break off one of the B-17s. It continued along for a second, as if determined to fly without a wing, then it fell off into a sharp spin and began its five mile fall toward the ground. The wing which broke free tumbled like a falling leaf, while the propellers on the two engines continued to spin futilely.

From beneath the airplane a German fighter suddenly popped up, going away. The ball turret, the nose gunner and the top turret were all able to track on target, and Martin watched as all three guns hosed into him. Smoke started streaming back from the fighter's engine cowl, and suddenly the blur of what had been the propeller turned into black bars as it slowed to the point that Martin could actually count the revolutions. He knew then that the plane was fatally hit. The fighter rolled over onto its back, and the pilot fell clear, rolling himself into a ball for the plunge through another bomber formation five thousand feet below. He was far from out of danger, as there were more than one hundred spinning propellers waiting for him should he hit one of the planes in his fall.

Then, in addition to the fighters, another danger presented itself. The anti-aircraft guns they had mentioned at the briefing opened up and the sky head became a sickening mass of exploding flame and smoke and jagged chunks of metal. The flak was everywhere. It tore pieces off wings, smashed out engines, and exploded inside fuselages to rip airplanes apart.

Martin's every sense was being bombarded with hyper-perception. Fire, smoke and exploding airplanes were before his eyes. There was a cacophony of sound as overrevved engines, exploding shells, screaming rockets and shouts of terror filled the air. He could smell the smoke and burnt oil, and he could taste the bile of his own fear. He felt the shockwaves of every explosion and his body itched with the pouring of sweat.

Martin tried to blot out all his senses and concentrate on flying. Finally they reached Schweinfurt. Smoke was already boiling up from the first wave. Martin turned the controls over to Greg Harris, the bombardier, who flew the plane with the bombing sight for a few moments until they crossed the release point. Greg called "Bombs away," and Martin shouted "Let's get the hell out of here!"

The German fighters followed them off their target for another fifteen minutes, then mercifully pulled away. They had survived.

Martin let out a sigh and settled back in his seat. His football knee had never fully recovered, and now it was jumping involuntarily, and every muscle in his body ached with the soreness of prolonged tension. He had never known such fear.

Suddenly a lone fighter plane appeared in front of them. It wasn't sharp-nosed like the ME-109s which had followed them back, it was square nosed like the P-47s. Martin wondered what one, lone, P-47 was doing this far in, but he figured it must be a scout plane, ahead of the others. The plane banked and then Martin saw the black crosses on the wings! It was a Focke-Woulfe 190!

As the German fighter made his pass, his wing and nose guns winked in orange flashes. There was an explosion in the nose of Martin's bomber, and a windstorm of hurricanic velocity whipped through, tearing papers off the navigator's table, and blowing everything out the open waistgun ports. The FW screamed passed, barely avoiding a head-on collision.

Martin leaned down to look into the nose compartment and saw what looked like a bloody pile of laundry, and knew that it was what was left of Greg Harris.

"Here he comes again!" the top turret gunner shouted.

The FW flashed by a second time, but this time he was caught in the deadly pattern of fire, not only from Martin's plane, but from all the others whose guns could bear on him. Flames raced back from the fighter, and it started to tumble, then, right beneath Martin's airplane, the German fighter exploded.

Martin must have passed out momentarily. When he came to, the B-17 was upside down, spinning round and round, falling toward the ground far below. He grabbed the wheel, and somehow managed to right the bomber, but by then it was too late to give the order to bail out. It was too late, even, to give the order to prepare for a crash landing, because there, right in front of him, was a ploughed field, and Martin forgot about everything except the need to hold his wings level, as he hit the field, bouncing and skidding, shearing off both wings, and sliding across the field like a toboggan sled gone mad.

Finally all noise and motion ceased, and the *Truculent Turtle*, or at least what was left of the *Truculent Turtle*, was down. Miraculously, Martin was uninjured. He looked over at Doug with a grin on his face, then saw that Doug was dead, not killed in the crash, but killed by the machine gun bullets from the German fighter's first pass.

Martin turned and looked into the dust filled area behind him. He saw Manny shaking his head.

"Are you all right, Manny?"

"Yeah," Manny answered. "Jesus, man, you ever think about landing on a runway sometime?"

"You mean this isn't Wimbleshoe?"

Manny grinned. "That was one hell of a flying job you did," he said.

Gradually the others of the crew began to call out to each other, then slowly, they all left the plane, and Martin took muster.

"We lost three, cap'n," the top turret said. "We lost Lieutenant Harris, Lieutenant Pyre, and Corporal Titus. He was in the ball turret and he couldn't get out when we landed."

"Oh, Jesus," Martin said, and he closed his eyes and fought back the sick sensation he felt. Titus had been trapped in the ball turret under the belly of the bomber. When Martin made the belly landing, the plane ground and crushed the ball turret, with Titus in there, knowing what was going to happen.

"It couldn't be helped, cap'n," the top turret gunner said. "The power was out, there was no way you could keep us up long enough for us to crank him out."

"Manny, where are we?" Martin asked his navigator.

"France," Manny said. "I make it about seventy miles from the coast."

"Cap'n, there are some men coming across the field over there," one of the men said.

"Quick," Martin said, pointing to a ditch which ran alongside the field where the plane had crashed. "Into the ditch. Anyone have weapons?"

"Just you and the Lieutenant," the top turret gunner said. "Only officers carry pistols."

"See if you can get Doug's and Gregg's pistols."

One of the men crawled back into the plane, then came back with two more pistols. He was ashen-faced. "Lieutenant Harris is pretty messed up, sir," he said in a shaky voice.

Martin looked toward the nose of the bomber, and he saw that it was buried in the dirt. He was glad that Gregg was dead before the plane hit.

"Okay, in the ditch!"

The seven men jumped into the ditch. The four who were armed stayed behind the ridge, looking in the direction from which the men were coming, and the three who were unarmed went down to the bottom, for cover.

"This is really great," Manny said dryly. "We're going to hold off an entire kraut army with four pistols. Add to that the fact that I couldn't hit a bull in the ass from five paces with this son-of-a-bitch." He held the pistol out and looked at it.

"Cap'n, how do you make this thing shoot?" one of the armed E.M. asked. "I've never shot a .45."

"You just slide the barrel assembly back," Martin said, demonstrating. "That puts a round in the chamber. When you pull the trigger, you make certain that the curve between the thumb and forefinger is depressing this. It won't shoot otherwise. Make sure the safety is off, and make sure it's not at half-cock."

"Here they come," Manny whispered.

"Don't shoot until I give the word," Martin said.

The crew grew quiet then and waited, nervously, as the men approached the wreckage.

The first thing Martin noticed about them was

that they weren't in uniform. Then he heard them speaking French, and he smiled broadly.

"If my high school French is accurate, they are from the underground," he whispered to Manny.

"Tell them we are here."

"No, wait, it might be a trick. Just wait."

"Ami," one of the Frenchmen called. "I am Colonel Miguel LeGrand, of the Free French Forces. I have come to help you back to England. The code word is Thor. Answer, please. Thor."

"That's it," Manny said. "That was the code word this morning at the briefing."

"What's our answer?" Martin said.

"What difference does it make? Hell, they can see we're Americans."

"And we can see they are French," Martin said. "But what if the Germans had gotten here first, killed us, then disguised themselves? Wouldn't that be a pretty good way of wiping out an underground cell?"

"Thor," LeGrand said again.

"The answer is hammer, Cap'n," one of the E.M. said. "I think," he added.

"You think?" Martin sighed. "Hammer," he called out.

There was a sudden, enthusiastic babble as the French realized that they had located the crew, and they ran over to the ditch laughing and extending their hands.

"Yes, hammer it is," LeGrand said, and he spoke English with a very little accent. "Come, let us help you out of there. Are any of your men injured?"

"No," Martin said. "We have three killed, no wounded."

"Then we can move quickly. Come, we'll take you to a secret landing strip and one of your Dakotas will come for you tonight. Tomorrow, Captain, you'll awaken in your own bed, ready to take another mission like the last one."

"Yeah," Martin said with dry humor. "I can think of nothing I would rather do than take another mission like the last one."

18

Martin read the *Officers' Guide to English Peerage, 1944.*

English Peers come in several degrees of importance. At the top of the order, are the 26 non-royal dukes. Next are the 42 marquesses. The next on this list are 210 earls, followed by 114 viscounts, 536 barons and 1,714 baronets

At the end of the book, there was a "who's-who" among the peerage, and Martin looked up the Earl of Dunliegh.

The Earl of Dunliegh's house is 130 miles from London, in the exact center of England. The earldom was created June 15, 1448. The family name of the Earls of Dunliegh is Cairns-Whiteacre (hyphenated at the creation of the earldom by Royal recognition of the legitimate claim of Arthur Cairns to being the bastard son of Henry Alton Whiteacre). The Whiteacre name is mentioned in the

Domesday Book, the list of England's landowners in 1086, as having title to nine "hides" of land.

Martin was reading about English peerage because he had been invited to Ingersall Hall, the Staffordshire seat of the Earl of Dunliegh, to meet General Percival Chetwynd Alexander Cairns-Whiteacre, who was the English General in charge of Allied Airfield procurement. But it was not on a matter of airfield procurement that Martin was invited. Martin was invited by Allison Cairns, the daughter of the Earl of Dunliegh.

"I don't use the Whiteacre part of my name," Allison explained after she confessed who she was, and invited Martin to meet her parents. "It makes things a little simpler for me at my work if everyone thinks I'm just 'one of the girls,' and of course, I really am just one of the girls."

Allison had invited Martin, right after they had made love, and while she was lying in bed with him with her head on his shoulder. She had heard of his being shot down through Elaine, who had heard it through Terry and Brad Phillips. Allison pulled every string her father's position would allow her to pull, until she found out that he had been rescued by a French Underground unit, and when the plane which landed on a secret field in France in the middle of the night returned to England, Allison was standing there to greet Martin as he stepped off. Over the next several months, Martin began spending as much time as he could with Allison, and they became lovers, with the understanding that they would be married after the war, and after Martin's divorce from Yolinda.

Allison knew of Yolinda, and of Charles, and of

Dottie. She also knew of the estrangement between Dottie and her parents, and thus could understand why Martin preferred to keep their relationship a secret from his parents until after the war, to spare them any more hurt. But Allison wanted to share Martin with her parents, and so she asked him to come out to the home at Ingersall Hall to meet them.

Ingersall Hall was a fine Jacobean pile started in 1608, and completed with the addition of a "new" wing in 1777. It sat in the middle of a fifty-five acre estate, amidst rolling green hills, with a verdant forest and a small lake. When Martin first saw it, driving up through the long road which led from the front gates, he felt his breath taken away. It was so awe-inspiring as to be overpowering.

A butler answered the door, and Martin was shown into a large room and asked to wait for a moment. Within seconds a maid appeared with tea and then he heard his name being called.

Allison was standing the the doorway, smiling. She was dressed in white shorts and a blouse and her hair was tied back with a white ribbon. "I'm glad you could make it," she said.

Martin looked around, at the high, vaulted ceilings, decorated with paintings, at the polished mahogany and leaded glass windows, and massive furniture. "It's a little different from your apartment," he said.

"Be it ever so humble," Allison said.

"All this house for just three people?"

"I have two sisters who are away now, and of course, there are the servants."

"Of course," Martin said. "And how many servants might there be at Ingersall Hall?"

"Just twelve now. Before the war, there were thirty."

Martin met General Cairns-Whiteacre, who looked very proper in his uniform, and with his walrus type moustache, though there was something about him, in his eyes, and in his manner, that caused Martin to warm immediately to him. The General asked Martin to walk with him.

"I know about the, uh, domestic problem you have," General Cairns-Whiteacre said when they were alone. "I'm not giving my approval, you understand, but human beings being human beings, I realize such things often occur. I'll leave that up to you and Allison."

"I appreciate your understanding, sir," Martin said. "I can only promise you that I will never do anything to hurt your daughter."

"Don't make a promise you might not be able to keep, son," the General said. "I only want you to do what is right to do . . . whatever that may turn out to be."

Lady Anne, Allison's mother, got Martin next, and she took Martin to the bedroom he would use. "Disraeli slept in that bed," she said. Only then did Martin get to be alone with Allison and she took him around the grounds. They walked around the lake and found a small lakeside cottage on the other side.

"This is my favorite place on the entire estate," Allison said when they went inside. She walked over to the bed, then turned around with a smile on her lips and her arms outstretched. "Come here, let me demonstrate this bed for you."

"Did Disraeli sleep here, too?" Martin teased.

"No. But then sleeping is not exactly what I had

in mind," Allison said, as she began to remove her clothes.

Martin stepped up to her and started helping. "Turn around," he said. "Let me unsnap your bra."

Allison turned around and Martin looked at the delightfully smooth skin of her back. He unsnapped the bra and she moved her shoulders forward to let it fall. Martin reached around and cupped her breasts in his hands, feeling the congested nipples with his fingers.

Allison turned her head back toward him and he kissed her open mouth, taking her tongue into his. Martin pushed her down to the bed, gently, then moved onto it with her. Her eager hands soon divested Martin of his clothes, then she pulled him over her and guided him into her.

They made love fully and completely then, and finally a burst of wet warmth filled her and made them as one.

"I know what you are going through," Dottie was saying to the young man who was sitting in the wheelchair of the hospital ward, looking morosely out onto the grounds. Behind them, on the ward floor, nurses and patients were decorating a Christmas tree, and tinsel and color brightened the room. Outside, where the soldier was looking, there was only brown grass and bare trees. The limbs of the trees rattled dryly in the cold December wind, and the gray sky was made even grayer by the smoke which curled up from thousands of coal fires as New York kept itself warm.

"Yeah? How do you know what I'm going through?" the soldier replied bitterly. He looked at Dottie. He was young, so terribly young, she thought, and yet, in that instant when a mine took off his foot, he had aged one hundred years. "You've got two arms, two legs"—he paused, then screwed his face up angrily—"two tits. How the hell do you know?"

Dottie wasn't shocked by his remarks. She had been working with the wounded and broken young men for three years now, and it was normal that they would lash out at someone near them, someone healthy, and try in whatever way they could to hurt them.

"Yes," Dottie said easily. "I do have all those things."

"Then don't talk to me about what I'm going through. You don't know."

"But I do know," Dottie insisted. "There have been hundreds, possibly thousands of young men through here, just like you. Some with worse injuries, some with injuries not as bad."

"And what am I supposed to do, be glad that I'm not wounded as badly as some of the others?" the soldier asked sarcastically. "What do you tell them? Is there always someone who is worse-off than the one you are talking to?"

"If I'm talking to him, yes," Dottie said. "At least they are alive."

"Oh, yeah, at least they are alive," the soldier said. "I spent one week in a choice-cut ward with some guys who had lost both arms and both legs." A choice-cut is what the amputees called themselves, macabre humor, referring to a butcher and the "choice-cuts" of meat. "Do you know what they spend most of their time talking about? Trying to figure out ways to commit suicide. Now, tell me that they are better off than the dead. Go away. Go away and don't come back and talk to me unless you've got a missing arm or leg. Then, I'll talk." The soldier wheeled himself back around to stare at the gray outside again.

Dottie stood there for a moment, then sighed, and turned and walked away.

"Don't let 'im get you down any, Dottie," one of the soldiers who was decorating the tree said, as she walked by. "You just keep fighting."

"Thanks, Mike," Dottie said, and she reached out to touch the soldier. The soldier had only one eye and one ear. His head was still swathed in bandages from the plastic surgery which had built half a face to replace the half he lost. He had been one of Dottie's toughest rehabilitative cases a few months earlier, and hearing words of encouragement from him now was a victory in itself. It took some of the sting away, but she still hurt for the suffering the soldier in the wheelchair was feeling.

Dottie left the ward and walked down the long hallway, then opened the door into an office. There, sitting behind a desk filling out some papers, sat Kenny Satterfield. He looked up and smiled brightly. "Hi," he said. "Is it time for lunch already?"

"No," Dottie said. She sighed and sat down. "It's Billy Baker. I just can't get through to him. You're going to have to go talk to him, Kenny. You're going to have to turn on your special charm."

"Let me guess," Kenny said. "He's missing an arm, right?"

"A foot," Dottie said. "He lost it in France."

"I see, one choice-cut to another, right?" Kenny didn't say it with bitterness, but with humor, and Dottie smiled with him, thankful deep inside that they could smile now at the wound to which it had taken Kenny so long to adjust.

Dottie followed Kenny back down the hallway

and into the ward. The tree was decorated now, and some of the patients and nurses were singing a Christmas Carol. Billy Baker was still staring morosely out the window.

Kenny walked right up behind him. "What did you do before the war?" he asked.

"I worked for Studebaker," Billy said. "I was a spot welder."

"Yeah? Did you do that with your feet?"

Billy turned around then and saw Kenny standing behind him. He also saw the artificial arm. "What kind of question is that?" he asked. "Hell no, I didn't do it with my feet."

"Were you any good at it?"

"I was the best on my line," he said proudly.

"Well, I was pretty good at something too," Kenny said. "In 1941 I had a .395 batting average, and I hit 34 homeruns. And I did it with my hands. Both hands."

"Satterfield!" Baker said. "You're Kenny Satterfield! Yeah, I saw you in a game in Chicago '41."

"You'll probably never see me play another game," Kenny said.

"Yeah," Baker said. "Yeah, I know what you mean. It's the shits, ain't it?"

"It's a fact of life," Kenny said. "I miss baseball, but there's nothing I can do about it. But you, you're a welder, and you say you were the best on the line. Were you really, or are you just shooting off your mouth?"

"I was," Baker said. "You can ask my foreman, or anyone who was with me."

"All right, I'll take your word for it. Now, in your league, I'd say you were probably batting at least .395, wouldn't you?"

"Yeah, I'd say that."

"Wouldn't you like a chance to bat .400?"

"What?"

"Four hundred," Kenny said. "I'd give anything if I could go back and have a chance to bat .400, but I can't. I can't play ball anymore. But you can still play in your league. There is nothing you were doing in your league before that you can't do now. And you can do it better if you put your mind to it. You still have a chance to bat .400, if you try."

"Yeah," Baker said. "Yeah, maybe I see what you mean."

"Let me talk to him for a while, Kenny," Mike, the soldier with only one eye and one ear said. He laughed. "That is, if my face doesn't scare him off."

Baker laughed, a small laugh. "From what I can tell of you, Dotson, you were an ugly son of a bitch before you got hit in the face. Whatever is under those bandages is probably going to improve your looks."

Dottie had been standing in the background watching and listening, and her eyes filled with tears when she heard Baker's attempt at a joke. He would be all right now. He was over the hump.

"You were pretty good in there," she said to Kenny as they walked back to Kenny's office. Kenny was Director of Rehabilitation, a special division of the Red Cross which had been set up to help severely wounded soldiers adjust. There was no such division before Kenny, and the division was created when Dottie talked the Senior Director into doing it. She convinced him that Kenny Satterfield, being a famous baseball player, would have a positive effect on others. What she didn't tell the director was that she hoped creating this

job would help Kenny. It had helped him even
beyond the fondest hopes of Dottie, and Bonnie,
and Kenny's mother and father.

"I'm going into spring training with the Dodgers this season," Kenny said. "I report to camp
April 5, 1945."

"What? You're going back into baseball?"

"As a hitting coach," Kenny said. "Of course, I
won't be making anything near the salary I was
making, but the pay is very good, and I'll be back
in the game."

"Oh, Kenny, that's wonderful!" Dottie said enthusiastically. "I am so happy for you!"

"I couldn't have done it without you," Kenny
said.

"Oh, don't be silly," Dottie said. "Of course you
could have. You've been wonderful these past two
years. You can read and count as well as anyone
else, you know how many letters we've received.
And, don't forget the article in *Life Magazine*."

"Oh, yes," Kenny said. "I know all that. But I
also know what few others know. I know that you
were rehabilitating me, while I was rehabilitating
the others."

"No," Dottie said. "You did it for yourself. All I
did was see the possibility of using your help,
that's all."

"That's all, the lady says," Kenny said. "Listen,
Dottie, I didn't think I ever wanted to even *see*
another baseball game, let alone get involved in
the sport again. And now, I'm actually looking
forward to this spring. Whether you want to admit
it or not, you gave me a new life, and I'd like to
thank you for it."

"All right," Dottie said. "If you insist on thanking me, then I will accept your thanks graciously," she teased.

"That's not all."

"Oh, there's more? Heavens, what more could there possibly be?" Dottie asked in a lilting tone.

"I want you to share in my life."

They had been walking down the hallway, talking easily, then, when Kenny said that, Dottie came to a complete halt. It was as if she had been hit in the pit of the stomach, and the breath was knocked out of her. It was a second before she could breathe again.

"Kenny, no, please," she said quietly. "Don't ask that, don't even think it."

"I love you, Dottie."

"I . . . I know," Dottie said. "And I would be lying if I said I didn't love you. But I love my husband, too. I love him and I miss him more than I can say."

"I thought as much," Kenny said easily. "You are too fine a woman to do otherwise." Kenny gave a short laugh. "In a way, I think I would have been a little disappointed in you if you had accepted my offer. Let us just pretend that the offer was never made."

"No," Dottie said. "Let's don't pretend that. A moment like this is very precious in anyone's life. I'm going to hold onto it, and keep it with me forever." She kissed him tenderly, and with love, though without providing an opening for the kiss to deepen, or go beyond control.

"Lieutenant Anderson!" the radio operator called.

"Yes," Jim answered. It was still difficult for him to adjust to being called lieutenant; his battlefield commission was less than one week old.

"Major Fieldgate wants you to send a patrol down to the road junction near Baugnez, and set up an observation post in the bombed-out church."

"Let me have the radio," Jim said, walking over and taking the handpiece.

"Mad Dog Six, this is Mutt Six. Do you want platoon strength?"

"Negative," the voice came back over the earset. "The Germans have broken through, Mutt Six. They are pouring everything through the Ardennes!"

"What? I thought they were moving back into Germany!"

"So did everyone else," Mad Dog Six said. "You've got to set up an observation post at the Baugnez Road Junction, and call back if you see a major Panzer thrust."

"Will do," Jim said. "Out!" Jim handed the receiver back to the operator. "You'll stay here," he said. "We'll take a walkie-talkie with us. It won't have the range to reach headquarters, but we can reach you here, and you can relay the information on."

"What do you mean we?" Mel asked. "Are you pregnant?"

"I mean we," Jim said. "I'm going."

"Jim, you dumb-assed hick, you are supposed to learn to think like an officer now," Mel said. "No self-respecting officer is going to take a patrol like this. You could get your ass shot off. That's what you have sergeants for. I'll take the patrol."

"You'll stay here with the platoon," Jim said. "I'll take the patrol."

"Like hell I will. I'm going down there. If you insist on going, the least I can do is try and watch after you."

"All right," Jim said. "Get two more men and let's go."

"What the hell is it with these krauts? Don't they know when they're licked? Don't they know it's damn near Christmas already?" Mel said, as they moved into position.

"Christmas?" Jim replied with a laugh. "You're worried about Christmas?"

"Hell yes, didn't you know it was the New York department stores who invented Christmas? The three wise men were named Macy, Gimbel and F.A.O. Schwartz."

Suddenly, Jim saw about thirty German soldiers approaching up the road. The Germans were walking with their weapons slung over their shoulders, as if totally unconcerned that they might encounter Americans here.

"Quick, into the ditch," Jim said, and the four Americans dived off the side of the road.

The Germans had seen them at about the same time they had seen the Germans, and they dived into the ditch on the opposite side of the road. The Germans started firing, and Jim and his men returned the fire.

"Call for help!" Jim said.

"Damn it, Lieutenant, when I dived into the ditch, I broke the walkie-talkie," the soldier replied.

"Let's try and make it back," Jim said. The ditch only went about forty yards, then it ended. When they tried to crawl out of it, the fire from the Germans was so intense that they couldn't leave.

The Germans charged across the road, yelling and firing their guns, but the four Americans, who had the cover of the ditch, were able to cut them down with deadly accurate fire. A second attack was beaten back as well, then, oddly, a white flag fluttered across the road.

"Damn, they want to surrender to us," Mel said.

"I doubt that," Jim said. "What is it?" he asked. "What do you want?"

"We want to get our wounded," a German voice said. "Will you allow us to do this?"

"I'm for shootin' the bastards," Mel said.

"They are soldiers just like us," Jim said. "They probably no more want to be here than we do."

"All right, you're the boss," Mel said. "Whatever you say."

"Go ahead," Jim called back. "Pick them up."

"We have a tank coming," the German warned. "If you surrender now, you'll save yourself."

"Just get your wounded," Jim said. "Then do your damndest, because we'll be waiting."

Jim and the others watched with almost detached curiosity, as the grey-clad German soldiers moved among the bodies, finding the wounded and dragging them back across the road to the safety of the ditch on the other side. Finally all movement stopped.

"The truce is over, Americans," the German voice called.

"Then take that, kraut!" Mel replied, and he stood up and fired an entire clip across the road. His fire was returned by blistering fire, but the Germans didn't try another attack.

A few minutes later they heard the distinctive clank and rattle of a tank, and then, around the bend, they saw it. It was a huge tiger tank, and the turret was traversing and the tube swinging down. There was a flash of light from the tube, then the entire earth seemed to explode around them.

Jim didn't know how long he had been out

when he opened his eyes. He was still in the ditch, but it was strangely quiet. He looked beside him and saw that Mel and the others were dead.

"Mel, my God," he said reaching for him.

"Your friend?" a voice asked, and Jim jerked around in surprise to see a German officer squatting at the top of the ditch. The soldier had a machine pistol pointed at him.

"Yes," Jim said. "He is my friend."

"I'm sorry," the German officer said. "Are you the officer?"

"Yes."

"It was you who let me retrieve my men?"

"It was all of us," Jim said.

"I lost many men here, too," the German officer said. "Your men put up a good fight."

"Thanks," Jim said.

"The fighting has gone too long now. I think it is time for the war to end. We are beaten."

"Yeah? You'd have a hell of a time proving it by me right now," Jim said.

The German officer stood up. "Lie down," he ordered, pointing his pistol toward Jim.

"What? What are you going to do?" Jim asked fearfully.

"Lie down," the German officer said again. "I have been ordered to take no prisoners, to kill all who surrender. I don't wish to kill you. I will shoot into the ground beside you. Pretend that you are dead. Do not move until the sound of the motors has gone, then you will be safe. Your army will move into here soon."

Jim didn't know whether to believe the German officer or not, but at this point he had no choice. He lay on his stomach, mouthed a quick prayer, then held his breath. The gun popped three times, and the bullets hit the ground beside him.

"Good luck, my friend," the German officer said quietly.

Jim heard him walk away, then he heard the sound of engines as trucks, tanks, and armored vehicles started back down the road. He lay quietly for the next three hours, afraid to move so much as a muscle. Finally he heard American voices, then he recognized the voice of one of his men. He was safe.

Nürnberg had cloud cover of seven-tenths, so the attack commander gave orders to divert to the secondary target which was only sixty miles away, but, according to weather reconnaissance had a cloud cover of only two-tenths. The secondary target was Schweinfurt, scene of repeated raids against the ball bearing plants, and a legitimate choice as an alternate. The truth was, however, that if there had been no alternate the bombers would have unloaded their bombs anyway, even if it meant bombing a farmers' field. That was absolutely necessary, for without reducing the weight of the bombs, the bombers would not have had enough fuel to get them back to Wimbleshoe.

Unfortunately for the men in the attacking bombers, the German Air Defense Command had correctly guessed that Schweinfurt would be the secondary target, and they were able to concentrate all their remaining fighter aircraft and flak batteries in such a way as to maximize their effectiveness.

The highway in the sky which stretched from Nurnberg to Schweinfurt became a pathway through the valley of death. Anti-aircraft artillery, manned by experienced gunners who wanted desperately to extract their pound of flesh from the flying devils who had turned their country into a living hell, knew the exact route and altitude of the bombers and that made their job easy. They launched welcoming cards into the formation in the form of exploding shells; angry, blinding flashes of light, flame, steel splinters, and red-hot chunks of jagged metal.

Martin was a little surprised at the violence of the sky. It had been several missions since the Germans had been able to mount a defense this tenacious. Shell fragments were everywhere, slamming into engine nacelles to interrupt the delicate balance of moving parts which had been machined to tolerances of thousandths of an inch, or puncturing fuel tanks to ignite gasoline, or tearing holes through the plexi-glass and aluminum skin to attack the men themselves, severing arms, and legs, and opening torsos to spill blood and intestines on the alclad.

One of the planes near *Truculent Turtle Two* took a direct hit in the bomb bay, and the thirteen five-hundred pound bombs went up instantly. There was a flash of light and a gigantic shock wave, but little wreckage, because the heat and shock very nearly vaporized a thirty ton machine and ten human beings.

Mercifully, the flak disappeared as suddenly as it had begun, and the angry puffs of white and black which littered the way, left the sky. Now it was blue, and clear and welcoming.

"We *made* it!" Kindig said with a great, relieved expulsion of breath. He laughed out loud. "By God, we *made* it!"

"Not yet," Martin said grimly. "Now come the fighters."

"The fighters?"

Martin pointed toward a rapidly closing swarm of black dots. "You wanted to see the jets," he said. "There they are."

"Why don't the Mustangs intercept them?" Kindig asked.

"The jets are traveling at 600 miles per hour. The P-51s top out at a little over 400. They aren't even close."

"But we have to do *something*," Kindig said in a frightened voice. "Can't we take evasive action, or something?"

"My friend, we can't do a damn thing except sit here and watch the show," Martin said.

Statistically, Martin knew, the anti-aircraft batteries brought down more bombers than the fighter aircraft did. And yet, the encounters with the fighters, especially with the seemingly invulnerable jets, were always more frightening.

The closing speed of the fighters was such that the dots grew quickly until they became the sleek Me-262 needle-nosed aircraft, with jet engines slung under each wing. The fighters approached in a line-abreast formation, with the wings and noses bright with the flashing fire of machine gun and cannon.

"Here they come!" one of the gunners called. "Eight, at ten-o-clock high!"

"I've got 'em, I've got em!"

"Look at those sons-of-bitches go! Look at 'em!"

"Lord, oh, Lord, help us!"

All the machine guns on the *Truculent Turtle* which could come to bear on the attacking fighters opened up, and the roar drowned out even the sound of the screaming engines. The first wave of jets screamed by, rolling over to plunge through the combat box and avoid the deadly cross-fire of the bombers they were attacking. The scream of their engines and the sounds of the guns, combined with the roar of the bomber engines and the cries of the men, to blend into a bizzare and cacophonous symphony which could have been orchestrated in hell.

Suddenly there was the sound of metal on metal, and the windshield was cracked. A shell fragment smashed through and landed on Martin's lap.

"Oh, my God, we're hit, we're hit!" Kindig shouted.

Martin looked down and saw the spent casing of a fifty caliber round. "Take it easy," he shouted. "We aren't hit, it's a spent casing from one of the planes above us."

Kindig, who had covered his eyes with his arm, looked at the shell casing, then he laughed. It was a wild, hysterical laugh, but one Martin recognized, for he had laughed in the same way on previous missions.

"Here they come again, the bastards!" the top turret gunner called, and almost immediately the guns opened up. Martin watched as the tracer rounds hosed into the approaching fighters, and though the first attack element slipped through without damage, two of the jets in this formation began trailing smoke.

Suddenly there was the chunking sound of sustaining a hit, then the right, outboard engine started going wild. Martin heard the banshee wail first, then felt the vibration as the engine threatened to pull out of the wing. He looked down at the tachometer and saw the RPM going through 3500 and still climbing. The prop governor was shot out and they had a run-away prop. To make matters worse, there was no way the propeller could be feathered.

"We're going to lose that prop," Martin said.

"It'll come right through the side of the ship," Kindig said anxiously.

"No, it won't," Martin said. "Keep your eyes on it. The moment it starts to go, let me know."

"What are you going to do?"

"Just let me know!" Martin shouted.

The runaway prop was on number four, on Kindig's side of the plane. He sat in his seat with his eyes glued to the prop, oblivious of the screaming fighters and exploding shells around them. Finally, he saw the tell-tale wobbling of the prop-shaft.

"It's going now," he shouted. "It's going now!"

Martin dropped the right wing just a little, then he twisted hard to the left on the wheel, causing the wing to flip up so that at the moment the propeller tore loose from the engine its momentum and the sudden upswing of the wing tossed it harmlessly over the top of the airplane.

"You did it!" Kindig shouted joyously. "You did it!"

Even as Kindig was shouting in relief over losing the prop without sustaining any further damage, number three started spewing thick, oily, black smoke. Fire leaped out from the nacelle, and began caressing the wing root, licking at the skin which was less than one inch away from a thousand gallons of high octane gasoline.

"Damn!" Martin swore. "Hit the fire-bottle! Feather number three!"

Kindig pulled the fire extinguisher and hit the

feather button. The smoke turned white even as the propeller spun to a stop. Finally the smoke cleared away and the twisted nacelle, white with scorching and residue from the extinguisher, told the graphic story of their predicament. Two engines out, and the airplane was losing altitude.

"We're sitting ducks now," Martin said grimly. "I can't keep us in the box."

"Look!" Kindig shouted. "The Germans! They are leaving! They are going away!"

"Well, well, well," Martin said, grinning happily. "One thing about the jets, my boy. They don't have that much range. It would seem as if they have exhausted their station time."

"Will they hit us again, going back?"

"I doubt it. They try and save their fuel now by striking only when we are heading for the target. Afterward, we are empty and they figure we can do no more harm."

"Is that Schweinfurt?"

"Yeah," Martin said. "That's Schweinfurt."

"You've been here before?"

"Five times," Martin answered. "I'm not sure, but I think I'm qualified to vote in their city elections now."

Martin looked down at the familiar triangular shape of the small city as it nestled along the Main River. Around the outer edges of the town, long, graceful roads passed through peaceful-looking fields, and by red-roofed houses in the small, surrounding villages. As they drew closer to the city itself, they saw that there were fewer red roofs. A close inspection showed that there were fewer roofs of any kind, because Schweinfurt showed the effects of being a frequent bombing target.

"There's no flak," Martin said.

"What?"

"There's no flak," Martin said again. "They must have concentrated all the flak in the bomber stream corridor. Walter, my boy, I think we have it made in the shade."

"I hope so," Kindig said. "Jesus, I've never been so scared in my life. Jesus!"

Martin smiled. "You've grown up in the last hour."

"Grown up my ass," Kindig said. "I've grown old. I'll bet my hair is pure white."

"Damn," Martin said. "We're losing altitude fast. There's no way we're going to make it all the way back to Wimbleshoe. We're going to have to pick out an emergency field somewhere in France."

"Can we do that?"

"We can now," Martin said. "We control France, remember?"

"Yeah," Kindig said.

"That's another advantage we have over the old days." Martin looked up and saw a bomber right over him. "What the hell? What's he doing there? Who is that, Walt, can you see his tail number?"

Kindig leaned forward in his seat and twisted around. "It's Four-six-three," he said.

Martin switched the radio to plane-to-plane. "Four Six Three, you are out of position."

"This is Four Six Three, who is calling?"

"This is Four Five Nine, I'm just below you with two engines out. I've moved to the tuck position, but you are in my way."

"I don't see you."

"Well, hell, tell your ball gunner to stick his arm out, he can shake hands with my turret gunner. Now get it over."

"Sorry," the other pilot said.

"Attention all planes, this is the flight leader. Drop your bombs now."

"No!" Martin screamed, too late as the thirteen bombs tumbled down from the plane just above him. One of the bombs sliced through the tail, cutting the airplane in half. With full power on the two engines on the left wing, no power on the engines on the right wing, and no control surface to overcome the pressures, the airplane went into an immediate flat spin. Martin's head was slammed against the steel frame of the armor-plated seat, and everything went black.

20

Thurman was tuning the radio, trying to get the little green light, the "magic eye" the manufacturer called it, at just the right intensity. He was looking for a St. Louis station, and the distance and the atmosphere made it somewhat difficult to get clearly. He thought he heard H.V. Kaltenborn's voice once, but he lost it under a deluge of static.

"Maybe Memphis," he said aloud, and he moved the dial across the band until he found Memphis, and the disturbance which was interrupting the St. Louis signal did not rob him of the Memphis signal, so he settled into his chair with a sigh to listen to the news.

"Yesterday, Sunday, January 23, the 7th Armored Division attacked toward Saint-Vinh. General Clarke had the honor of being the first to enter the town, and thus it came full circle, for it was General Clarke's command which put up such a stubborn defense one month ago when the German offensive began. The Germans gambled heavily in the Ardennes, and they lost. Ah, there's good news, tonight."

Dennis walked over to the radio and put his

finger on the little green light light, then reached for one of the dials.

"No, no, Dennis," Thurman said. "Don't touch the radio. Come here, sit in grandpa's lap."

Dennis looked toward Thurman.

"Come on, sit in grandpa's lap," Thurman said, patting his knee. Thurman grinned, then ran toward him, holding his arms up. Thurman picked him up. "I want to hear the news about your daddy," he said.

The front door opened and closed, and Nancy started removing her coat and hat. "It's cold out there," she said.

"How was your meeting?" Thurman asked.

Nancy looked at Thurman and smiled. She walked over and kissed him on the cheek. "I don't know why I ever wanted to get in to the Twentieth Century Club in the first place," she said. "It was boring."

"Can I quote you on that?"

"Don't you dare. Is Yolinda gone?"

"Again," Thurman said dryly.

"Thurman, you don't think there's anything to the gossip, do you?"

Dennis had taken a pencil out of Thurman's pocket, and now he was studying the little pocket-hook slide, trying to make it move. Thurman looked at him for a moment before he sighed.

"I don't know, Nancy," he said. "I just don't know. Whatever the case, I just don't think it is our place to say anything."

"But surely, with such gossip, there almost has to be something to it."

"At least Dr. Chambers has left to take an appointment in Chicago," Thurman said. "So if there was anything to it, it's over now by virtue of geography, if for no other reason. Yolinda got a letter from Martin today, by the way. It's over on the lamp table."

"Did you read it?" Nancy asked, starting for the letter.

"Yes."

"What does he have to say?"

"Oh, the usual kind of thing the censors will let through," Thurman said. "It's not what he did say that's important, it's what he didn't say."

"What do you mean?"

"You read it. Does it sound like a man who's been away from his wife for three years? I don't know what kind of letters Yolinda sends him, but on the basis of the ones he sends her, I'd say their marriage is in difficulty."

"Yes, but you aren't being fair," Nancy said. "Any marriage would have a strain on it under these conditions. I feel that they will work out their problems, if they just get the chance."

"We did, didn't we?" Thurman said.

"What do you mean?"

"Leah Davis," Thurman said.

"Leah Davis?"

"She wrote me a letter about five years after she left Mount Eagle," Thurman said. "She told me she came to visit you the day she left, and she told me what the two of you talked about. I loved you before, Nancy, but when I found out that you had faced up to that, alone, I loved you more than words could ever express. I was a fool, and I nearly jeopardized everything I held dear. It's twenty years late, but, I want to ask for your forgiveness."

"I didn't realize you knew she had come to see me," Nancy said. "I'm glad I didn't know, I had a difficult enough problem with my self-image at that time as it was. And you did nothing which requires forgiveness. Whatever you did, I drove you to it."

Nancy walked over to the chair where Thurman was sitting and put her arms around him, hugging him tightly. Her eyes were moist, and she sniffed. "Look at me," she said. "I'm about to cry.".

"I didn't think I had it in me to get you all teared up anymore," Thurman teased.

Nancy laughed, and the doorbell rang. "You'd better get it," she said. "If anyone sees me like this they'll think we've had a fight."

"They couldn't think too much about it," Thurman said. "I don't even have a black eye."

Thurman was still laughing when he opened the door. Albert Watson was standing on the front porch, and in the driveway his yellow cab stood with the door open and the engine running.

"What's up, Albert?" Thurman asked. "No one here called a taxi."

"I'm sorry to be the one to deliver this," Albert said. He handed Thurman a small, yellow envelope.

"What is it?" Thurman asked.

"Thurman, oh my God, no, it's a telegram!" Nancy said.

"I'm sorry," Albert mumbled again, and he turned and went back to his taxi.

Thurman stood in the doorway watching as the taxi backed out. He had the strongest feeling that whatever was in the telegram should not be shared with anyone else. He didn't want the driver anywhere close when he and Nancy opened it.

"What is it?" Nancy asked.

Thurman looked at the small yellow envelope, and at the address visible through the cellophane window. "It's for Yolinda," he said quietly.

"Open it," Nancy said.

Thurman opened the envelope with trembling fingers, then unfolded the small yellow sheet of paper.

NA362 29 GOVT-WUX WASHINGTON DC 28 701P

MRS YOLINDA S HOLT

TAXI PAID 427 ELM AVE MOUNT EAGLE ILL RTE HE

REGRET TO INFORM YOU YOUR HUSBAND CAPTAIN MARTIN W HOLT WAS SHOT DOWN OVER SCHWEINFURT GERMANY ON FIVE JANUARY MISSING PRESUMED DEAD LETTER FOLLOWS WITH DETAILS

MANNING ACTING THE ADJUTANT GENERAL

When Charles received the letter it had half a dozen postmark and censor stamps imprinted on the envelope. No doubt many were curious as to what kind of correspondence a foreign national would have with the secret-most base in the world. The letter was from Allison Cairns-Whiteacres, with the return address of Ingersall Hall, the Staffordshire, England.

Dear Charley,

I know Martin is the only one who ever called you Charley, but it is the way he always spoke of you, and so it is the way I think of you too. Martin told me all about you, you know. I know how gentle and sensitive you are, and how terribly smart you are and how understanding. I think it is that I am

*looking for now, Charley, understanding I mean. I
can't very well write to your mother and father, nor
do I think it would be proper to write to Dottie. But
I do want to reach out and touch someone, to share
my grief with someone whose grief is as great as
mine. It is a lonely and frustrating feeling being in
love with someone, when all the dictates of society
condemn that love. And it is even lonelier when
that love is torn away, and you have not even the
frame and structure of propriety to help ease the
pain.*

*I talked with Brad Phillips about the mission
on which Martin was lost. Brad said that after all
the large raids over Schweinfurt, that this mission
seemed like a piece of cake, to use his words. There
was very little flak, and practically no fighter aircraft. Schweinfurt was only a secondary target for
them anyway, as their primary target, Nuremberg,
was covered by clouds. Of course, I can tell you all
this now that Germany has surrendered . . . before
now, mention of the targets would have been cut
from this letter.*

*Martin's airplane was not shot down, it was
bombed down! According to Brad, one of the upper
level bombers released their bombs too soon, and the
string of bombs fell through Martin's airplane, breaking off the tail. The airplane went into a flat spin
and crashed, with no parachutes observed. Since the
Germans surrendered, it has been confirmed that
Martin was killed, and his body has been recovered
by the Allied graves registration service. I will not
get to see the body, nor even the coffin, as I am sure
it will be sent back to Mount Eagle for burial. But
my prayers will go with Martin, while some of*

*Martin will stay with me for, you see, I am preg-
nant with his baby.*

*I will not write again, dear Charley, for I
have no wish to cause embarrassment, or pain or
discomfort. I thought only to share my grief with
you, and to tell you that some of Martin lives on. I
wish you the best of luck, now, and forever more.*

Allison

Most of the news in Allison's letter was already
known to Charles. A follow-up notification from
the War Department gave the actual details, even
admitting that Martin's ship was inadvertently hit
by bombs from his own group. Then, after Germany surrendered, the War Department informed
the Holts that Martin's body had been found, and
would be shipped back to the United States on a
space-available basis. First Lieutenant James Anderson had been selected as the escort officer.
Lieutenant Anderson, the War Department informed them routinely, was the brother-in-law of
the decedent.

The phone beside Charles' chair rang, and he
picked it up. "Yes," he said. "This is Holt."

"Charles, this is Hans. Sunrise at 05:30. Be ready
to go."

"Are you sure?" Charles asked.

"Goldfire confirmation."

"All right," Charles said. "I'll be ready." Charles
hung up the phone, then looked at it for a few
minutes, drumming his fingers on the table. He
wanted to call his parents, and he wanted to call
Dottie. He knew phone calls were monitored, and
though he wasn't concerned about giving away
any secrets, even inadvertently, he did not want
strangers listening in now. Not at this moment.

He tore out a sheet of paper and started to write his parents, then he wadded it up and tossed it aside and started one to Dottie. He tossed that one aside too, and started a third letter, this time to Allison Cairns-Whiteacre. Finally he tossed that one aside as well and abandoned the whole idea. He decided he would just go to bed. There would be an early sunrise tomorrow.

The site was called Trinity Site, and it was located in the middle of the desert, in an area called *Jornada del Muerto*, or Journey of Death. There were fewer than 50 present, including the 15 who were aware of the total implication of Manhattan Project from the beginning. Dr. Oppenheimer was passing out very dark glasses to everyone. In the distance stood a one hundred foot tall tower. From where the fifty people stood, the tower, despite its height, wasn't even visible.

"Are we safe here, doctor?" someone wanted to know.

Dr. Oppenheimer looked at the questioner, and smiled wanly at him. "I wish I could guarantee that we are," he said.

"Gentlemen, one minute," General Groves said, looking at his watch.

"Everyone put on your goggles!"

Charles slipped the goggles on and faced toward where he knew the tower to be. The goggles were so dark that he could see absolutely nothing, and he had a desire to slip them up, but his own calculations had told him that it would be foolish to do so.

"Ten seconds."

Charles tensed, and listened as the seconds were

counted down: five ... four ... three ... two ... one ... zero.

At that instant a light, more brilliant than any light which had ever been seen on the face of the earth, turned the pre-dawn shadow into the sunniest afternoon, even through the extra-dark glasses. It was a light which could have been seen from any planet within the earth's solar system and it was fed by a temperature of 100 million degrees.

After the light a tremendous ball of fire, with a diameter of more than a mile, began shooting upwards. The fireball changed colors, going from deep purple to orange, growing bigger, and bigger still, rising as it grew.

When the fireball subsided, it left behind a tremendous black cloud which formed a gigantic mushroom.

"You can take your goggles off now!" someone called, and everyone did, then stood there looking in stunned silence. Even those who had been part of the Trinity 15 had no idea of the power that would be unleashed, and they were shocked beyond the ability to express their feelings in words.

Charles couldn't get over the eerie silence, the long, long period of absolute, total, dead silence.

And then it hit, the shock wave and sound waves traveling together. The concussion, even this far away, nearly knocked Charles over, and a whistling hurricane came up, with sand thrown before a wind which had the searing heat of a blast furnace. There was a roar, louder than any roar Charles had ever heard, and he closed his eyes and prayed in fear, for it seemed as if they had, somehow, tapped straight into the forces of hell itself.

When the smoke finally cleared away and the scientists could go to the site for a closer examination, the awesome power they had sensed earlier became even more graphic. The one-hundred-foot steel tower upon which the device had sat was gone, completely vaporized by the heat of the explosion. The explosion had left a giant 1,200 foot wide dish in the sand, forming a pure, jade-green glass from the action of the heat on the desert sand. All animal and plant life had been destroyed within a radius of one mile.

"It is finished," Hans Werfel said solemnly, and Charles didn't know whether he meant the Manhattan Project, or mankind itself.

21

The destruction of Schweinfurt was nearly complete. Streets were blocked by rubble, only the narrowest paths were cleared to allow a minimum of traffic. Brick walls stood starkly black against the sky, and the buildings they once enclosed were gone. Trolley tracks were twisted, and bridges were down. People walked around as if in a daze, though it had been six months since the last bomb fell on the city.

The U.S. Army had taken over the two military bases which had been in Schweinfurt: Ledward Barracks and Conn Kaserne. Conn was located close to the huge ball-bearing factory, the target of the many air raids, but, amazingly, Conn wasn't too badly damaged. Jim approached the gate of Conn, having driven from Nuremberg along the marvelous, and virtually undamaged Autobahn.

An M.P. stepped out of the guardhouse, and Jim stopped. The M.P. saluted.

Jim showed the M.P. his orders, authorizing him to claim Martin's body.

"The graves registration section is straight ahead, Lieutenant," the guard said. "There is a big yellow building on the left side of the road. You can't miss it, it has a big eagle and swastika on it. The remains are kept there."

"It seems rather inappropriate to keep American bodies in a building marked with a swastika, doesn't it?" Jim asked.

"Yes, sir, they's lots of people that agree with you," the guard said. "I hear they are gonna take off all the swastikas, but they just ain't got around to it yet."

Jim drove through the camp which had once been the headquarters for the German Panzer Corps, and he saw the Officers' Club with a fresh, new sign out front, announcing that it was "Under New Management". Then he saw the building the M.P. described, and he stopped and went inside.

A sergeant was sitting at the desk and he took Jim's orders, then led him into a large, gymnasium type room. There were well over two hundred coffins, and Jim stopped and whistled softly. "So many?" he asked. "Where did they all come from?"

"Lieutenant, this isn't half of them," the sergeant said. "Don't forget, we lost over fifteen hundred airmen on the Schweinfurt raids. As it turned out, we had as many airmen killed as there were krauts killed in the city. And for nothing. It broke down to about one aviator per ball-bearing."

"What? What do you mean? I thought the ball-bearing production was just about halted," Jim said. "That was what we heard."

"That was what we thought based on the photographs," the sergeant said. "What we didn't know was that there is an entire network of tunnels under the city. The people went down there and they weren't even scratched by the bombs. On the first raid, 1100 bombs fell on the city and only 80 fell in the factory compound. Of the eighty, only six fell near the the critical machinery. They didn't even scratch the machinery. As it turned out, we dropped some incendiary bombs as a nuisance factor, and they did the most damage. High explosives knocked the machinery over, but Jerry just took the machines into the tunnels and went right back to work. The firebombs ignited the oil in some of the machinery though, and then the rollers and guides would warp, and the machine would be useless but there weren't many of those. We bombed the hell out of this place, and we didn't interrupt production any more than a wildcat strike would at home."

"How do you know all this?" Jim asked.

"I've been here since the week the war ended," the sergeant said. "One of the airmen who went down over Schweinfurt was my brother. I took an interest in what he might have accomplished."

"I'm sorry," Jim said. Jim looked at the quiet rows of coffins. "Is your brother one of these men?"

"No," the sergeant said. "His body hasn't been located yet. I volunteered to stay here until we do find him."

"Do you think you will?"

"Yes," the sergeant said. "I've got to hand it to these German bastards," he added begrudgingly. "They are so thorough that they have pinpointed the exact location of every bomb strike, and the location, date, and time of day of every plane that went down. They recovered all the bodies, catalogued them, then buried them in carefully marked graves. Our job here hasn't been a search, as much as it has been retrieving, then cross-referencing their filing system with our information to confirm identification. We haven't found Buzzer yet, but we will. You can rest assured, Lieutenant, that if you have come after"—the sergeant looked at the orders—"Captain Martin W. Holt, then that's who you are getting. The identification is thorough."

"That's comforting to know," Jim said.

"He's over here," the sergeant said, leading Jim among the many gray boxes, until they stopped by one. It had a number, and beneath the number, an information card.

HOLT, MARTIN W., CAPT.
02124390 Air Corps
Shot down 1430, 5 January
1945 over Geldersheim

"Is he a relative?" the sergeant wanted to know as Jim read the card, then looked at the box and touched it lightly.

"He's my wife's brother," Jim said. "And a friend. I've known him all my life. I took classes under his father."

"That's tough," the sergeant said sympathetically. "Martin Holt, that name sounds a little familiar for some reason."

"He made All-American football team in 1941," Jim said.

"Yes," the sergeant said. "Yes, he played for some school in Indiana or Illinois or something like that, didn't he? I remember reading about him. He was a halfback, wasn't he?"

"Yes," Jim said. "Standhope College, in Mount Eagle, Illinois."

"Son of a bitch," the sergeant said softly. "The poor son of a bitch."

Jim sighed. "What do I do next?"

"You go over to transportation and arrange for an ambulance to transport the body to the *banhhof*, that's the railroad station, then you get travel orders for you and the remains to Bremerhaven. There you'll get on a ship and it'll take you to the States, and then, Lieutenant, you are out of the war."

"Thanks," Jim said. He turned and started to leave, then he looked back at the sergeant. "I hope you find your brother soon."

It was amazingly simple to get the travel orders and arrangements made. Jim had grown used to the red tape and the bureaucracy which caused everything in the army to move at a snail's pace, and the efficiency of this operation surprised him. It was another touch of irony, he thought, that a person had to die to find such efficiency.

"What was that area just outside?" Jim asked the clerk who was processing his paperwork.

"What area is that, sir?"

"The big fenced-in area, with the barbed wire? Was there a concentration camp here?"

The clerk laughed. "The only concentration camp here is ours," he said. "We've got a bunch of the Nazi bastards prisoner there. The word is there are going to be trials in Nuremberg, and some of these birds will be going there."

"Good," Jim said. He had not been in on any actual liberation of the camps, but he had already heard of the death camps, and he had seen the results of some of them. He was even more sensitive to it because of Mel. "I hope they hang every son of a bitch who had anything to do with it."

"If they did that, they'd hang every German in the country," the clerk said.

Jim took his orders and walked back out to the jeep. He looked over toward the enclosure, and some impulse caused him to walk over to it. As he approached the fence, the three or four Germans who had been near turned and sullenly moved away. Jim went up to the fence and stood there, looking in. There were about forty prisoners visible, all of them were wearing gray fatigues with big white letters PW painted on their backs. They stood in groups of three or four, talking quietly among themselves, paying no attention to the Americans who were occupying what had once been one of their camps.

"You did this to yourselves, you bastards," Jim muttered under his breath. "You killed Martin, and you killed Mel, and you killed forty other good men that I knew persona!ly, and you killed millions of innocent people, and you caused death and destruction among your own people. You deserve everything you get."

Jim turned and started to walk away, when one of the German prisoners called out to him.

"American Lieutenant," the prisoner called.

Jim continued to walk, ignoring him.

"American Lieutenant, please, I must speak with you."

Jim stopped, and squeezed his hands into fists. He didn't look around. "I have nothing to talk to you about, you Nazi bastard," he said.

"Please, Lieutenant, you recognized my flag of truce once before, won't you do so now?"

Jim was shocked by the German's statement, and he turned and looked toward the fence with that shock registered on his face. The German had come all the way to the fence and was standing just on the other side. "Please," he said again. "I must talk to you."

Jim returned to the fence. "Are you?" he started, then he looked at him. The man was thinner, with a drawn, gaunt face, and old, old eyes, but it was the same man. "You are the German officer at the ditch," he said. "You are the one who fired into the ground beside me."

"Yes," the German said. He smiled. "I see you took my advice and lay quietly until your own men came."

"Yes," Jim said. "Yes, I did. They came within a few hours."

"Ah, how different our fortunes became after that," the German officer said. "I was a Panzer officer, without tanks, a commander without men, a warrior without hope. I reached my own truce on Easter Sunday, 1945. For me, the war ended on that day, for on that day I returned home, to Schweinfurt."

"Why are you in here?" Jim asked.

The German officer smiled. "My American friend, that is where you can help me," he said.

"Wait a minute," Jim interrupted. "Listen, I'm grateful to you, whatever your name is,"

"*Hauptman* Rudi Rodl," the German officer said, clicking his heels together automatically.

"Yes, well, Captain Rodl, I'm grateful to you for saving my life on that day. But I don't think I can do anything for you here, this all—"

"Do you remember the date?" Captain Rodl asked.

"I beg your pardon?"

"Do you remember the date I saved your life?"

"Yes," Jim said. "I remember it well, because that was also the date you killed my friend, Mel."

"It was an act of war, Lieutenant," Captain Rodl said. "You killed many of my friends on that day as well. Do you remember the date?"

"Yes," Jim snapped. "I remember the date. What is so damned important about the date?"

"I am only charged with one crime," Captain Rodl said. "I have been identified as the German officer who executed a Polish Catholic priest in Warsaw. The day the priest was killed was 19 December, 1944."

"Nineteen December?"

"Yes."

"You couldn't have been in Warsaw," Jim said. "You were in the Ardennes. Can't you prove you were there?"

"How?" Captain Rodl asked. "I was attached to a rover unit. We were supposed to capture our supplies from the Americans, our fuel, even our food. We were independent of any major command, so I cannot verify my whereabouts by official orders."

"But surely, one of your men—"

"Dead," Captain Rodl said. "Every man you saw with me on that day is dead. I am the last survivor of an army that never even existed as far as anyone is concerned. Lieutenant, you are the only person alive who can put me there on that day. Will you do it?"

Jim looked at the German captain, and he remembered that cold, terrifying day in the ditch on the road near the little village of Baugnez. He remembered the last, terrifying second, just before the gun went off, then the relief which almost couldn't be believed, as the bullets hit the ground beside him.

"Yes," Jim agreed. "I'll do it."

"Danke," the German said, smiling broadly, and with obvious relief. Then, realizing he had spoken in German, he said again in English. "Thank you."

Jim turned to leave, then he stopped and looked back toward Captain Rodl. "Good luck, my friend," he said, parroting what Captain Rodl had said to him that day in the ditch.

The cruiser *Indianapolis* was anchored off Tinian Island, and several large metal containers were being off-loaded and put gingerly onto an LST. Charles had already climbed down the net, and was in the LST, watching the off-loading process. Hans Werfel, who had flown to Tinian the previous day, had come out to meet the cruiser.

"How did it take the voyage?" Hans asked.

"Better than I did," Charles admitted. "I was seasick the entire distance."

One of the nearby sailors laughed. "Doc, I never saw anyone feed the fishes like you done."

"Feed the fishes? What does that mean?" Hans asked.

"Believe me," Charles said, still not looking well. "You don't want to know."

"Okay, take it away!" the loading officer shouted, and the crane which was extended over the side of the cruiser was withdrawn, lines were cast off, and the LST operator opened the throttle. The diesel engine exhaust let out a plume of foul-smelling blue smoke, and the little boat, bobbing and weaving, started toward the island.

"The modified B-29s are already here," Hans said. as he and Charles stood near the edge of the LST, watching the island approach, and feeling the water spray in their faces. They were able to do this only because they were standing on a platform half way up the side of the vessel.

"What do the crews know?"

"Only that they are going to fly some sort of special mission. The commander knows everything of course, but the rest of the men know nothing."

"It's better that way," Charles said. "It's a little like having one blank round in one of the rifles of a firing squad. Every member of the firing squad can believe that his was the weapon with the blank round. The men of this aircrew will always have the comfort of not having known beforehand they were dropping a device from hell."

"Stand by to dock," someone up front called, and the boat engine raced a few times, then there was a scrubbing feeling as the LST ran ashore and let the front gate down.

"Where do you wish to go first?" Hans asked, as they stepped off the boat.

"Let me see the airplane," Charles said. "I want to assure myself that there is no way an errant electrical or radio signal could predetonate the bomb."

"It's been checked out," Hans assured him.

"I want to check it again," Charles said.

"Very well," Hans said. "It's over here, in the first hangar."

As Charles walked across the scrub grass, and then the oiled sea shells which made up the airfield, toward the hangar, he saw dozens of newspaper, newsreel, and radio reporters.

"What are all these people doing here?" he asked.

"The War Department has given them the word that something big is about to happen," Hans said. "But they have no idea what. I guess they had to be told, but they have made things rather difficult for us, trying to find out what is going on before the official release-date."

"When will that be?" Charles asked. "The official release date?"

"The first day weather permits," Hans said. "Oh, you'd better put this on or the guards won't let you into the hangar." Hans handed Charles an identification card to pin onto his pocket.

The guards honored the cards, and Hans and Charles stepped into the large hangar. There they saw the B-29 that would carry the first atomic bomb. The airplane was long and slender, with graceful wings and beautifully tapered engine nacelles. It was one of man's most noble creations, a machine capable of flying nine miles high, at nearly 400 miles per hour, over miles and miles of ocean, mountain, or any other obstacle on earth. And it was going to be used to deliver an instrument of death such as the world had never witnessed.

"What is that?" Charles asked, pointing to the name on the nose.

"Enola Gay," Hans said. "It's named after Colonel Tibbets' mother."

"Let's take a look inside," Charles said.

They went into the airplane and there they saw a Naval ordnance officer whom Charles had come to know quite well. It was Captain William Parsons, the man responsible for the final arming of the bomb.

"Captain Parsons is going on the mission," Hans said.

"Yes," Captain Parsons replied. He ran his hand through his hair, nervously. "I got to thinking about it. You know, I once saw four B-29s in a row crash during takeoff. If that happened with the bomb, well, we could just kiss this island and everyone on it good-bye. I've decided that the bomb shouldn't be armed until after we are aloft."

"That may not be a bad idea," Charles agreed. Charles made a final check for electrical or radio signals, then left the plane and went with Hans to his quarters, to await the mission.

Five days after he arrived, Charles was lying in his bunk looking at the August issue of *National Geographic*. One of the advertisements showed a picture of a mother, father, and little boy looking at a large television screen. The headline of the ad read; "Coast-to-coast television . . . through radio relay".

It held the promise of a bright new tomorrow, after peace was won. Charles could only hope and pray that the promise came true.

"Charles, it is time," Hans said, sticking his head in the room. "Colonel Tibbets is now going to brief his crews. Come."

Charles put the magazine down, then hurried over to the quonset hut which was designated as the briefing hut. There he slipped inside and took a seat in the rear of the building. He looked into the intense faces of the men who would drop the bomb.

Colonel Tibbets walked up to the platform in front, then looked out at the men. He cleared his throat, and began to speak.

"Tonight is the night we have all been waiting for. Our long months of training are to be put to the test. We will soon know if we have been successful, or failed. Upon our efforts tonight it is possible that history will be made. We are going to drop an atomic bomb. That is a bomb which uses the same source of energy that the sun uses, and it will be equal in destructive force to 20,000 tons of TNT."

There were a few low whistles and murmurs of amazement.

Colonel Tibbets completed the briefing, then Chaplain William Downey led the men in prayer.

After the briefing and prayer, the crews went for a midnight supper of eggs, sausage, apple butter, milk, bread and coffee. Then they went out to their airplanes. The first airplanes to take off were the weather planes, and they started up and taxied out amidst the popping and flashing of flashbulbs.

Next, came the *Enola Gay* and two escort planes. The *Enola Gay* revved up her engines, then started down the runway. It gathered speed slowly, then moved faster and faster, though still on the ground. Charles held his breath until, at the far end of the runway with precious little of it left, the *Enola Gay* lifted off. Charles looked at his watch. It was 2:45 on the morning of August 6th.

22

As the plane circled Charles looked with wonder at the scene below. Within a few days after Japan surrendered, Charles requested, and was granted, a C-47 aircraft in order to go to Hiroshima to check on the effects of the bomb.

"Dr. Holt," the crewchief said, coming back to Charles' seat. "The pilot said to tell you that this is Hiroshima."

"My God," Charles breathed softly.

Charles had seen pictures of cities laid to waste by bombing, and he was familiar with the blackened, skeletal remains of gutted buildings and rubble-filled streets. But what he was looking at now defied all the senses. There was no rubble, there weren't even any streets. There was nothing down there but a vast, lifeless desert. It was as barren as the Trinity test site.

Charles' plane wasn't the first one into Hiroshima, there were others before it, so the pilot was able to find what had been the airport. He landed gently and rolled across a wide open field. From down here, the total destruction seemed even more complete, because Charles could see all the way across what had been the city, a totally unobstructed view. Now, too, he could see that there were some survivors, pitiful groups of maimed and deformed people who sat around stoically, waiting to die.

The pilot cut the engines and the propellers ticked over a few times, then stopped. The crew chief opened the side door and lowered the steps, and Charles climbed down to set foot on the site of the world's first city to be destroyed by an A-Bomb.

An American major walked over toward the plane and watched as Charles and the others stepped out.

"Reporter?" the major asked, when he saw that Charles' uniform had no military insignia.

"Scientist," Charles replied, looking around him. The major checked Charles' badge and nodded confirmation.

"Come to check out the city, huh?" the major asked. He chuckled. "Well, I'll tell you, doc, there's not much left to check out, that's for sure."

"Such unimaginable destruction," Charles said. "My God, what have we done?"

"Are you one of the guys responsible for this?" the major asked.

"I am ashamed to say that I am," Charles said.

"Look here, doc, there ain't nothin' to be ashamed of," the American major said. "The way I look at it, the Japs brought it on themselves. Besides, if you hadn't set this thing off here I'd probably be writin' my last will and testament about now, gettin' ready to invade the main islands. Don't think I wasn't sweatin' that."

"I know all the justification for it," Charles said. "Still." He let the word hang. "What is that?" Charles asked, pointing to a large shape on the ground.

"That there is a pink horse," the major said.

"A what?"

"He had all his skin burned off by the bomb," the major said. "He lived for a couple of weeks, just sort of wandering around here like he didn't know what happened to him, then this morning he just keeled over dead."

"Are you just going to leave him there?"

"Doc, we still got thousands of human corpses to get rid of," the major said. "I can't be worried about a horse."

"I'm sorry," Charles said. "Of course you are right."

The major softened. "Look, it'll take you a while to adjust to everything you are going to see here," he said. "And then you won't adjust, you'll just find some way to put it out of your mind. You have to, or it'll drive you crazy. Now, I hear you want to meet Dr. Nakamura."

"Yes, he is a well known Japanese physicist, and I understand he is here," Charles said.

"He's here, alright. He's been here since the very first day," the major said. He pointed across the field. "You'll find him in the aid station over there. The truth is, there's not very much anyone can do for any of these people now, but he stays over there all the time anyway."

"Thanks," Charles said. Charles reached back into the plane and took out a bag which contained a geiger counter, plus several medical supply items. He walked across the field to the aid station the major had pointed out. The aid station was made of several pieces of corrugated tin which the survivors had pieced together. There were literally hundreds of patients inside, lying on the ground, as there were no beds, and moaning quietly, almost discreetly, as if their injuries were embarrassing to them.

The injured were pitiful in their wounds. Some had their eyebrows and hair burned off, others had badly burned skin, and some even had the patterns of their clothes burned into their skin. Charles saw one woman with flower patterns all over her body, and he realized that she must have been wearing a kimono which had dark flowers on a light background. The dark flowers absorbed the heat and conducted it to the skin.

Dr. Nakamura was busy applying bandages and ointment. Charles recognized him from pictures he had seen. Dr. Nakamura, Charles was told, spoke excellent English, and had actually studied under Dr. Oppenheimer. Dr. Nakamura was one of the addressees of a special letter which had been dropped before the bomb, warning Japan and begging them to surrender before it was too late.

"Dr. Nakamura, my name is Dr. Charles Holt. I bring you greetings from a mutual friend. Dr. Oppenheimer sends his regards."

"I am pleased to be remembered by so great a man," Dr. Nakamura said, bowing to Charles.

"I am here to assist you if I can."

"Are you a medical doctor?"

"No," Charles said. "I'm sorry, I am not. I am a physicist."

"Ah," Nakamura said. "You are one of the men responsible for the bomb." It wasn't an accusation, or even a denunciation. It was merely an observation.

"Yes," Charles said. "God help me, I am."

"You should not feel too badly about it," Dr. Nakamura said. "The blame is not yours alone. It is with everyone whose action brought on this war. It is good the war is finally over, even if it required such a devil-device as the atomic bomb."

Nearby, someone began retching, and Charles looked over at them with a sense of helplessness.

"Many are suffering from the radiation sickness now," Nakamura said. "They do not understand the disease, and many think the Americans spread a poison which will last for seven years. I have tried to calm them by telling them their fears are false."

"I hope their fears are false," Charles said. "I hope we have not unleashed a lethal radiation which will linger for seven years."

"Your testing did not discern what the effects would be?" Dr. Nakamura asked.

"No," Charles said. He made an apologetic gesture with his shoulders. "I'm afraid we were so dedicated to making it work that we paid no attention at all to the after-effects."

"Then we will work on it together," Dr. Nakamura said. "Come with me, I have found the epicenter. I will show you."

Charles followed Dr. Nakamura away from the aid shelter and across the quiet, desolate plain which was once a city.

"The power of the bomb was such that it marked its place for us," Dr. Nakamura explained. "I was able to locate the epicenter by examining the pattern of scorching on the telephone poles and concrete walls. I used a method of crude triangulation and it brought me here."

Charles looked around. He could see a graveyard nearby. Perhaps even those who lay here had been disturbed by the blast. He saw several pieces of green glass on the ground, and he wondered what window could be so large as to leave so much. Then he remembered the scene at Trinity. Here, as in the desert, the bomb had made glass of the sand in the earth. What must it have been like at the exact moment?

"What is this place?" Charles asked. "Or rather, perhaps I should ask, what was it?"

"It was the Torii gateway of the Gokoku Shrine," Dr. Nakamura said. "Notice, if you will, some of the oddities of the bomb." Dr. Nakamura pointed to a concrete building which was still, amazingly, standing, though it had been completely gutted. The building was of reinforced concrete, built to be earthquake resistant.

There, on the roof of the building, Charles saw a permanent shadow of what had been a tower.

"It is as if a photograph were made," Dr. Nakamura said. "Such shadows are also found in other places." He pointed to some of the granite tombstones within the graveyard of the shrine, and Charles gasped, for on one he saw clearly the imprint of a man, crouched and holding his arms over his head. He must have died in that instant, but his picture stayed behind to tell his story.

Charles took out his geiger counter and began taking readings. The intensity of radioactivity was higher than normal, though low enough that the danger had passed. That was a relief to Charles. He really didn't know how long the radioactivity would linger in the dangerous state. It had dissipated quickly at Trinity, but there had been no buildings or structures at Trinity to capture it and hold it, to allow it to trickle out slowly.

A Japanese woman approached them then, seemingly from nowhere, because Charles had not seen anyone down here. She stopped a respectable distance away and bowed, then spoke in her native tongue.

"What is it?" Charles asked. "What does she want?"

"She has found a child," Dr. Nakamura said. "She wishes help with it."

"Let us go, at once," Charles said. "What is wrong with the child?"

"The child appears to be unhurt," Dr. Nakamura said. "It is a little girl, about two years old. Her name is Ohka. That means Cherry."

"I don't understand," Charles said. "If the child is not hurt, what help does the woman want?"

"The child has no one," Dr. Nakamura said. "Its mother and grandparents were killed in the bomb blast. Its father and brother were killed in the war. She is all alone. This woman has many others to care for. She wishes to find someone to care for the little girl."

"I will care for her," Charles said quickly. "Tell the woman to bring the child to me."

Dr. Nakamura laughed quietly. "You are kind to say such a thing, but it cannot be done."

"Why not? Is there anyone who would object? Would the government authorities object?"

"The Japanese government is no longer in authority," Dr. Nakamura said. "Surely no one here would object to such a kindness. But I fear you will have difficulty with your own government."

"I will handle my government," Charles said resolutely. "Tell the woman to bring the child to me. I will take her and raise her as my own."

"Perhaps you should not," Dr. Nakamura suggested gently. "Perhaps you will always be reminded of this place when you see her. It will be difficult for you."

"Dr. Nakamura, I assure you, I will never forget this place, or what I have seen here for as long as I live," Charles said. "And that is with or without the little girl. Now, if you would be so kind as to ask the woman to bring the little girl to me, I will take her back to the plane, then I shall return to help you. We have much work to do here."

"Yes," Dr. Nakamura said. "Much to do, but little that can be done."

"There is something that can be done," Charles said. He watched as the woman returned, carrying the little girl in her arms. "We can fully document the horror of this place, and we can let the world know what it was like. With God's help, mankind will understand the fullest ramifications of such a weapon, and never again will it be used as it was used here."

23

The staff sedan stopped in front of the New Grand Hotel in Yokahama. The New Grand had weathered the war, and was now headquarters for the Allied Occupation force, to include General MacArthur. Charles had a room in the hotel, though for the last five days he had been in Hiroshima and Nagasaki, conducting tests.

"Here it is, sir, the New Grand," the American military driver said to Charles.

"Thanks," Charles said. He reached for Cherry, and she put her arms around his neck and let him pick her up.

"I don't know what they are going to say about—" the driver started to say, but Charles cut him off.

"About what?" he asked, sharply.

"Nothing," the driver said.

Charles walked through the front door of the hotel, carrying Cherry, and before he had gone fifteen steps across the lobby, an American sergeant, wearing a black armband with the word "Billeting", came up to him.

"Where do you think you are going with that, mac?" the sergeant asked gruffly.

"I am going to my room," Charles answered.

"Not with that, you ain't."

"Sergeant, this is a little girl," Charles explained patiently. "She is a two-year-old girl, she is not a 'that'."

"Whatever she is, you ain't takin' her to your room."

Charles reached into his pocket and pulled out his identification card. It was coded class-12. Though that was a civilian code, it was equal in protocol treatment to a general. The sergeant looked at it, then gulped.

"I beg your pardon, sir," he said. "Of course you may take her to your room."

"Is General MacArthur still in his headquarters?" Charles asked.

"The General? No, sir, he's out on the battleship *Missouri*. They're gonna sign the surrender this morning."

"I've got to get out there," Charles said. "Please arrange for some transportation, and find a woman to stay with the child."

"Yes, sir," the sergeant said.

Charles went to his room, bathed quickly, and had just stepped out of the tub when there was a light knock on the door. He wrapped a towel around himself, then walked over to open the door. A Japanese woman stood just on the other side, with her head bowed.

"Do you speak English?" Charles asked.

"Yes," the woman replied quietly.

"Please, come in," Charles said, stepping back and motioning the woman inside. "I want you to look after this child for me. I'll be back later today. Whatever you need, order from the sergeant at the desk in the lobby. Tell him it is for Dr. Holt."

"Yes, Dr. Holt-san," the woman said.

Charles walked over to the closet and pulled out the clothes he would wear, while the Japanese woman sat beside the little girl who was now sleeping peacefully on the bed.

It was five minutes until nine, on the morning of September 2, when the Japanese delegation started up the gangway to step aboard the battleship *Missouri*. On board the ship, waiting for the Japanese, were the gathered officers and officials of the Allied Powers, as well as the sailors and soldiers who were fortunate enough to have wangled a place. Also present were hundreds of reporters and special observers. Charles was classified as a special observer, and as such, had a front row position. But his unique window on history was not what had drawn him to the ceremony. What had caused him to go to the ceremony was a two-year-old Japanese girl, a survivor of the atomic bombing of Hiroshima.

After the Japanese delegation was in position, General MacArthur arrived, walking quickly across the deck to the table which would be used to sign the surrender instruments.

General MacArthur made a few remarks, then the Japanese officials, one at a time, came forth to sign the official act of surrender. The first to sign was Foreign Minister Shigemitsu, limping forward on his artificial leg and fumbling around so much that MacArthur had to show him where to sign. Next was General Umezu, and then came the allies: MacArthur and Nimitz for the U.S.; Yungchang for China; Sir Bruce Fraser for England;

Derevyanko for the Soviets, Moore-Cosgrove for Canada; and half a dozen others, until the documents were completed.

Shortly after the last signature was affixed to the document, thousands of American airplanes roared over in an awe-inspiring fly-by. Then MacArthur stepped up to the microphones which carried his words back to all America.

"Today the guns are silent," he began. "A great tragedy has ended. A great victory has been won. The skies no longer rain death ... the seas bear only commerce, men everywhere walk upright in the sunlight. The entire world is quietly at peace. The holy mission has been completed."

Charles listened to the words of MacArthur, and one sentence was particularly meaningful to him, for he believed it with all his heart.

"The utter destructiveness of war now blots out this alternative. We have had our last chance. If we do not devise some greater and more equitable system, Armageddon will be at our door."

Charles had hoped to be able to speak to General MacArthur after the ceremonies, but he was unable to. Instead, he found himself standing on the deck of the *Missouri* watching General MacArthur and a special party of other high-ranking Allied Officers return to shore.

"Charles," Hans greeted, coming up to him. "I thought you were still in Hiroshima."

Charles turned to see the man with whom he had worked so closely, over the last three years, in developing the threat of Armageddon.

"I flew back this morning," Charles said.

"What's the latest count? How many killed in Hiroshima?"

"Anywhere from 75,000 to 200,000," Charles

said. He shook his head. "The truth is, we may never know. It is a wasteland, Hans. Hiroshima resembles the impact area at Trinity. It is one vast desert."

"We can be thankful the war was ended before we had to use any more of them," Hans said. "The suffering those people have endured is beyond belief."

"Hans, I'm taking one of the survivors home with me," Charles said.

"What? You mean for study?" Hans asked.

"No, not for study," Charles said. "For love. I'm adopting her, Hans. It's a two-year-old girl. Her name is Ohka Saito. Her mother was killed by the bomb, her father was killed on Okinawa, and her brother was a Kamikaze pilot. I found all that out from a Japanese doctor. The little girl has no one left, no known grandparents, uncles, aunts. No one. She was going to have to go to a home for unclaimed children."

"There are thousands of children like that all over Japan," Hans said.

"I know, I know," Charles said. "And I know there is nothing I can do about all of them. But there is something I can do about this child, Hans. Don't you understand? All her suffering is the result of what I did. I *have* to take her."

"Charles, you alone can't assume the guilt of all mankind," Hans said. "If you had not come to work with us, the Manhattan Project would have been completed anyway. You know that."

"Yes, I know," Charles said. "Nevertheless I'm going to take this little girl home with me, and I'm going to adopt her."

"What do the Japanese think about that?"

"They think it is a wonderful idea," Charles

said. "It's the American military government that is causing me problems. The province governor, a colonel, says he won't allow me to do it. That was why I came here today. I thought I would make a personal appeal to General MacArthur, and get him to overrule the colonel. But he left before I could see him."

"Then go higher," Hans said easily.

"Higher? There is no higher," Charles said.

"You can still use the code word Goldfire," Hans suggested.

Charles smiled. "You once said that Goldfire would pull Roosevelt away from a dinner date to talk to me. Do you think it will get President Truman out of bed?"

"You'll never know until you try," Hans said.

Allison Cairns-Whiteacre sat in the Lloyd George chair in her bedroom and watched the sunset. The disc was blood-red, and no longer painful to the eyes, and it spread its red and gold color over the grounds of Ingersall Hall, backlighting the beautifully scuptured hedgerows, statues and fountains of the grounds. Its beauty was all the more poignant now, because Allison was looking at it alone. She would have given all she possessed to be able to reach over and take Martin's hand. But Martin wasn't here. He was in a flag-draped coffin, enroute to the United States.

There was a discreet knock at the door, and Allison heard Smythe call her quietly. Smythe was evidence, if evidence were needed, that the war was finally over. He was the third generation of Smythes to enter "the service" at Ingersall Hall, but he had been absent for the last five years, fighting in the war. He had only been back a short time, and his return had been celebrated as much as the return of any of the members of the family.

"Yes, Smythe, come in," Allison called.

Smythe opened the door and stepped into the room. "I beg your pardon, Lady Allison, but there is an American officer here to see you."

"An American officer? Who is it? Did he give you his name?"

"No, Lady Allison. He simply said he was a friend."

Allison got up from her Lloyd George chair—so called because Lloyd George was reputed to have once used this room, and the chair was the only piece of original furniture remaining—and she reached for the back of the chair to support herself. Her pregnancy was quite advanced now, and if she moved too abruptly, it caused a pain in her back. There were those who were scandalized that Allison was going to have a baby out-of-wedlock. But they didn't understand the significance of the baby. To Allison it was the one link she had with Martin, a piece of him she could keep and love forever. Give up the baby? She would die first.

"I am Allison Cairns-Whiteacre," Allison said as she stepped into the parlor a few moments later. A tall, handsome American lieutenant had been standing by the unused fireplace, and he turned as she entered. When he noticed her advanced pregnancy, he hurried to offer her a chair.

"No, it's good for me to stand some," Allison said. She smiled in confusion. "Lieutenant, you'll have to forgive me. Have we ever met?"

"No," the lieutenant said. "Is the baby Martin's?"

Allison gasped and raised her hand to her mouth. "Who *are* you?" she asked.

"Oh, please, forgive me," the lieutenant said. "I am Jim Anderson, I am—"

"You are Martin's brother-in-law," Allison said quickly. "Martin has spoken of you often. Could I get you some tea, or coffee?"

"No, thank you," Jim said. "I'm afraid that I only have a few minutes. The ship leaves France tomorrow, and I must be back there to be on it. By luck, I found out there was a courier plane coming to Wimbleshoe, and returning tonight, so I hopped a flight. I . . . I just had to see you, that's all."

"I see," Allison said, hedging a little.

Jim smiled easily. "Don't be nervous," he said. "I'm not passing judgment or anything like that. It's just that . . . well, here, you might want these." Jim handed a package of letters to Allison. "They are your letters to him, and a couple of letters he had written to you, but didn't get mailed. There is also a letter he was writing to Yolinda, telling her about you. He didn't get it finished."

Allison looked at the packet of letters, and her eyes teared.

"He loved you very much, Allison," Jim went on. "And I just wanted to come by . . . to give you some contact with the family. I know your position hasn't been an easy one."

"No," Allison said, smiling through her tears. "No, it hasn't been easy at all."

"I'll be taking Martin home," Jim said. "I'm sorry we can't come through here. I guess your only contact with him is through me. It's a poor substitute, I know, but the only thing I could think of."

Allison moved across the room and into Jim's arms. Jim cushioned her head on his shoulders as she cried softly. Finally, after a long moment, Allison pulled away and looked up at him.

"You are a dear, dear man to think of this," she said. "I shall never forget you for it. Thank you, Jim. Thank you so very much."

24

Dottie was in a 1940 wine-colored Mercury, driving from New York to Mount Eagle. She had traded the old '35 Chevrolet for it, because Kenny had warned her that the Chevy wouldn't hold together for the trip. Kenny knew a retired baseball player who now owned a car dealership, and they found a very clean, low-mileage car with good tires and at a reasonable price.

Dottie clutched the steering wheel with both hands and stared through the windshield at highway 40, which stretched out in the darkness before her. The interrupted white line in the center of the highway rushed toward her, each white bar being picked up by her headlights, then slipping by quickly, as if they were missiles launched by some unseen foe. The drone of the car engine was soothing, and when she looked in the back seat, she could see Holt, sleeping the sleep of the innocent.

Dottie's eyelids were heavy and sleep pulled at her. Oh, how she wished she had a bed, a couch, or even three minutes when she didn't have to hold her eyes open. It would be so peaceful and restful, just to close her eyes and drift, drift as if she were lying on a raft in a quiet pool, listening to the whispering sigh of the wind in the trees, feeling the gentle ripple of the water, drifting and sleeping, sleeping and drifting. . . .

Suddenly the hum of the tires changed to a crunching sound and Dottie realized that she had let the car drift all the way across the highway and onto the opposite shoulder of the road. She snapped out of it and jerked the wheel sharply, causing the tires to squeal in protest, as she got back onto the highway. She had gone to sleep at the wheel!

Dottie reached down to turn on the radio. Maybe a little music would wake her up.

"*It's three a.m. in Terre Haute, and time for the news,*" the radio announcer was saying.

Dottie twisted the dial to find some music. She was sick of news. She had listened religiously for the entire war, and now that the war was over, she didn't want to know what was happening in Germany, or France, or Japan, or anywhere else, for that matter, except right here and right now.

The war was over, and Dottie had prayed for this time to come for the last four years. She had dreamed about it, and looked forward to it, but not like this. In her dreams she would meet Jim on the docks in New York. The ship would come in, the flags would wave, the bands would play, children would laugh and people would cheer. She had stayed in New York for the entire war, working in the veteran's hospitals, just so she would be there on that great day.

But Jim wasn't coming home to the port of New York, he was coming into the port of New Orleans. At New Orleans he would board a train for

Mount Eagle, and Dottie would meet him at the depot. There would be no bands playing, or people cheering, and the only flag would be the one draped over Martin's coffin.

Dottie saw a sign which read "40 Truck Stop", and she pulled off the highway and up to the side of the building. There were about four trucks on the lot. One was getting gasoline and Dottie could hear the bell dinging with each gallon which went into the truck's tanks. Dottie looked through the window of the truck stop café, and she saw a couple of men sitting at the counter, while a woman was behind the counter, working over a griddle.

A juke box was playing in the corner as Dottie went in, and she walked over to sit by the window so she could keep an eye on the car. Holt was still asleep in the back seat. The woman behind the counter looked toward her, and the expression on her face told Dottie she was irritated that Dottie sat so far away, necessitating her having to walk over to her.

"I'm sorry to make you walk," Dottie said. "But my baby is asleep in the car and I wanted to sit here so I could keep an eye on her."

The woman's expression softened, and she smiled. "I know how it is, honey, when you are havin' to raise a kid alone."

"We won't be alone much longer," Dottie said. "My husband arrives in Mount Eagle tomorrow."

"Mount Eagle?"

"It's in Southern Illinois," one of the two men at the counter said. "Not too far from Cairo."

"Do you know Mount Eagle?" Dottie asked. She gave a little laugh. "I've been living in New York for the entire war, and no one I met there had ever heard of the place. I was about to decide that it may not exist at all. Maybe it was just something I made up."

The driver laughed. "It exists, all right. I'll be rolling through there at about seven o'clock in the morning."

"Are you going there?"

"I'm going to Cairo, I'll be going through Mount Eagle."

"Oh, would you mind, that is, would it be all right if I follow along behind you? It's been such a long, lonesome drive, and I'd just like to know there's someone else on the highway."

"I'll tell you what, little lady," the driver said. "You lead the way. That way if you happen to have any trouble, I'll be right behind and I can see it. Is that a deal?"

"You've got a deal," Dottie said with relief.

Dottie had a cup of coffee, then, when the driver asked her if she was ready, she followed him outside.

"I'm in that red Reo over there," the driver said.

"I don't know a Reo from a bicycle," Dottie admitted with a little laugh.

"The trailer has Ben-Hur Fence painted on the side. You can't miss it. I'll flash my lights when I'm ready, then you pull out onto the highway in front of me."

"All right," Dottie said, slipping into the car and starting it. "And I thank you."

The coffee helped Dottie hold off the sleep until the sun began to come up, then when the darkness rolled away, it was easier to stay awake. Finally it was bright enough for the lights of the truck behind her to go off, and she turned her own lights off. She cracked the window a little, and a bracing breath of cool fall air came in.

"Where are we, Mama?" a little voice asked from the back seat.

Dottie smiled cheerily. "Well, well, well, good morning my little sleepyhead," she said. "Did you have a nice sleep?"

"Oh, is it daylight already?" Holt asked, looking outside. "Mama, I was just going to take a little nap, and then stay awake and talk to you. My eyes must have glued shut."

"Yes, I'm sure that is what happened," Dottie said. She patted the seat beside her. "Climb over the seat and sit beside me. It's been awfully lonesome without my Holt to talk to."

Dottie passed a roadsign. It informed her that Mount Eagle was only 14 more miles.

"Oh, Mama, there's another poem. Read it to me, Mama, please?" Holt said. Holt was talking about the Burma Shave signs which were posted alongside the highway, each sign part of a limerick, until after a distance of half a mile, the entire limerick was complete.

"Here's the first one," Dottie said. "There was a man"—she waited for the next sign—"who was such a grouch....everytime he shaved....he gave a big ouch....then came Holt....to save the day....making him shave.... the Burma Shave way."

"Oh, Mama, did it really say Holt?" Holt asked, squealing with delight.

"Well, it said Mary," Dottie said. "But the dumb person who painted the sign just didn't know any better."

"Will I see Daddy today?" Holt asked.

"Oh, that you will," Dottie said.

"Will he like me?"

"Will he like you? Of course he'll like you. He's your father."

"And I'll see grandma and grandpa too?"

"Yes, and Aunt Yolinda and your cousin Dennis, and Uncle Charles and Cherry."

"Cherry," Holt laughed. "That's a funny name for a girl."

"Oh, I think it's a very pretty name," Dottie said. "Her Japanese name was Ohka, but Ohka means Cherry, so Charles changed it to Cherry. Besides, little lady, there might be some people who think Holt is a funny name for a girl."

"Grandma and Grandpa are named Holt, aren't they?"

"Yes," Dottie said. "That was my name before I married your Daddy."

"Will they like me?"

Dottie put her arm around Holt's shoulder and squeezed her. "Darlin', I have no doubt in my mind," she said.

Dottie crested a hill, then before her she saw the campus of Standhope College, ablaze now with the yellow and red leaves of fall. She saw the stadium, and she laughed. "There it is," she said. "Shaky Jake."

"What?" Holt asked.

"We're here," Dottie said. "This is Mount Eagle, where Grandma and Grandpa live."

The truckdriver honked his horn behind her, and Dottie rolled down her window, then stuck her hand out to wave her thanks to him. At the first light she turned right, went three blocks and turned left onto Elm, and pulled into the driveway of her parents' home. She stopped and sat there for a moment, just looking around. This was the first time she had seen the place since that night she eloped with Jim.

"Aren't we going to go in, Mama?" Holt asked. "Aren't we going to go in and have breakfast?"

"Yes, darlin'," Dottie said. "Give me just a moment. We're going in."

The side door opened, and Dottie saw her mother step out onto the porch and look curiously toward the car. Dottie felt a quick spasm of fear. What if her mother didn't accept her?

Nancy took a few tentative steps toward the car, straining to see who it was, then Dottie opened the door and got out.

"Dottie?"

"It's me, Mom," Dottie said.

Nancy let out a little squeal of joy, and ran toward her daughter, holding her arms open. Nancy met her halfway and they embraced and kissed, and alternately laughed and cried, then Thurman was outside too, and all three of them were embracing and crying. Standing by the car, Holt looked on apprehensively, while just inside the screen door to the house, Dennis looked out.

Holt, Dennis, and Cherry were playing together near the side of the depot. Thurman, Nancy, and Yolinda were sitting solemnly on the outside bench, while Charles and Dottie stood on the brick platform near the tracks, waiting for the train to arrive.

"She seems to be playing quite well," Dottie said, speaking of Cherry.

"Yes," Charles said. "Dennis has been good for her, and now, of course, Holt will help as well. Yolinda has been a big help. I think she's trying to make up for something."

"Do you think Cherry is going to have any problems? I mean, any long-range problems?"

"I don't know," Charles said. "It's hard to say, she is very young, but how anyone, even a baby, could come through that unspeakable horror without problems, I'll never know. Still, the human mind is an amazing thing. It may well be that there is some genetic ability to bear the unbearable which is bred into us from the beginning of time."

"How about Mom and Dad? And Yolinda? How are they taking things?"

"You mean Martin? Well, it's been ten months now, so the terrible shock is over, I'm sure this is difficult for them, seeing Martin come home like this. But they are prepared for it. They're tougher than we gave them credit for, I think, Dottie. And more flexible, too." He smiled. "It will be a melancholy moment, but Jim will be welcome, not only by you, but by everyone. At last the long nightmare is over."

Dottie heard a train whistle, and she looked south, down the track. The train came around the bend, huffing and steaming, throwing a large billow of black smoke up from the stack to drift over the rolling fall foilage of the town. The crossing gates dropped down and the cars stopped to allow the train to pass. A moment later, it reached the station, and the steam began to gush and the wheels began to squeak as it gradually slowed to a halt.

The station attendant slowly pushed a large, four wheel cart down toward the baggage car. The steel wheels rolled loudly over the brick, then the attendant stopped and waited for the door of the car to be opened. The cart was for the coffin, and the man pushing the cart was the same one who had loaded Martin's suitcase onto the train that cold, snowy morning, almost four years ago. Martin had been the only one to get on that night.

The door opened, and a tall, handsome officer stood at attention, saluting, as a flag-draped box was transferred onto the cart. Only after the transfer was made did the officer drop the salute, then he jumped down from the baggage car and looked up toward Dottie. Dottie let out a little cry and ran toward him, meeting him halfway and smothering him with hugs and kisses.

Thurman walked out to the cart and stood there for a moment with his head bowed. Nancy watched, but she didn't move. She just stood there, looking toward Charles, then at Thurman and Martin's coffin, and finally toward Dottie and Jim. She felt the tears streaming down her face. Her family had come home.

THE END

Author Robert Vaughan talks about himself and wars he has known

I was born November 22, 1937 in Morley, Missouri, a tiny settlement on the Missouri side of the Mississippi River, just across from the location of the fictional town of Mount Eagle, Illinois (the hometown of the Holt family in *The Brave and The Lonely*).

I grew up in Sikeston, Missouri, a somewhat larger community, and, as a boy during the war, I watched the trains pass through loaded with soldiers, trucks, guns and tanks. I also remember the scrapmetal drives, the newspaper collections, ration points and air raid blackout drills.

When my father was drafted we followed him to army bases in Arkansas, Alabama and Oklahoma, before he went overseas. Thus, I was exposed to army camp life, particularly the housing shortage, to say nothing of the money shortage of an enlisted man's family.

I joined the army in the middle of the 1950s, entering army aviation, where I became a Warrant Officer, flying helicopters. I served, or traveled in, 30 countries, including Germany, France, England and Japan. Because of my interest in history, I studied the war in those countries, including visits to the libraries and archives, and had lengthy conversations with the people.

When the war heated up in Vietnam, I went over for my first tour in the early part of 1966. I flew helicopter recovery missions during this period, and over the next 18 months I saw a great deal of combat.

The most hazardous operation I participated in was one called *Junction City*, a major search and destroy operation. Near an area called "The Iron Triangle" I was part of a 13-ship element. Eight of those ships were shot down, and, as recovery officer, I had to recover each of them. It was for this mission that I was awarded the Distinguished Flying Cross. During my tours in Vietnam, I also received the Purple Heart, the Bronze Star, the Air Medal with several oak-leaf clusters, the Meritorious Service Medal, the Army Commendation Medal, the Vietnamese Cross of Gallantry, and several lesser awards. I served eighteen months during my first tour and eighteen months on a later tour, for a total of three years in Vietnam.

My early writing reflected my military background. My first novel was a story of the U.S. Army along the DMZ in Korea. I have also done three books about Vietnam: *Brandywine's War, The Valkyrie Mandate*, and, under a pseudonym, *Junglefire*. Over 9,000,000 copies of my books are in print, most of them under various pen names.

I played football in my younger days, and I love all sports. I am now quite active as a football and track and field coach in Sikeston, Missouri, where I live with my wife, Ruth Ellen, and young sons, Joe and Tom.

In life, he was lover and friend,
father and son—
in death he would be but another
faceless victim
of the human folly
called war

Jim didn't know how long he'd been unconscious when he opened his eyes. He was still in the ditch, but it was strangely quiet. He looked beside him and saw that all his men were dead, victims of the German tank.

There was a noise from behind him, and Jim turned to see a German officer squatting at the top of the ditch, a machine pistol in his hand.

"I'm sorry about your friends," the German said in English, his eyes moving briefly to the bodies of Jim's fallen comrades. "I lost many men here, too. You put up a good fight."

"Thanks," Jim said.

"The fighting has gone on too long now. I think it is time for the war to end. We are beaten."

"You'd have a hell of a time proving it by me right now," Jim said.

The German officer stood up. "Lie down," he ordered, pointing his pistol at Jim.

"What are you going to do?" Jim asked. His voice was choked with fear.

"Lie down," the German said again. "I have been ordered to take no prisoners . . ."